Caleb looked at Grace. "I don't want to lose you."

"You won't." She smiled, but he still felt the tension between them. It had been a long day.

"Things might get even messier," he warned. "I hope you'll bear with me."

Grace stepped toward him. "If you're honest about your intentions, you won't be able to get rid of me."

"I'll take that as a yes." And he drew her closer to kiss her.

Her lips were soft and she wound her arms around his neck. For a moment, the day's problems and irritations melted away. Grace felt so good in his arms. He wished they never had to return to reality.

Dear Reader,

In *Home for Keeps*, a couple characters are frustrated by parents who don't support them in working at what they love in life. Both of us, the coauthors of this story, were warned by our protective parents that making a living in a creative profession was impractical.

Patricia wanted to work in theater...then in television production...then as a romance writer. Because she'd had similar youthful desires, her mother empathized. Even so, she urged Patricia to get a teaching degree so that she always had a job. Patricia didn't exactly follow that dictum, but she did work in educational television for nearly two decades, even as she wrote romances and became a published author...and eventually, a college-level fiction writing teacher, as well.

Linda wanted to be an artist and a writer. Although nobody else in her family had graduated from college, they urged her to pick up a teaching degree as a backup plan. She started out as a high school art teacher, went on to write romances and then got into teaching writing at the college level. Throughout, she has done artwork and used the creativity she developed in art classes to make life more interesting.

We believe that people should do what they love... *and* that it never hurts to have a practical option to earn a living. Hopefully, you'll see something of yourself or someone you love in Grace and Caleb's story.

Good reading!

Lynn Patrick

HEARTWARMING

Home for Keeps

—

Lynn Patrick

◆ **HARLEQUIN**® HEARTWARMING™

Recycling programs
for this product may
not exist in your area.

ISBN-13: 978-0-373-36788-7

Home for Keeps

Copyright © 2016 by Patricia Pinianski and Linda Sweeney

This edition published by arrangement with Harlequin Books S.A.

For questions and comments about the quality of this book, please contact us at CustomerService@Harlequin.com.

® and TM are trademarks of Harlequin Enterprises Limited or its corporate affiliates. Trademarks indicated with ® are registered in the United States Patent and Trademark Office, the Canadian Intellectual Property Office and in other countries.

Printed in U.S.A.

www.Harlequin.com

Lynn Patrick is the pseudonym for two best friends who started writing together a few decades ago. Linda is a professor with a reading specialty, and Patricia writes as Patricia Rosemoor. Together they enjoy creating worlds that are lightened by the unexpected, fun and sometimes wonderful vagaries of real life.

Books by Lynn Patrick

Harlequin Heartwarming

Shall We Dance?
The Marriage Assignment
Home to Sparrow Lake
A Forever Home
The Long Road Home

Harlequin Superromance

Good Vibrations

Visit the Author Profile page
at Harlequin.com for more titles.

PROLOGUE

JUST AS NELLIE MARTIN opened the kitchen door to empty her garbage, her glasses slipped down to the tip of her nose. Stopping to punch them in place, she jerked when a ball of fur streaked through her legs. Her fifteen-year-old cat had just gotten out! There she went, all twenty pounds of her tottering straight into the dark.

"Olive!" Trying not to panic, Nellie dropped the garbage bag and followed.

She'd moved from a two-story home to a first-floor apartment in Sparrow Lake's new green community only a week ago, and her cat had never been outside here. Oh, dear, what if she got lost?

Her pulse pounding, Nellie yelled, "Olive, you naughty girl, you come back here!"

How could such a rotund cat move like that? With her arthritic knees complaining, Nellie couldn't move fast enough to catch up to the old girl. And where did Olive think she was going anyway? The area outside the apartment building was woodsy. Wisps of fog rose from the ground, making it a little scary at night. Imagining a coyote darting from the dark and snatching her beloved pet for dinner, she forced her legs to go faster. Even so, the cat slinked around a tree and then simply disappeared.

"Olive, sweetheart, please!"

Where had she gone? Nellie's heart was in her throat as she slowed to scan the area. Nothing! Then through the fog, she saw movement.

"There you are," she muttered, heading in that direction.

But the shape ahead turned into something other than a cat. A pale, floaty figure shot from one tree to another.

Oh, dear, it looked like…like a…a…!

Starting, Nellie couldn't take her eyes from the vision, not until her foot hooked on something hard and heavy. Then she went flying, arms waving, but unable to regain her balance.

"Ohhhhhh!"

Landing on both hands and knees, Nellie saw stars from the pain. She couldn't see anything else because her glasses had flown off her face and everything was a big blur. She gasped for breath. Tried to move. Sobbed from the pain as she felt around for her glasses.

Sobbed some more for the loss of her cat.

"Oh, Olive, how am I ever going to find you now?"

"Meow..."

Nellie's eyes widened. "Olive?" She found her glasses and put them on just as her cat strolled up to her and gave her a full-body rub.

Grabbing Olive, Nellie kissed her head and clung to her furry companion with all her strength. Now all she had to do was figure out how to get to her feet without letting go. If she put Olive down, the naughty girl might take off again.

Fog swirled around them both, reminding Nellie of the distraction, the cause for her fall. She knelt there, cradling a now-purring Olive, her gaze scanning the area. She saw nothing amiss...yet...

Could the rumors be true?

Did a ghost really haunt the new development?

CHAPTER ONE

RUMOR HAD IT that Walworth Builders was responsible for Nellie Martin's fall while chasing down her cat the night before, and there was speculation that Nellie was going to sue.

Sue for what? Grace Huber wondered, zooming out of Sparrow Lake proper and heading for Green Meadows. She hadn't heard the nature of Nellie's injuries, but the woman was up in years and a little frail. Concerned that Nellie might be more hurt than she'd let on, Grace wanted to make sure she was all right in person. And she wanted to take care of Green Meadows, as well. She'd found a new passion in building with the environment in mind, having talked her father into developing the "green" community, which combined condos, rental apartments and semidetached homes, all constructed with sustainable materials and heated with solar energy.

So it was no wonder that she wanted to deal with the problem herself.

Green Meadows didn't need bad publicity, and she didn't want her perfect community ruined by a lawsuit. She needed to work this out so Nellie was properly taken care of without the development being in jeopardy.

Turning off the main road, she entered Green Meadows and headed straight for the community center, where Nellie had agreed to meet with her. She was almost there when she realized a crowd had gathered outside in the parking lot. Because Nellie *had* been badly hurt? Worried, she pulled into the lot, left her car and made her way through the throng, only to stop when she saw the reason for the commotion. Taking a good look at the previously blank side wall of the building, Grace started. The community center had been constructed using repurposed wood plus stone from the local quarry, and the stuccoed side wall now boasted a large mural. In it, a woman walked away from prison bars separating her from the girl who was reaching for her.

"You ruined our community center!" a man cried.

"You two ought to be arrested!" a woman added.

It took Grace a moment to realize residents had surrounded two teenage girls. One looked like a wild punk rocker with dyed black hair, black eye makeup and lipstick. The other appeared more subdued, naturally dark hair pulled back from a makeup-free face that hinted of a Native American heritage. She held a paintbrush in hand.

"C'mon, let's get out of here," the punk rocker said. "They don't appreciate your talent, Summer Storm."

The girl did seem stormy when Grace stepped closer for a better look.

"Talent?" a woman said. "She defaced our property! Someone call Police Chief Novak!"

"What's so wrong?" the young artist protested. "The development will look better with a mural! And they don't even have to pay me for it."

The sound of a truck squealing to a stop made Grace turn away for a second. She watched as a man with a rugged profile and blue-black hair worn to his shoulders jumped out. He was probably six feet and appeared powerful, if not broad. His tan shirt, sleeves rolled up to his elbows, revealed arms roped with the muscle of someone acquainted with hard work.

"Grab the girl," a woman called out. "We can bring her to the police ourselves."

That pulled Grace's attention back to the situation. "Wait a minute, no one is grabbing anyone!"

Now that she was closer to the artwork, she was stunned by the ferocity of emotion in the mural and knew it had nothing to do with beautification. The teenager herself wore a defiant expression, but Grace couldn't miss the haunted look in her eyes. What had happened to make her so angry?

Before she could do anything to find out, the man from the truck stepped in. When he took the girl's arm, she protested, "Dad!"

She struggled, but he didn't free her. His dark-eyed gaze aimed straight at Grace when he said, "Don't worry, I'll be back later to make sure this mess is taken care of."

"Mess?" Summer Storm jerked her arm to no avail. "Taken care of? What do you mean, Dad? You're going to ruin my mural, aren't you?"

As he hauled his daughter off to his waiting truck, the man said, "I'm not the one who has explaining to do."

Grace stared after them, wondering why she'd never noticed the attractive man around town before. He was definitely unforgettable.

"Are you going to let her get away with

this atrocity?" someone in the crowd asked Grace. "Do something!"

Grace sighed and tried to muster a smile. "It's time for everyone to go about your business. Don't worry, I will get everything in hand."

As the group dispersed, another person muttered, "You need to have both of those girls arrested."

Girls. What happened to the other one? Grace wondered as she looked around. The punk rocker was nowhere to be seen. She'd disappeared while the going was good. Pints of different-colored acrylics that Summer Storm had used to paint the mural had been left behind in a carry carton, along with painting knives and brushes on a tray.

Several of the residents remained, undoubtedly waiting to see how she would solve the problem. Not knowing what to do with the girl's paint supplies, Grace gathered them together and set them on one of the outdoor tables.

"Do any of you know the girl's father?" she asked the onlookers.

"Name's Caleb Blackthorne," a man said. "He and his daughter live a half mile right down the road." He pointed east. "They have one of them fancy new type A-frames set back from the road. Look hard to the left. You can just see it through the trees."

"Thanks."

The Blackthornes lived so close, she would deliver the supplies in person. And maybe get a bead on what was troubling the girl. Painting that mural on the development's property made it Grace's business. Then she spent the next several minutes rounding up a couple of workers and a neutral-color paint. Her chest tightened as she watched the men start to obliterate the mural that obviously must have meant something to Summer Storm. Once again, she wondered what had made the girl express her unhappiness so publicly.

Not that she had long to think about it. A van pulled up, its side scribed with *Kenosha Journal* in fancy lettering. Oh, great. What a terrible time for a reporter to show up. It took everything Grace had to smile at the man who alighted from the vehicle. She assumed the reporter was interested in the green community—it had already been featured in news reports in southern Wisconsin. Surely no one had called in the story about the mural.

"Hi. I'm Grace Huber with Walworth Builders. Green Meadows is our development. Can I help you?"

"Hope so. You can tell me about the latest ghost sighting."

Grace had to scramble mentally to change subjects. "Ghost sighting?" She'd heard the rumor about there being a ghost flitting around the complex at night, but of course that was ridiculous. Why would a newspaper be interested?

"Nellie saw it last night," an elderly woman stated. "That's why she took a tumble."

Nellie? The name jarred Grace into remembering why she'd come to the community center in the first place. She managed to sputter, "Nellie didn't say anything to me about seeing a ghost."

"Well, she did!" the woman's companion added. "That's why she fell on that rubble your crew left in the area. She told me she was distracted by something weird moving through the trees and her foot caught on a piece of discarded flagstone."

The reason people were talking about Nellie suing Walworth Builders.

"Maybe Nellie has a few problems with her sight," Grace said, remembering the older woman's large glasses. "She's probably confused if she thought whatever startled her could be a ghost."

"How do you know?" another man asked. "There were rumors about the old farmhouse that used to be here being haunted."

"Really," the reporter murmured, zeroing in on the man.

Grace got between them. This was ridiculous. "There's no story here. One of our residents had a little mishap chasing her cat last night. That's all."

"That's all? I'd like to talk to her myself."

Holding back a moan of dismay, knowing she couldn't stop the annoying reporter, Grace forced another smile. She'd wanted to speak to Nellie alone, to get the whole story without an audience to egg her on. Now that was out of the question.

"All right, then. Come with me."

Though reluctant, she led him inside the community center, where she hoped she could run interference if the situation got out of hand.

CALEB BLACKTHORNE WAS royally ticked at his daughter getting into a mess again with her edgy little friend Kiki Johnson. He might feel sorry for the foster kid, but he wished Angela would stay away from her and what he saw as a negative influence. Kiki was always getting into some kind of trouble, and lately, so was Angela.

"Are you ready to explain yourself, young lady?"

He gave Angela a quick glance, long enough to see her mouth tighten before she turned her head away from him to stare out the side window in silence.

"What were you thinking, defacing private property?" Surely she would have something to say in response to that.

But no, the silence continued.

"And why would you go to Green Meadows in the first place? You don't know anyone there." The development was so new that only half of the units were even in use at this time.

More silence. Obviously his daughter didn't mean to speak to him. Something that was becoming very familiar lately. This talk would have to be continued. She couldn't go around doing whatever she wanted. He would be lucky if she didn't get arrested this time, a distinct possibility. Something he would do anything to avoid.

What happened to his little "Angel"? His daughter had changed, especially lately, and he didn't know what to do about it. Maybe he deserved this. His karma for giving his mother so much grief when he was a teen. Maddie Blackthorne had been and was a great mother and person, a social worker who helped the homeless on the local Chippewa reservation find housing and health care and jobs. He'd never met his father, who'd disappeared without even knowing his mother was pregnant. Though she'd been on her own, his mother had given him a settled, safe life.

Despite his trying to do the same for his daughter but with more money than his mom had been able to make, Angela was as wild as he had been at her age. Now that she'd done something illegal, how long would it be before the local police came to pick her up? Was there any way to avoid that happening?

He couldn't stop himself from asking, "Whose idea was this stunt? Yours or Kiki's? Why do you want to hang around with her?"

That did it—Angela came out of her silent funk, shouting, "No! I'm not going to stop seeing her. She likes the same things that I do. She understands me. Kiki is my best friend!"

He knew both the girls thought of themselves as artists. "And you're the only friend she has. That girl is a bad influence on you."

"I don't care what you say. I won't stop seeing her. You can't take someone else away from me!"

"I didn't take anyone away from you."

"What about my mother?"

Caleb gritted his teeth at that. Angela had seemed okay that it had been just the two of them all these years. What had brought this up now?

"I didn't make your mother leave." At sixteen, he'd been a too-young father with an irresponsible baby mama. "She wanted you…" And then she hadn't. Lily had run away, leaving a month-old baby girl in his arms. "…but she was really young and scared."

"You always tell *me* what to do and make me do what you want. You could have made *her* stay."

"I only wish that was true. Lily made a bad decision because she was so young, Angel. I'm sure she's regretted it a million times over the years." At least he wanted his daughter to believe that.

"Then why didn't she come back for me?"

A question he'd never been able to answer.

And then it came to him. The mural. The woman walking away from the jailed girl— Lily walking away from Angela and Angela feeling helpless to do anything about it. That had to be it. Something had brought up a hornet's nest of emotion in his daughter. Not hard to envision. Angela was fifteen now, questioning everything, especially him and anything he wanted for her. But why was her absentee mother suddenly so important to her?

He flicked a look over to his daughter, who once more was staring out the side window, her shoulders set so tight he knew she wouldn't answer if he asked. He wondered if she would talk to her grandmother, tell *her* the truth. Mom was his go-to person when it came to Angela. His daughter never resented her grandmother the way she did him. He would call Mom as soon as they got home, then he would settle this mural mess.

But how to do that other than manage the cleanup?

The woman who'd told everyone that no one was grabbing his daughter had appeared to be in charge at Green Meadows. She seemed like a decent sort. Attractive, too, he thought, remembering her lush dark hair and the spark in her pretty blue eyes as she'd controlled the situation. A strong woman. One who didn't shirk from responsibility.

When he went back to take care of the mural, he would look for her. Talk to her. See if she could help.

He would do it for his daughter.

Still, the thought of getting to know a woman like that was extra incentive.

CHAPTER TWO

IT WAS STILL MORNING, and Grace felt wrung out from the stress of everything happening at once. At least the reporter looking for a ghost story had spent only a few minutes with Nellie before leaving in disappointment. Thankfully, Nellie hadn't been able to give him any details other than having seen some kind of faint movement through the trees. Just as Grace had expected. Apparently some of the other residents had blown up what they'd heard into something more exciting.

The community center had an area with tables for the residents to get together. Sitting opposite the older woman, Grace winced when Nellie raised her soda can with a bandaged hand.

"That's quite some experience you had last night, Nellie. I'm very sorry you were hurt."

"I was just so worried about Olive disappearing. And I let myself get distracted." Nellie shook her head and her big glasses wobbled on her nose so that she had to punch them back in place. "I don't believe in ghosts. It probably was just fog and wind."

Relief washed through Grace. But not because of Nellie's disbelief in ghosts. It didn't sound as if the older woman wanted to sue the company.

"Are you sure you don't want to have a doctor check you out?" Grace asked her.

"For a bruised knee and scraped palms?" Her surprisingly sharp blue eyes, magnified by thick lenses, gave Nellie an owlish expression reinforced by small tufts of silver hair around her face. "Really, no, but thank you for your concern."

"Of course I'm concerned about all the residents of our new community. I'm going to make certain that area around your apartment is cleared of any debris."

Nodding, Nellie said, "That would be good. Now if that darned cat of mine will get it into her head to appreciate her new home, we'll be fine." She glanced at the clock on the opposite wall. "Uh-oh, it's time for me to go. I need to get to my shop. Nellie's Treasures opens in half an hour." She gathered up her things. "I don't know what else I can tell you anyway."

Grace still hadn't been to Nellie's consignment shop and now vowed to do so as soon as she had some free time. "I don't have anything else to offer. I just wanted to find out what happened and to be sure that you were all right."

Nellie got to her feet. "Like I said, I hope Olive doesn't try to escape again. The new apartment is nice, but it's so small compared to our old house. At least there are no stairs," she said, putting a positive spin on the complaint.

The woman didn't have a car, so Grace asked, "Can I give you a ride to your shop?"

"That's nice of you, but I'm good. Walking is the only exercise I get these days."

Grace followed Nellie out of the building and headed straight for the parking lot, where she picked up the abandoned art supplies from the table. By the time she carried them to her car, she was a little breathless. Just walked too fast, she told herself. Nothing to do with looking forward to meeting the impressive-looking Caleb Blackthorne. Wondering if she was also going to meet Mrs. Blackthorne, she drove out of the parking lot and onto the road.

She was doing this for Summer Storm. The supplies were simply an excuse. What she really wanted was some insight to the girl. Grace hadn't had a perfect past herself, so she could recognize a kindred spirit. She didn't know why that seemed so important to her. Didn't know what she could or would do about it. Community residents wanted the young artist arrested. Grace wanted to know if she needed help.

Once past the development property, she slowed the car and began peering through the trees near the road, looking for a house.

She almost missed it.

A glimpse of windows made her hit her brake just as she came to the driveway. Her stomach fluttered as she turned in toward the house. Built of cedar and stone, the building blended well with its natural surroundings despite its wall of windows. A large deck around the front and east sides of the house. The steep roofline dotted with solar panels met straight vertical walls, so the modified A-frame had a second story. A beautiful home, one she would be proud to have as part of Green Meadows.

Grace parked and fetched the art supplies. By the time she got to the front door, it opened to reveal Caleb Blackthorne on the other side. He'd changed into worn jeans and an old T-shirt. Though he stood straight and still, the energy he gave off seemed dynamic. His expression was serious, brows seemingly ready to segue into a scowl, but Grace refused to let that intimidate her.

Her smile feeling a little stiff, she said, "Mr. Blackthorne, I've brought what's left of your daughter's art supplies. Is she home?"

"No, her grandmother came and got her. Let me take that from you." He removed the supplies from her hands and nodded toward the inside of the house. "Come on in."

Grace followed him into a great room—it went the full two stories, and she could see a loft area above. "Wow, this is much bigger than I imagined for an A-frame."

"The new multistory designs are." He set everything on the dining table. "Thanks, but you didn't need to trouble yourself. I could have fetched all this when I took care of the mural. I was just getting ready to head back to Green Meadows."

"Already looked after," she told him. "I came because I wanted to talk to you about Summer Storm."

"Her name is Angela."

His expression did become a scowl now,

though Grace wasn't sure if his irritation was with her or with his daughter.

"Okay, Angela, then," she said.

"I only recently learned that she's calling herself 'Summer Storm.' My daughter feels she needs a more exotic name to identify her as an artist."

Grace heard the increased tension in his voice on the word *artist*. So he didn't like his daughter's ambition? Looking around at the art on the walls—her work, Grace assumed—she would never know it. Painted in broad, thick, colorful strokes that gave the paintings a life of their own, the artwork depicted the moods and intense beauty of nature. Some paintings seemed to be semirealistic landscapes; others were birds, a few with outstretched wings. The style wasn't exactly abstract, but the artist had gone for emotion, not photographic reality.

"She has talent, that's for sure," Grace said sincerely, noting the tone of these paintings was far happier than the mural Angela had done that morning. She was glad she'd taken an art appreciation class so she had some basic understanding of expression in various mediums.

Caleb snorted. "Art, ha! How will my daughter make a living? She has no respect for my wishes or my hopes for her future. Whenever I tell her she needs to do something practical for a career and do her art on the side, she simply gets angry with me." Making an exasperated sound, he pushed a wild strand of long hair back from his face. "Hey, I just made some iced tea. Can I get you a glass?"

"Sure. That would be great." A reason to stay a little longer, so she could have a more in-depth conversation about Angela with him.

He moved into the open-concept kitchen area and grabbed two glasses from a shelf and filled them with ice from the refrigerator door. "Before Angela started calling herself Summer Storm, she was 'Sights Lightning' and before that, 'Snow Falling.'" He poured the tea. "As far as I'm concerned, she's 'Looking for Trouble.'"

One look at his expression and the raised eyebrow and Grace grinned. She liked a man with a dry wit, especially when he could use it to counter his own feelings. He was obviously upset by his daughter's action and was dealing with it in his own way. He handed her one of the glasses, and when he indicated the high chairs at the island, she slid onto one.

She sipped her iced tea. "I think all teenagers go through an identity crisis of some sort."

"Yeah, that." His voice was gruff. "I'm sorry about what happened this morning. My daughter has some issues, but why she went to Green Meadows to resolve them, I have no clue."

"Is she unhappy about something in particular?"

"She's fifteen." He left it at that as if it would explain everything.

Which it sort of did to Grace, though she was certain there was more to it. But she was a stranger, and Caleb Blackthorne didn't seem to be a man who liked to air his dirty laundry. He had his back up, but still, she couldn't let it go.

"I was fifteen once, too. I did some things that made my dad a little crazy. But I had good reason." Not that she wanted to tell a stranger her life story, either. "So I expect Angela had good reason for doing something so daring."

Giving her an intent look, he said, "You seem to be in charge over there."

"Sort of. Well, temporarily. I'm sorry, I didn't introduce myself. Grace Huber. Walworth Builders is the family company. I'll be in town overseeing things until Green Meadows is completed and more residents move in."

He nodded. "About what happened, then… have you called the authorities?"

"No. I don't want to handle it that way. I could see how upset your daughter was and I feel for her." When Caleb gave her a questioning look, she said, "Remember, I was fifteen once, too."

He heaved a sigh. "That friend she was with—Kiki—she's always in trouble. It was probably her idea, convincing Angela to deface your property."

"You really believe that?"

"Unfortunately, I do. The girl's a problem. She doesn't have anyone to stop her, either. Her dad overdosed on drugs and her mom's in jail. She's in a foster home."

Grace couldn't help but feel a pang. "How terrible!" But she wanted to talk about Angela. "Why does your daughter want to hang out with that girl? She was angry about something. And hurt. I could see it in her expression. In her eyes. Whatever her reason, it goes deeper than an irresponsible friend egging her on."

Caleb sat stone-faced. She remained silent, hand tensed on her glass. Was he going to ask her to leave?

CALEB BIT BACK the urge to ask Grace to leave.

It wasn't in his nature to open up to people he didn't know well. Or to anyone, really, other than to his mother.

Grace Huber seemed to be a kind woman, concerned about his daughter. The ring of truth was in her words and her expression was sincere. She said she didn't want to see Angela arrested. What *did* she want? Apparently something or she wouldn't be here. No doubt, the truth to start.

It nearly choked him, but he said, "I think the girl behind bars in the mural was Angela, and the woman she couldn't reach was her mother."

Grace's eyebrows rose. "So her mother's not here. A recent divorce?"

He shook his head. "Never married. Lily ran off after Angela was born."

"Oh." Distress shadowed Grace's expression, but she recovered quickly. "Then your explanation of the mural makes total sense."

"Why now, though?" Caleb still couldn't fathom it.

Had someone been talking to Angela about her mother? Lily's parents had moved to a warmer climate after she'd disappeared.

And there were no other relatives in the area. So who?

He said, "She's rarely asked about her mother in all these years."

"But now she's fifteen. A fifteen-year-old girl needs a mother."

Hearing a catch in Grace's voice, Caleb started. She didn't even know his daughter. "That's something I can't do for her. I've never heard from her mother since she ran off. I have no idea where to find her. And I can't even make Angela realize what she did at Green Meadows was wrong."

"I guess all you can do is keep trying. Talk to her. Support her."

"Exactly what I've been doing all these years!" He hadn't meant to show his irritation, and he could see his flare of anger threw Grace off. "Hey, sorry. I'm just at my wits' end with all these changes in Angela."

"Obviously this is a more difficult time in your daughter's life than you've experienced before."

Which was true, Caleb thought. Calmer now, he said, "Hopefully my mother can get through to her. She has more influence with Angela than I do these days." He took a slug of his tea, but it tasted sour going down.

"Whatever it cost to remove the mural, I'm good for it. Just let me know how much."

"Don't worry about it."

"I pay my own way."

"If you insist."

"I do." He toyed with his glass, spinning it halfway around on the island. They were done here, but for some reason, he didn't want Grace to leave yet. Didn't want to be alone to torture himself with what-ifs about his daughter. So, he said, "I want you to know I admire the work you're doing at Green Meadows."

"Thank you. It's been a challenge, but very rewarding."

"How did you get interested in green living?"

"I've always enjoyed the outdoors. Hiking. Biking. Boating." Things her father didn't care about and didn't like her doing. "So I started looking for ways to help keep the planet healthy. Recycling. Composting. Adding little things to make my place earth-friendly."

"Sounds like a great start. Not everyone is open to change." Another thing to appreciate about her.

"Until now, our company built single-family homes and moderate-sized apartment buildings. Then Dad got this idea to create a whole development in an area that had open spaces but was still commuter distance from cities like Kenosha and Milwaukee. A place where people could live while they worked and then could retire in comfort. He's been thinking about that a lot lately—retiring."

Caleb realized her tone shifted on that last thought, as if it bothered her. "And he wanted it to be a green community?"

She shook her head. "That was my doing. I'd been reading about ways to build green, and I got on board. Not everyone in Sparrow Lake seems to be in love with the idea of the new development, but I think most people are coming around."

"I was eager to see what would happen when I heard about the proposal. I teach environmental studies at the community college."

"Really. Oh, I love it! I should take one of your classes."

Her sudden enthusiasm made him smile. "We're two-thirds of the way through spring semester now, but you can sign up for a course this summer. They start at the beginning of June. Well, if you'll still be here then."

"I will be here, at least until fall, so I'll keep that in mind," she said. "We're just completing a half-dozen town houses. And starting the landscaping with an environmental company. The woman in charge lives in Sparrow Lake. Maybe you know her. Heather Scofield."

"I do. I mean, I don't know Heather well, but she took a couple of my classes, and we've talked a bit at some regional environmental meetings."

"Have you taken a personal look at Green Meadows?" Grace asked. "I mean, other than this morning."

"No, haven't had the opportunity."

"Let me know when you have some time available. I'd be happy to give you the grand tour."

"Thanks. Real nice of you." He noticed her glass was empty. "Can I refill that?"

"Thanks, but no. I should get going." She slid off her chair. "I need to get to the office."

Caleb rose and walked her to the door. "Thanks for bringing Angela's supplies. And for taking care of the cleanup. And most of all, for being concerned about my daughter."

"No problem. If there's anything I can do to help…"

"…I'll let you know."

She left. Caleb remained at the window and watched as she got into her car and drove away.

An interesting and compassionate woman.

One he hoped to see again.

Soon.

GRACE LEFT THE Blackthorne property but couldn't get thoughts of Caleb out of her mind. He intrigued her. He seemed to be a strong man, one who would do anything to protect his daughter. Not unlike what her father had done for her when she was a teenager.

Despite the fact that it was a Saturday, she headed for the office, admiring an open field full of dandelions as she passed. She bet that the country roads around here sported wildflowers and all kinds of new growth. Birds would be making nests. She only wished she had time to drive around and look. The weekdays were so busy. There was always so much to catch up on.

They'd rented a storefront with offices for both her and her father in Sparrow Lake proper, directly on Main Street. She passed Nellie's Treasures and a little farther down, Sew Fine, the quilting shop. The Walworth Builders satellite office was on the next block, directly across from The Busy Corner, which served a great breakfast and a decent lunch. After parking in a reserved space behind her office building, she entered, wondering if her father had heard about that morning's excitement at the development.

"Morning, Carol," she said.

"Grace, there you are, thank goodness."

The receptionist wore a worried smile. Then again, Carol worried about everything and everyone, said it was the result of having raised five kids. Blamed them for the gray in her hair, though she was barely forty.

"Is something wrong?" Grace tried to keep tension from her voice, but Carol's brows were knit together.

"Mr. Huber wants to see you," she said in something just above a whisper. "He told me to send you in the moment you arrived."

Oh, great. Wearing a forced smile, she entered her father's office. Sitting behind a massive desk loaded with paper files, Henry Huber appeared every bit the successful businessman he was. His stocky build was minimized by tailor-made suits, which he wore even when visiting the construction site, and his dark hair laced with silver was professionally trimmed every other week.

"Hey, Dad, I heard you wanted to see me."

He glared at her and looked as if he was ready to pop a cork. "Where have you been?" he demanded. "I've had people calling me the past couple of hours to complain."

Uh-oh, he knew about the mural. Grace tried to divert him by asking, "You mean they're bothering you about the ghost sighting? I talked to Nellie Martin. She really didn't see anything other than some faint movement through the trees, maybe fog, but people are convinced the land is haunted."

"Ignore them." He carefully arranged a stack of paper in one of the trays on his desk. "I did hear a rumor about a murder...or similar in that old farmhouse we tore down. Whitman. That was the name of the old couple that lived there."

"A murder?"

"Something that happened back nearly a century ago. Nobody could offer any proof, though. Probably just gossip."

"A hundred years ago, huh?" Grace felt a bit relieved. "Yes, probably gossip." People in small towns loved to talk.

"Whatever. It's not important. What *is* important is taking care of our project now. I heard how well you did that this morning.

Residents are complaining that you wouldn't call the authorities and have those girls who defaced the property arrested."

She should have known better. When her father had something he wanted to say, it was like a mission to him. "I did speak with the artist's father—"

"Artist? You mean vandal!"

"She's a kid, Dad. Her mother ran off and left her, and she's upset about that. You remember what *that* was like, don't you? You would have totally gotten it if you had seen the mural she painted."

Her father's mouth tightened.

She went on. "Caleb Blackthorne has taken this very seriously. He's about out of his mind with worry for his daughter. I think he was terrified that I would have her arrested."

Her father's visage changed. He looked a little haunted himself. She knew he remembered the trouble she'd gotten herself in. It was a time in their lives that neither of them would ever be able to forget.

"Dad?"

"All right, all right! As long as they stay off the Green Meadows grounds."

Grace was certain Caleb would do what he could to make sure Angela stayed in line.

But she didn't know about the other girl, Kiki. Still, she said, "They will," with more certainty than she actually felt.

"Good. Then concentrate on the job. On what's important, so you can slide behind my desk when I retire next year."

Grace's throat tightened. "You're not going to retire, Dad. You would be too bored." And thinking about whether he would retire or not was making him uptight.

"I want the pleasure of seeing what I've built become an enduring legacy for my family."

"I understand you do." Though Grace was not happy with the future he expected of her, she never could tell him that. "Now, I've got work waiting for me."

While she enjoyed the public part of her job—dealing with people—she wasn't so crazy about the executive part of it, particularly the never-ending meetings and financial planning for the future. The endless paperwork made her crazy, and she would do anything to avoid it. She wanted to expand her knowledge and get more personally involved in the green community, an idea that Dad continually criticized, making her keep her wishes to herself and resent him for it.

Her father waved her away, and she traded his office for her own, where she pulled out the proposal Heather had drawn up for the landscaping. Though she looked it over, she couldn't focus. She kept glancing out the window, watching sparrows play tag as she thought about her future.

About her father telling her she was born to be his right hand, that her purpose in life was to run Walworth Builders when he was done serving his time.

She knew that position would have gone to her twin brother, if Michael had lived past thirteen. His death in a tragic boating accident drove her parents apart, and her mother had divorced her father and abandoned *her* when she'd moved to Minneapolis. She and her father had been left to go it on their own. That's when she'd started acting out, getting herself into trouble. Like Angela, she'd been a handful, but her father had both protected her and put her back on the straight and narrow. And so, grateful, she felt very protective of the man who'd lost so much in life.

If only he wasn't so demanding and grumpy. If only he didn't tell her what she needed to do and how to do it. Her father really would retire one of these days. He expected her to take over as CEO at Walworth and, though it was the last thing she wanted, Grace knew she would do as he wished. Reaching up to close the blinds, she forced herself to stare at the papers in front of her.

CHAPTER THREE

"AREN'T YOU AFRAID your dad's gonna kill you?" Kiki asked Angela on Monday morning, halfway through building a semitraditional sweat lodge a hundred yards from the house.

Angela glanced at her friend, who was decked out in her usual black clothes and makeup, but with new purple extensions flowing from her hair. "Dad grounded me, he said I had to stay home, but he didn't say I had to stay inside." It was her spring break, after all. The community college had been off the week before, so Dad was at work and she was theoretically alone. He'd probably have a cow if he knew Kiki was here. "Besides, he'll have to see I'm doing something worthwhile."

Even if her father wasn't into Chippewa culture the way she was. And even if her true intention was to have a place to get away from him. She could come out here to avoid his lectures about how she needed to be practical, to plan for her future, about how she was always doing things the wrong way—which really meant she wasn't doing things *his* way.

"What if he asks why you decided to build a lodge?" Kiki asked.

She wouldn't tell him the truth. "I'll say I was inspired the last time I stayed with Gran Maddie. He never argues with his mother about anything. He just can't know you were here helping me. By the time he comes home from work, we'll be finished. Too late for him to tell me to forget it."

Kiki circled the half dome of saplings they'd tied together with twine. "Um, I hate to say it, but it looks a little crooked."

Sighing, Angela agreed. "It does, but it's my first try. It'll have to do for now. Let's get this stuff up." She indicated the pile of tarps and blankets she'd collected from the house. "Blankets first. The tarps will keep them from getting wet when it rains."

"Yeah, if you get to keep it up that long."

Angela's chest tightened. Dad had better not make her take her sweat lodge down! She didn't know what she might do if he did.

They spent the next twenty minutes carefully aligning blankets and securing them to the frame, leaving an opening facing east, but with a flap she could lower for complete darkness. And privacy.

"So what did you do yesterday when Dad dragged me away from the mural?" Angela asked.

"Something fun."

"What?"

"I got back at them—the creepy Green Meadows residents who wanted us arrested."

"Kiki, what did you do?"

"I called someone who would be interested in murders and ghosts. Hopefully, he'll scare them to death!"

Angela rolled her eyes. Wasn't the mural enough for one day? "Are you sure you should have done that? If anyone finds out, you're going to get yourself in trouble."

"So? I've been arrested before. No biggie."

Arrested. Angela shuddered as they began gathering large stones. She knew Kiki had been arrested for shoplifting once and had spent a day behind bars. She didn't want that fate for herself. She'd hoped they could disappear before someone discovered they were painting a mural on that wall, and when they were caught, she'd really been afraid someone *would* call the cops.

Having borrowed the portable fire pit from

the deck, she'd set it on its pad a dozen feet from the lodge. She layered the bottom with wood and covered it with the stones they'd gathered before starting the fire. They really should be volcanic rock, but she didn't know where to get those, so fieldstone would have to do. While she filled a bucket with water and set it inside, Kiki dug a hole in the ground under the dome. Then they used shovels to move the hot rocks into the hole.

"That's it. We're ready." Feeling a sense of accomplishment, Angela crawled inside, careful not to get too close to the heat.

Following suit, Kiki turned on a battery-operated light and lowered the flap.

"Ready?" Angela asked.

"I am if you are."

Angela lifted the bucket and poured water onto the hot stones, filling the dome with steam. Wow, it really did get hot in there fast! She was already beginning to sweat. Then it was time to start the ceremony that would bring them closer together, as Native American tradition dictated. She'd researched sweat lodges. They weren't going to strip off their clothes, but they'd worn tank tops under their shirts and bicycle shorts to help with perspiration. Kiki was already taking off her black cotton blouse.

On to the ceremony. According to the sources Angela had found on the internet, they were supposed to conduct a "talking circle."

"Kiki, you start. Speak from your heart about your life and concerns."

"What life? You know what I have to deal with. I guess that's my concern, too."

Angela knew that Kiki had drawn the short straw when it came to family, but somehow she'd held up under the negativity and was a good-hearted person anyway. And a really good friend.

"Isn't there anyone out there for you?" she asked. "An aunt or an uncle? A cousin?"

"A grandmother. Somewhere."

"You never told me that before!"

Kiki shrugged. "Why would I? It's not like I know her. The last time I saw her I was seven. We were living in Chicago at the time. She and my mom had a big fight, and Mom told her she was leaving town and Grandma would never see either of us again."

"Sorry. I didn't know that." And that meant Kiki's grandmother didn't have any idea her granddaughter was in trouble and needed her. "What's her name?"

"Elizabeth Hartl. Why?"

"Maybe we could find her."

"Why bother? She won't want me around. No one does."

Angela was sure Kiki's foster mother had convinced her of that. "Well *I* want you around." There had to be a way to find Kiki's grandmother. Surely the woman wouldn't want her granddaughter in some terrible foster home. Wanting to get her friend's spirits up, she said, "Why don't you speak about your dreams. Or anything that comes to you that puts a smile in your heart. What would make you really happy?"

"Okay… I wish… I wish I had a father like yours."

"Like mine?" Angela choked out. Still angry with Dad, she was aghast. "But he's always ordering me around!"

"Because he wants the best for you. He takes good care of you. You have a great bedroom and an art room, too." Kiki's voice rose to a squeak. "The only nice thing I have is my tattoo."

"It really is beautiful," Angela said, thinking of the roses tattooed on her friend's hip.

Despite being underage, Kiki had found someone to ink her.

"Most of all," Kiki went on, "your dad's *here* with you. And he *loves* you."

"I'm sure your mom loves you. Your *real* mom, I mean."

"A lot of good that does me with Mom locked up."

"But she'll get out. You'll see her again in less than a year."

"I hope so, but I don't know," Kiki said, sounding forlorn. "Sometimes I think it'll never happen. I'll never see her again."

Angela could really identify with Kiki on that one. Both girls were silent for a moment.

Then Kiki asked, "What do *you* wish for?"

Angela took a deep breath. "Pretty much the same as you. I wish I had a mother who cared about me instead of running away from me all my life." Her chest tightened and her stomach started to ache as she thought about it. "Even now, she can't come to see me."

"Are you certain your dad didn't make it impossible for her?"

"Pretty certain." After the talk they'd had the night before. Maybe Dad wasn't to blame for her mother leaving her as she'd always believed. "So that means she just doesn't want anything to do with me."

"Well…if it's true. Your mom being back could just be a rumor."

"You're right. Ever since I heard Gran Maddie's neighbor talk about 'that Lily Trejo having the nerve to show her face on the rez again,' I've been asking around. No one will admit to actually having seen my mother except for old Jasper, who sits outside the municipal building most days, and he's not the most reliable person."

"Do you think he lied when he said he saw your mom on Green Meadows property?"

"No, not lied. But Jasper has his good days, and other times…" She shrugged. Something in her wanted to believe…

The real reason she'd painted the mural had been to send a message to her absentee mother, assuming she really was back and had gone to Green Meadows.

Another purpose for the lodge: she could come out here to simply think about the mother she'd never met and without interference figure out what to do next to try to find her.

MONDAY MORNING WAS BUSY, as usual, but after showing a potential buyer to the office door,

Grace glanced out the windows just as Caleb Blackthorne entered The Busy Corner across the street. He looked every bit the confident male in his jeans and leather jacket and boots. His long hair was tied back with what appeared to be a strip of leather. A little breathless, she had to fight the urge to leave the office and visit the restaurant for some take-out coffee as she often did. Instead, she decided to make a fresh pot.

"Oh, I didn't see the pot was empty," Carol said as Grace carried it to the restroom to get water. "I can do that. You have more important things to take care of."

"No problem, Carol." Grace raised her voice over the already running water. "I needed an excuse to stretch my legs anyway."

An excuse to get away from more important things—that wretched paperwork that was waiting for her on her office desk. She would love, for example, to give Caleb that grand tour of Green Meadows she'd promised him. Hmm…

Setting up the coffee took only a few minutes. Carol was now on the phone with one of their suppliers. As she thought about the possibility of that tour to get her away from the office, Grace couldn't resist the temptation to walk back to the windows. She was staring at The Busy Corner as if she could conjure Caleb Blackthorne again, when an old minibus rattled up and parked in front of the restaurant. Out stepped the odd-looking driver, who appeared to be wearing a costume of sorts. Short and chubby with a Van Dyke beard, he sported a bowler hat and a frock coat that had seen better days.

As he walked around the vehicle to let passengers out of the back, she noted the cartoon-like ghost painted on the side of the bus along with Spooky Tours... Hosted by Vincent Pryce.

What in the world...?

And then it hit her—this was a ghost tour operation. And it had come here, no doubt, because of the rumors at Green Meadows!

The odd little man was guiding a dozen people inside The Busy Corner.

"The coffee is ready."

Carol's voice jerked Grace around. "What?"

"Your coffee." The receptionist indicated the coffeemaker.

"Right. Thanks." She glanced back through the window as the man followed his customers inside. What in the world was he telling them about the development? And with all those people in the restaurant—potential residents—within hearing distance. "I think I need something to go with the coffee. If anyone asks for me, I'll be back in…well, a while."

Grace left the office and raced across the street. She opened The Busy Corner door. All the passengers on the tour had taken seats around tables, and a busboy was distributing menus and water. Grace glanced past them to the far wall where Caleb sat alone enjoying a piece of apple pie. She wanted to wave at him, but he didn't seem to notice her. Or anyone for that matter. He was too busy reading his newspaper.

One of the people from the minibus said, "What I heard happened on that farm is even better than the Milwaukee beer baron story. C'mon, Vincent, don't make us wait any longer. Tell us about the farmhouse murder!"

Grace clenched her jaw so she wouldn't interrupt. She wanted to hear what this guy had to say, as well. Her father had told her there had been a murder on the Green Meadows property, but he hadn't had the details.

The tour leader—Vincent, apparently—stood in the center of the room, bowler hat still firmly in place as he puffed out his chest and cleared his throat. "Right after the First World War, that farm was owned by a mean old couple with a crazy grown son. Really weird folks, the Whitmans, who made their neighbors uncomfortable, made friends with no one. They were farmers who should have had responsibility to their animals, but they got up whenever they wanted and made the cows wait to be milked."

"Was that bad?" asked another member of the group.

Vincent said, "Yes, it was bad. They should have been milked at sunrise. Those poor cows suffered. And then they didn't milk the cows again until after dark. The neighbors were horrified when they saw the lanterns lighting up the old barn late at night. Horrified, too, when the crazy son who served in World War I marched around the property carrying a shotgun and looking for Germans."

"Plenty of Germans in these parts," a local woman said. "Did he ever shoot anyone?"

"He did. One of their cows who wandered away from the herd. Shot it in the head and killed it dead."

Several gasps made Grace realize everyone in the restaurant other than Caleb was captivated by the story. Finally looking up and spotting her, he shot both eyebrows up high and shook his head.

"What happened then?" came another question.

"Son got taken away to an asylum, where he stayed for the rest of his life."

"That's it?" a man groused. "A *cow* was murdered?"

People grumbled as if disappointed.

"No, no, that was just the beginning," Vincent went on, embellishing. "Then the rumors started about a cow with blazing red eyes appearing. Soon after, the couple was found dead. Old Whitman sprawled across the kitchen floor, his head smashed in…blood on a rolling pin in the sink."

"What about the woman?"

"Found facedown outside as if she'd been running from something fearsome and had a heart attack. Rumor had it the murdered cow's ghost was possessed, and no one wanted to go near the property because it haunted the fields."

"Oh, come on!" Appalled, Grace moved toward the tour guide. "Where did you get that information? What proof do you have that anything you said is true?"

Vincent puffed himself up but still had to

tilt his head to look her in the eye. "Are you a ghost hunter?" he demanded.

As if his calling himself a ghost hunter gave him unique qualifications, Grace thought. "No. Green Meadows is my community, and I don't appreciate your tall tales meant to scare people or make them uncomfortable."

"I'm not doing anything illegal. And just because *you* don't believe in ghosts doesn't mean the story isn't true."

"A ghost cow?" she asked.

"With blazing red eyes. And it still wanders the area, sometimes on deserted country roads…"

Grace had had enough. She started to open her mouth again.

"Oh, come on, lady," one of the group interrupted. "Don't spoil our fun!"

Fun? Could this man really just make up a bunch of lies and people would pay to hear them? Distraught, she looked around and noted irritated expressions on several faces. Obviously these tourists were getting what they wanted and didn't appreciate her interference.

"Fine," she muttered.

Paying no attention to her, the tour leader started explaining how the cow chasing old

Mrs. Whitman was reenacted on the Green Meadows property whenever there was moonlight.

Disgusted, Grace turned to leave and nearly ran into Caleb, who had his bill and some cash in hand.

"Don't let him get to you," he said softly as they reached the cashier and he set down his money, then went on without waiting for change. "It's ridiculous, but it isn't meant to hurt anyone."

"Plus it brings in business," added the cashier, nodding to the group, most of whom seemed to be ordering sandwiches or full meals.

"Come on." Caleb held the door open for Grace.

Once outside, she said, "But what if it hurts the new community? People can be superstitious. If they believe him, they might not want to go anywhere near Green Meadows."

"Yes, levelheaded people around here are going to believe there's a ghost cow with blazing red eyes roaming the property." His tone was serious but laugh lines crinkled around his eyes.

Despite her irritation with the tour leader, Caleb made her laugh. "Okay, okay."

"If I know people around here, they'll be snorting over that guy's story for days to come. Until someone else comes up with a more outrageous tale."

"Hopefully Green Meadows is safe then." The idea of going back to her paperwork made Grace desperate enough to ask Caleb, "Have you thought about taking that tour of the green community with me?"

"You were serious?"

"I was."

"Then I would love it. Are you busy now?"

Thinking about the paperwork waiting for her in the office, she said, "Now would be a perfect time."

SINCE CALEB LIVED so close to the development, it made sense for them to drive separately and meet at the community center. Arriving at Green Meadows before Grace, he took a good look at the wall his daughter had defaced a few days ago. Already painted over. Part of him regretted Angela's work being destroyed, especially since it had such emotional significance to her. What she had done was wrong, but maybe it was his fault. In the past, he'd avoided discussing Lily with his daughter. He'd had no idea that she'd thought he had somehow taken her mother away from her, the antithesis of the truth. When he'd fallen in love with Lily, he'd been young and naive and had thought they would be together forever.

"How is Angela doing?"

Caleb started. He'd been so deep in thought he hadn't heard Grace's car pull up. He turned to face her. The breeze caught her dark hair, creating a lovely cloud around her face. "She's coping, I guess. She's still avoiding me as much as she can."

Grace nodded in what seemed like understanding. "Let's walk this way."

She indicated the sidewalk that would take them past one of the condo buildings, plus several duplexes. Caleb was glad to note that all the buildings sat on large pieces of land and backed onto a forested area. So while people did have neighbors, they also had enough room for gardens and outdoor activities and a wonderful backyard view of something other than more buildings. The solar panels that heated and cooled the dwellings were cleverly inserted into the roofs.

He asked, "How big is the development?"

"Almost four acres. Half of that is common land, never to be built on. Phase 1 is only about an acre, similar to the size of a football field."

"So there will be a Phase 2?"

"Down the road. Maybe. Assuming Phase 1 is successful. So far we're about half-full and still working on completing a half-dozen town houses. Let's hope that tour operator didn't scare away people who might have been thinking of moving in."

"I doubt that's likely. He was just too outrageous for anyone with sense to buy into his story."

"Hopefully you're right. At any rate, if we went ahead with the second phase, we would probably add some single-family homes."

"That would be good to bring in families with kids."

"Exactly what we're hoping to do. We want the community to be multigenerational, with the option for our more mature residents to age in place."

As they walked through the network of winding streets, Grace talked about their objectives. "We want to protect occupant health by using safe building products, including what we can of mold- and fire-resistant materials. And we hope to reduce the impact to the environment by using energy and water resources more efficiently." Grace sounded apologetic when she said, "But I'm preaching to the choir. You already know all that."

"That may be true, but it's nice to hear someone else talk about it."

Caleb appreciated that Grace knew her stuff. Despite the fact that she claimed to be an amateur, she'd gotten so much right. He liked the walking paths carved through the forest so that residents could experience nature just outside their door. He particularly liked the chance to walk through the area with her.

"This is the rental building where Nellie lives," she pointed out, taking a path that led behind it toward a stand of trees. "Let me know if you see any ghosts, okay?"

"A cow with glowing red eyes?"

They laughed together as they got on the walking path that cut through the trees behind the housing.

Caleb loved the near silence surrounding them. He could pick up welcome noises. A bird's wings flapping. A small animal foraging for something to eat. A squirrel racing from one tree to the next. Grace seemed equally happy just being one with nature for the moment, not having to keep a conversation flowing. The expression on her face looked as serene as if she were meditating on the outdoor beauty. He liked that, plus he felt comfortable with her. As if he'd known her for months or years rather than a few days.

"Angela would love this trail," Caleb said. "She would find dozens of places to hunker down and sketch."

"I noticed how much she used nature in her art at your place the other day. If you wanted to bring her out here sometime, I have no objection."

"I don't think she wants to go anywhere with me at the moment."

"She knows you love her. She'll calm down."

"I can hope." Then Caleb reminded her, "I want to pay for the damage. Did you figure out how much I owe you?"

"Not yet. How about I send you an email when I tally it up."

"Sounds fair. What I should do is find a way to make Angela pay for her own bad choices before she does something worse. I had a rough go of it myself when I was her age." Surprisingly, Caleb found himself opening up to Grace, probably because she'd been so concerned for Angela and Kiki. "I was reckless. Got into all kinds of trouble. I didn't expect to end up being a Dad at sixteen."

"Oh…wow…you were a kid yourself."

Rather than shocked, Grace sounded compassionate, which made Caleb appreciate her even more.

"I had to grow up fast. Thankfully, I had a terrific mother, who helped me make a U-turn with my life. I took custody of Angela, got myself through high school and into college. Took me a lot of years going to school while working in construction and other hard labor jobs. I had to make a decent living while getting my degrees."

"But it was all worth it."

He nodded. "I did it for Angela. Not that she sees it. She has no idea of how hard it was for me to give her the comfortable life she's had. I wanted to be a good example, so that she would make better choices for herself than I did at her age. Lately it hasn't seemed like I succeeded."

"You can't blame yourself. Every teenage kid goes through something. It's part of growing up. What you did for her…that was everything. Give her some time, and she'll realize that."

Caleb hoped Grace was correct. Drawn

to her caring nature, he didn't miss the fact that she was a fine-looking woman. A little fancy for him, wearing what he thought was a designer dress and heels so high they were practically eye-to-eye. The look suited her, though, appearing…effortless.

Caleb wouldn't mind getting to know Grace Huber better.

If only Angela wasn't having an absentee-mother crisis.

Realistically, he couldn't have met the appealing woman at a worse time.

CHAPTER FOUR

GRACE HUMMED TO herself as she got ready for her meeting with Heather Scofield about the landscaping for Green Meadows. She kept playing the time she'd spent with Caleb the afternoon before over and over in her head. It had been a simple walk, but she couldn't remember when she'd had such a good time with a man. She'd been so focused on work since Dad announced he was contemplating retiring, that she hadn't even thought about dating in some time.

Well, now she was thinking about it!

There was a lot she appreciated about Caleb Blackthorne beyond his good looks. His devotion to his daughter touched her deeply. She liked the fact that he taught environmental studies. He was a man of principle. She'd meant to forgo billing him for the repaint job on the community center, but his reminder had convinced her she needed to let him make up for his daughter's actions.

Most of all, she'd loved just being with Caleb on that walk. They had a like appreciation of nature. She was always trying to identify birds and often spent free time reading nature magazines, so she'd been aware of everything around her, and he hadn't cut in with forced conversation. They both had been comfortable just being together, listening to the sounds of birds flying and small animals scurrying around. She couldn't have had a better time.

She was smiling to herself just thinking about it when Heather appeared at her office door.

"You certainly look cheerful this morning."

The smile turned to a grin. "I have a lot to be cheerful about."

That's when she noticed Heather's expression was just a little distressed. And, in addition to her portfolio, Heather held a sheet of paper gripped tightly in one hand.

"Uh-oh. What's wrong?"

Heather crossed to her desk. "Sorry." And set the paper down in front of her.

It was a flier.

SPOOKY TOURS... HOSTED BY VINCENT PRYCE shouted at Grace from the top of the flier, and it took her a moment to read the rest. *See the old Whitman farm-stead, where ghosts were responsible for the deaths of an old man and his wife! Now* they *are haunting the grounds, too.*

Choked up, she said, "If only there was something I could do to stop him!"

"I don't know on what grounds as long as he stays off yours," Heather said. "I mean, he can drive down the street and say whatever he wants about the area. I don't know that anyone can stop him unless he's defaming someone who is still alive and who can sue him."

Grace's stomach tightened at the thought of instigating a lawsuit. Not that it would go anywhere under the circumstances. "Well, maybe no one will want to go on that tour. At least not potential residents."

"The best way to calm people down is to get to know them personally," Heather said.

"I haven't exactly had a lot of time for socializing this past year."

"I know you were really busy. But things at Green Meadows are winding down now."

Grace immediately thought about checking out Nellie's Treasures as she'd vowed to do the other day. Then again, Nellie was only one person. And she was already a resident.

"Any suggestions of where I can meet a lot of people at once?"

"There's a fund-raiser social being given by the Ladies Auxiliary of First Presbyterian Church the weekend after next. They're raising money for a new air-conditioning system for the church offices. And this Wednesday is Pancake Day. You definitely should go to that to meet people."

"Pancake Day?"

"The Sparrow Lake Creamery and Dairymen's Association have a Pancake Day every year during the kids' spring vacation so everyone can come. It gets townspeople invested in supporting the local dairy industry—the butter and cream and milk produced in this area."

"So it's a breakfast?"

"All-day breakfast at the Sparrow Lake Farmers' Co-op."

Grace scribbled a note to herself even as she wondered if she would fit in at this kind of social event. "At the co-op?"

"Right. The building has offices and meeting rooms. That's where the Dairymen's Association is located. I'm going around noon. If you like, we can go together, as long as you don't mind that I'll be bringing the twins. I can introduce you to people you haven't yet met."

"Great. And I would love to see Addison and Taylor again."

Heather eyed Grace's designer suit. "You might want to…um…dress down a little."

"So I fit in. Got it. Now at least I have a plan to influence people more than some transient ghost hunter. I can hope, right?"

Heather's expression remained cautious.

Uh-oh. That didn't bode well, Grace thought. "Is there a problem I don't know about?"

"Just a little one. There's another reporter going around town, trying to dig up a story about the ghost sightings."

Grace groaned. "And I was just thinking what a nice day I had yesterday on the 'haunted' property. I say we get down to work before I lose my mind over this nonsense."

At her invitation, Heather took a chair on the opposite side of the desk. As always, she was dressed casually compared with Grace, today in pale green chinos and a matching spring sweater. Her light brown hair streaked with blond was pulled back in a ponytail, and her face was makeup free other than a swipe of tinted lip gloss.

"So…yesterday…" Heather cleared her throat and with an interested expression lighting her pretty face asked, "What was going on?"

"Oh. I, um, gave Caleb Blackthorne a tour of the area." Grace tried to keep her tone casual.

"Ah, I see."

She simply blinked at the other woman's knowing tone.

Heather went on. "Caleb Blackthorne is considered quite a catch to the unmarried women in these parts, you know. Good-looking, great job, beautiful home. Lucky you."

"It wasn't a date," Grace was quick to assure her. "The other day, his daughter, Angela—or Summer Storm, as she calls her artist self—created some problems at Green Meadows."

"So I heard."

Sparrow Lake was a small town with an active rumor mill, Grace reminded herself. Probably *everyone* had heard. "I wanted to talk to Caleb about his daughter, to see if I could get some insight on why she painted that mural, and I learned he teaches environmental studies at the community college."

"I know. I took a couple of his classes. Great teacher."

Grace thought about telling Heather she'd been considering taking his classes, too, but something stopped her.

"At any rate," Grace went on, "Caleb asked me about why we went green with the new community, and I offered to give him a tour of the place."

"A tour that put a big smile on your face."

"I enjoyed myself," Grace admitted, then before Heather could question her more indicated the table along the wall. "That should give us enough room to spread out your blueprints, don't you think?"

"That it does."

Part of Grace wanted to continue discussing Caleb with someone who knew him—she wanted to learn more about him if she could—but she didn't want to seem too enthusiastic about a man who didn't necessarily feel the same way about her.

ANGELA WASN'T SPEAKING to him again, and Caleb was ready to pull out his hair.

He still couldn't believe he'd come home the day before to find a rickety structure that passed for a sweat lodge in his yard. Not that he objected to the idea of his daughter building one, but she had been grounded for the entire spring vacation. Apparently she'd chosen to interpret what that meant for herself. He'd given her a stern lecture about following rules and taking responsibility. He'd been sorely tempted to order her to tear down the flimsy shelter before it fell down, especially when he'd learned she'd used their winter blankets to build it. But his daughter's tearful, accusatory expression had torn at his heart. He'd merely told Angela she couldn't use her sweat lodge until her punishment was over at the end of the week.

She'd refused to have dinner with him.

Or breakfast.

What was he going to do with her? They'd never been at odds like this until the past few weeks. He needed someone to talk to about his daughter—someone who could give him some guidance. A good reason to visit his mother. Angela wasn't speaking to him anyway, so he was simply spinning his wheels walking through the house.

Stopping at her closed bedroom door, he raised his voice. "I'm going out for a while."

No answer.

No big surprise.

"I expect you to stay inside the house." He waited for a moment, then said, "I need to know that you heard me."

"I heard you."

Still sullen. What was he going to do with her? Hopefully Mom would give him some good ideas of how to handle his daughter. How to get her to open up and not simply in anger. He thought about calling Mom first, then just decided to surprise her.

Maddie Blackthorne was a member of the Sparrow Lake Chippewa Band on what was the smallest reservation in Wisconsin. The land was a little more than seven hundred acres, supported by three tiny family farms surrounding a single village. The band that had broken off from its Lake Superior cousins had fewer than a thousand members, only half of whom actually lived on the rez itself.

It was beautiful land, with a couple of hundred acres of meadows and unharvested old forest that he'd explored throughout his youth. His love of nature had inspired him to become an environmentalist. And a professor of environmental studies.

The Blackthorne family house was situated on a quarter acre halfway between the village proper and the untouched land. It was a simple two-bedroom with a living room and eat-in kitchen, but the garden surrounding the house would be spectacular in full bloom, the flowers intermixed with rows of vegetables. Caleb had helped his mother start the garden when he was a kid, before he'd begun finding ways to get himself into trouble.

He'd barely parked the truck before his mother came out of the house to greet him. She smoothed back the silver wings of her long blue-black hair, caught in the back with a clip. She was wearing her usual jeans with a long-sleeved pullover sweater. Mom's clothing was always practical. A social worker, she spent her life taking care of other people rather than fussing over herself. He appreciated her dedication but wished she would fuss just a little. She deserved it.

"Hey, Mom." Stepping up to the porch, he threw his arms around her.

She gave him a big hug. "This is certainly a surprise."

"I needed to talk to someone with more wisdom than I have."

"Angela?"

He nodded.

"C'mon in. I have a fresh pot of coffee to go with the acorn bread I made this morning."

Caleb's mouth was already watering as he followed her inside. "Any of that rhubarb ginger jam left?"

"Of course. You know I always make enough to last until the next rhubarb crop comes in."

The acorn bread must have come out of the oven a short while ago, because the wonderful smell still filled the air. The kitchen was old-fashioned, a combination of wooden cabinets and shelves with speckled laminate countertops and ancient white appliances. Caleb loved Mom's kitchen, because it felt like home. She'd said it felt like home, too, when he'd offered to buy her a new stainless steel stove and refrigerator, saying that would be a waste while the old ones still worked. While his mother sliced the bread, Caleb poured them mugs of coffee and fetched half-and-half, butter and the jam from the fridge. When everything was on the table, they sat opposite each other in comfortable silence for several minutes until they'd spread thick slices of bread with butter and jam, and Caleb had taken a big bite.

"Delicious," he murmured as he chewed. "Your cooking always makes me feel better."

"What did Angela do this time?"

Caleb took another bite and washed it down with coffee before answering. "You know I grounded her, which by that I meant study. Instead, she went outside and built a sweat lodge that looks like it would fall over if someone bumped into it."

"Well, I would say that's educational."

"She wasn't supposed to leave the house."

"Perhaps she thought 'house' included the property, too."

"Mo-o-om."

"She's so much like you were before you became a father." His mother grinned at him. "It's kind of just retribution."

Caleb scowled. "That isn't helpful."

"But just a little satisfying to me, honey."

Finishing the slice of acorn bread, Caleb muttered, "What am I going to do with her? She keeps defying me and getting into trouble. I'm afraid that if I can't find a way to reason with her, she's going to go too far." He sighed. "What is it with teenagers?" Including his younger self. "Why do they all seem to go crazy?"

Maddie laughed. "It's called hormones. A body that's mostly adult combined with a mind that's mostly child." She added, "Maybe you're taking the wrong approach." Her smile faded into a more serious expression.

"Wrong approach?" Was she going to place the blame in his corner? He couldn't help feeling defensive. "What is that supposed to mean?"

"You're so demanding with Angela that it surely backfires on you. You need to *listen* to your daughter, to understand what it is *she* wants. What is important to *her*."

"You mean this new kick about her becoming an artist?"

"It's not new, Caleb. She started drawing the moment she could use a crayon. You've been displaying her artwork for years."

"That's what you do when your kid creates something for you."

"Even if you don't like it?"

"I never said that. I love it. She has incredible potential. But thinking you can make a living as an artist isn't practical."

"So you dash her dreams."

"What should I do? Encourage her to live in poverty? Being an artist doesn't bring in a regular income. I keep trying to tell her she needs to have a real job and that she can do her art on the side."

"Which makes her dream sound unimportant. An afterthought."

"If I could make it work for her, I would."

"Then try to help her find a way. There are jobs with regular incomes for trained artists. Help her see that she can channel her creativity to something that will support her like graphic arts—or *teaching* art—while she creates a portfolio that she can take to art shows or galleries. When you tell her to do art on the side, it sounds…dismissive. Be positive and supportive instead of demanding she do things your way all the time."

Mom had a point. He could be gruff, he supposed. "All right. I'll think about how I can do that."

"Good." Mom held out a plate to him. "More bread?"

"Did you think I might say no?" He took another piece.

As he spread the butter and jam, he realized his mother was staring at him intently. "Something on your mind, Mom?"

"So what's going on with you lately? Terese Kistler said she saw you with the Huber woman walking through Green Meadows yesterday. Were you making peace over Angela?"

The reminder of their private walk through the development warmed Caleb inside. "As a matter of fact, Grace offered to give me a tour of Green Meadows, so I could see how it's progressing. I was very impressed."

"With the development or with Grace?"

He didn't hesitate. "Both, actually." Though he'd already realized his attraction to the woman was hopeless until he straightened things out with his daughter.

"Oh, I see."

"No, you don't." He quickly tried to backtrack before his mother made a big deal of it. "We simply have a lot in common. Environment-wise, that is."

She raised her eyebrows and gave him a challenging expression. "So you don't actually like Grace? As a woman, I mean."

"Yes, I like her."

"Then you'll ask her out."

He shook his head. "The timing is all wrong."

"Because she's seeing someone else?"

"No. Well, maybe. I don't know. I didn't ask. It's not her, it's me." He sighed and set his acorn bread back on the plate. "Rather, it's Angela."

"So Angela doesn't like her."

"Angela doesn't really know her." But that didn't prevent Caleb from assuming the worst. He couldn't count on anything when it came to his daughter these days.

"Then what's the problem?" his mother asked.

"Lily is the problem. I told you about the mural. When I tried to talk to Angela about defacing private property, it turned into something else. She admitted she thought I took her mother from her. I explained what happened, but at the moment she's obsessed with feeling abandoned. I have no idea where this is coming from. Teenage imagination, I guess. I just don't see how I can bring another woman into the mix right now."

"Angela might not like it at first, but she'll come around. She has before. You dated several women while you were in school."

"None were serious."

"So this Grace Huber…" His mother cleared her throat. "You could be serious about *her*?"

Caleb started. Not a question he'd asked himself. Not one he wanted to explore too deeply right now. "Mom, you're jumping the gun. I like her, but I haven't even asked her out on a date."

"Then maybe it's time you did something about that."

CHAPTER FIVE

"I WANT A big stack of pancakes with lots of whipped cream," Taylor announced as they left Heather's van parked just down the street from the co-op. "With cherries on top."

"I'm not sure they have whipped cream, sweetie, and I know they won't have cherries," Heather told the child. Then she explained to Grace. "Cherries on top are her new thing. Rick bought a big jar of maraschino cherries to put on everything...mashed potatoes, broccoli, cottage cheese." She grinned, probably thinking of her hunky new husband. "He's spoiling both twins."

"We're not spoiled." Addison slipped her hand into Grace's and smiled up at her like a little angel. The eight-year-old looked incredibly cute with a missing tooth. Grace smiled back and squeezed. "I just want mine completely plain," the girl said. "Not even syrup."

Taylor made a face. "Yuck."

"Come on," chided Heather. "People have

different tastes. Just because you like whipped cream doesn't mean Addison has to like it."

"O-o-okay." Taylor flounced along, then tossed her head. "But pancakes are better with whipped cream."

"No, they're not," singsonged Addison.

Heather frowned. "Shh!"

They stepped up on the sidewalk and walked toward the co-op about a block away. There were so many cars parked in downtown Sparrow Lake that they'd had to hunt for a space, because of the festival. Heather spoke to several people they met on the way, introducing Grace, who appreciated the friendly gesture. Not that she would be able to remember all the new names.

A whizzing sound made all of them glance behind them. A boy on a skateboard approached swiftly, drawn by a very large, spotted Great Dane on a leash. As the dog and skateboard whizzed past in a flurry of huge paws and wheels, Heather drew Taylor closer, keeping her out of the way.

The little girl stared openmouthed. "Wow!"

"We could do that with Kirby!" cried Addison.

"No, we're not getting a skateboard so you can hitch it to the dog," Heather told them firmly. "It's too dangerous." She turned to Grace. "And that kid is a danger, too. He could have knocked us off the sidewalk!"

Grace merely nodded, smiling, but the twins continued to jabber about the big dog until they reached the co-op building, an old storefront with an entrance refinished with brick. A line of people stood outside, waiting to go in.

"Wow, Pancake Day must be popular," murmured Grace. She'd dressed down for the occasion, as Heather had suggested, forgoing her usual business attire for loose black trousers, a short-sleeved blue cashmere sweater and a leather moto jacket.

Heather nodded. "Free food. Don't worry, the line will move fast. There are at least two pancake stations set up."

"Ooh," said Addison. "I smell sausage."

"And bacon," added Taylor.

"Yes," agreed Heather. "You can have both if you want. Consider this 'dunch' or 'linner,' okay? We won't need anything else but a small snack before you go to bed tonight."

The line did move quickly and they were soon inside, heading down a hallway toward the main room. There, long tables had been set up for people to sit and eat, and other tables formed a barrier near the walls where grills were being manned to cook mounds of pancakes and breakfast meats. As they approached the nearest pancake station, Grace glanced back at the townspeople already eating, laughing and chatting. All the cooks were men, people she'd seen around town and who Heather had said were employed by the co-op or the creamery. Two tables were set up with butter and cream… but no whipped cream. Taylor stood on her tiptoes and looked around. Addison laughed and did a little whirl.

Grace grinned. "They sure have a lot of energy."

"You'd think some of it would wear off as they get older, but the girls just seem to find more," Heather said with a laugh.

"There's ice cream over there," Taylor told her mother. "Vanilla soft-serve."

"Well, maybe we can get you some of that," said Heather.

The twins stopped talking as they both got plates of pancakes. Addison ordered a stack of two but Taylor wanted three.

"Honey, I think two will be enough for you. Those pancakes are pretty big."

"I want three!"

"You'd better eat them." Heather lowered her voice in an aside to Grace. "Or not. I don't want her to get sick."

Grace just laughed and ordered a stack of three for herself. She also got three strips of bacon and three sausage links.

Then they turned toward the tables in the center of the room, most of them already full. Apparently the whole town turned out for Pancake Day, so Grace looked for the one face she would be happiest to see.

Disappointed.

Apparently the whole town had turned out except for Caleb Blackthorne.

As they sat down, Heather began introducing her to the people around them, and if they owned or operated a business, she included that information, as well. Grace tried to mentally keep track of everything Heather told her, but she feared she'd already forgotten half of what she'd been told. Then Heather realized they'd forgotten drinks and got up to fetch glasses of milk for the girls and two cups of coffee for themselves.

Taylor dug into her food hungrily. She'd gotten a cup of soft-serve ice cream, which she dumped on top of her pancakes. Addison cut her plain pancakes into dainty pieces and chewed equally daintily. Grace wondered how two sisters born at the same time could be so different.

"Slow down," Heather told Taylor, "or you might end up with a tummy ache."

Grace spread fresh creamery butter on her pancakes and laced them with syrup. "Yum. I can see why so many people turn out for Pancake Day."

Heather bit into a piece of crisp bacon. "It's not just the food, it's the sense of community, of everyone taking a short break from work to celebrate spring with friends and family and catch up with people they don't often get to talk to."

Looking around, Grace saw so many smiles, heard so much laughter, that she couldn't help but grin. Never having experienced anything like this in Milwaukee, where neighbors didn't necessarily even know each other—Grace was acquainted with only one other woman in her condo building—she responded to the positive energy in the room. There were a lot of things she liked about Sparrow Lake, and the feeling of community just went to the top of her list. She imagined that even if you lived alone, you would never have to be lonely in a friendly town like this.

Heather had been right about her coming to the event. Several people wanted to know how the green community was faring, and others asked what her plans for the future might be. Lots of interested questions from potential residents or simply people who might help spread the word to friends in nearby towns. People came and went, but the twins went back for second helpings, so, content to stay awhile longer, Grace fetched another cup of coffee.

Just as she brought it back to the table, she looked up to see a familiar face. Three familiar faces, in fact. Caleb had arrived with Angela and Kiki. They had just filled their plates with food and were looking around for a place to sit. As if he knew she was staring at him, Caleb turned in her direction. Their gazes met and her stomach did a little flip when his lips turned up in a big smile aimed her way. She waved. Then Angela saw her, and the girl's lips tightened.

"C'mon," Grace heard Caleb say to his daughter and her friend. "There's room over there."

Over there was across from her and Heather and the twins. Grace sent him a welcoming smile. "Hi, Caleb."

"Grace, Heather…good to see you, both," he said as he set down his food.

"You, too, Caleb," Heather said.

Grace's pulse thrummed. "I was hoping we might run into each other."

Caleb took the seat directly across from Grace, Angela and Kiki reluctantly joining him. Caleb introduced the women to the girls. Angela didn't say anything, simply slapped down her plate and threw herself into her chair. Kiki avoided looking at anyone.

Oh, great. Talk about awkward. Grace figured the teenagers recognized her from the mural incident.

As if he didn't notice his daughter's attitude, Caleb gave her cup of coffee and empty plate a quick look. "I take it you already ate."

"More like overate," Grace said. "But it was delicious, worth every calorie."

He eyed her more thoroughly. "Not that you need to worry about it."

Grace started to laugh until she noted Kiki's sour expression. Definitely aimed her way.

A loud *bam* startled them all, and Grace turned to see the twins near a food table, an entire bowl of butter turned upside down at their feet.

"Oh, no," Heather groaned, pushing herself away from the table. "I knew something had to happen. Things were too peaceful."

Grace laughed. "It's probably an accident. They didn't mean to cause any trouble."

But then she noticed Addison stooping to pick up a glob of butter with one finger and promptly flinging it at her sister. Heather bore down upon the pair and Grace turned back to her food, not wanting to watch the twins get reprimanded. Even an angelic-looking child could be naughty, she guessed.

Caleb grinned and gave his daughter a penetrating look. "They can get into trouble no matter the age."

At which point Angela turned her back on him and went forehead to forehead with Kiki, whispering. Caleb merely rolled his eyes and continued smiling at Grace, who felt a sudden attack of butterflies whirl through her stomach.

She said, "I understand Pancake Day is a tradition."

"I've been here every year since I moved into town."

"I can understand why. It's a lot of fun, and you get to see people you probably don't see often." Like him. She was definitely glad she'd run into Caleb. She hadn't met a man who interested her this much in ages. "Are there other community events like this?"

"The big Memorial Day picnic. Fourth of July fireworks over the lake. The cow parade. Labor Day, when everyone pitches in to spruce up the town square and other public areas, then take part in a potluck. We have a Christmas party…Valentine's Day…Easter egg hunt…"

"Got it. Sounds nice. Not that we don't have holiday activities in Milwaukee. We have lots of them, but it's not like the whole city can come together as you do in a small town."

"So you like Sparrow Lake?" Caleb asked, the personal timbre of his voice getting to her.

Swallowing hard, she met his gaze directly. "More and more every day."

"Ever think about staying?"

"Permanently?" Surprised by the thought, Grace said, "Milwaukee is my home. I've lived there all my life other than when I went to college in Chicago." An even bigger city. "And for the past year, I've been splitting my time between home and here." Though lately, she hadn't even made it back to her condo every weekend. "I rent an apartment here in town."

"You could build yourself whatever kind of home you want over at Green Meadows."

"I suppose so, but our main office is in Milwaukee." Now Grace was getting a little nervous. She realized Angela's eyes had widened as if in alarm. What was the teenager's problem? She focused on Caleb. "I—I know it's commuter distance, but I've really enjoyed the lack of traffic and getting to work in five minutes most days."

"If Phase 2 becomes a reality, you should consider it."

There was an appeal to living where she worked…but was it realistic? Dad would probably throw a fit if she suggested it. He would demand to know how she was going to run the company long distance. Grace wouldn't disappoint her father by arguing the point that she didn't want his job. And yet… she realized Caleb sounded as if he wanted her around. The idea warmed her through and through. Too bad it seemed as if Angela didn't agree with her dad. The girl's expression had closed, but Grace sensed she was seething inside.

Her smile fading, Grace murmured, "Something to think about."

Angela popped out of her chair, Kiki following suit.

"Getting seconds?" Caleb asked.

Now Angela glared at *him*. "Getting out of here."

"I'm not ready to leave yet."

"Fine with me." The girl whipped around and headed for the door with Kiki.

"How are you getting home? Walking?" When his daughter didn't answer, Caleb reluctantly rose. "I'd better go after her," he told Grace. "She's still grounded. I made an exception for Pancake Day. My mistake."

Grace forced a smile to her lips. "Well, it was good seeing you."

Nodding, he took off after his daughter.

Leaving Grace feeling a little empty and alone.

WHAT NOW? CALEB WONDERED, as he dodged several townspeople carrying loaded plates in one hand, cups of coffee in the other.

"Oh, Caleb, there you are." Margaret Becker stepped in front of him. "I wanted to talk to you about possibly co-teaching a limited workshop or two this summer. Combining art forms with conservation. That would give us opportunities for field trips."

Retired but now teaching part-time as an adjunct professor, Margaret was a vibrant seventy-year-old with bright red hair and an eye-popping colorful wardrobe. She was one of his favorite people from the college.

"I would love to talk to you about it," he said, slipping around her, "but I have to catch up to Angela. I promise I will call later!"

Margaret nodded. "I understand. Go get your girl."

Which was exactly what he tried to do. But as he hit the street and looked around, he didn't see Angela. Or Kiki. He stood there for a moment. Where had they disappeared to so quickly? An engine revved nearby and a moment later, a motorbike shot out from the south side of the building and spun around the corner, Angela clinging to Kiki, who was driving the thing.

"Angela!" he yelled.

She heard him, because she glanced over her shoulder for a second before turning her face away from him.

Caleb clenched his jaw and turned his body to steel so he wouldn't race for the car to go after them. That would be a sure way to cause an accident. If he went home, would she be

there? Though they were headed in that direction, he sorely doubted it.

"You didn't catch up to her?"

Grace. He turned to her as she moved
closer, a concerned expression on her pretty
face.

"She got away on a motorbike with Kiki.
I didn't even know Kiki had one, or I would
have forbidden Angela from riding with her."

"No helmets?"

"They had helmets. And I'm assuming
Kiki has a driver's license since she's older
than Angela."

"Well, I'm sure they'll be fine, then," Grace
said agreeably.

"Angela won't be. I'll ground her until her
eighteenth birthday!"

Grace placed a hand on his arm. "I think
you need to take a breath, Caleb. A really
deep one."

"Will it help the situation?" he asked,
thinking her touch was calming him down.

"I would guess it'll help your skyrocketing
blood pressure."

Caleb sucked in a lungful of air and let it
go with a whoosh. Clueless as to his daughter's behavior, he shook his head. "What was
that all about, anyway?"

"They were probably bored."

"I'm sure you have a point. That's the very reason I let Angela come today. She begged me to let her out of the house just for a little while. Then when we got here, Kiki was waiting for her. I think they had the escape planned out."

"Maybe."

But Grace didn't look so certain.

"What else would have driven her away?" he asked.

"Well, um, truthfully...maybe...*me*?"

"You mean because you took charge the day of the mural debacle?"

"Partly. She, um, didn't look thrilled when you were talking to me."

He'd been asking Grace if she'd thought about moving to town...mentioned Phase 2... said she should consider it. Hmm. It seemed that Angela was jealous of his interest in Grace, no matter that he hadn't even asked the woman out. He remembered the conversation with his mother about his daughter feeling abandoned...his reluctance to bring another woman into the mix...his mother's telling him that Angela would come around...

Ask her out...now...

The thought wouldn't go away.

Kindhearted and with their passion for the environment, Grace was exactly the kind of woman he would like to get to know better. He hoped Angela wouldn't do something purposely to ruin this chance for him.

So he said, "I was wondering if you were busy on Saturday."

"Saturday evening?"

"Late afternoon, early evening?"

"Um, well, no. I mean, I'm free." Grace's expression went from bemused to pleased. In a very cute way.

Making Caleb grin at her. "The weather is supposed to be unusually warm this weekend, and I was thinking we could take a boat out on Sparrow Lake."

"You want to go fishing?"

"Not exactly. I was just thinking about circling the lake, maybe having a picnic dinner in the nature center there."

She smiled and her whole face lit up, and in response he lit up from the inside out.

"Sounds nice," she said, eyes shining as they met his. "I would love to do that with you."

"Great."

The fact that Angela might be annoyed flicked through his thoughts, making him wonder how he could bring her around. Grace had Angela's best interests at heart. If only his daughter could see that.

"ARE YOU SURE you want to do this here?" Kiki asked.

"Positive. This is exactly the right place."

They got off the motorbike Kiki had "borrowed" from her ex-boyfriend Viper. Angela suspected Viper didn't know that Kiki had it, but she didn't care any more than she cared about being on the rez where Gran Maddie lived. She wanted to make sure her mother got this message, and the big public bulletin board to the side of the recreation center would be perfect for it. While residents shopped in the village stores, no one was around here at the moment. Now she simply had to work fast before anyone spotted them.

"Let's hurry."

They unloaded the cargo bag. Kiki had brought another set of acrylics and brushes that Angela had paid for with her allowance. Then Kiki pulled myriad posters and notices from the bulletin board as Angela opened containers.

"What are you going to paint this time?"

"My mother." At least that would be the focus of the painting.

"Yeah, but the photo you have of her was taken a million years ago, before you were born. She might not even recognize herself. And you might get into big trouble this time."

Angela gritted her teeth. "You can leave if you don't approve."

"I wouldn't do that." There was a slight note of panic in Kiki's voice. "You know I'm your friend."

"And I'm yours, Kiki, no matter what."

"Well, I'm staying."

"Then let's get this thing done." Angela rummaged in the bag of paints. "I want plenty of black and acid blue. Then white. For lightning. We're gonna paint a great big goth 'spirit buffalo' with smoke coming out of his nostrils and lightning shooting out of his sides."

Kiki found a big piece of discarded cardboard they could use as a palette and laid it down on the ground.

"I thought this was about your mother."

"She's going to be riding the buffalo."

After watching Angela sketch out the basics, Kiki picked up a brush and followed her lead.

"Wow, the white you're using for your

mom's face makes her look like a zombie. That's so sick!" Kiki said admiringly. "Maybe she should be wearing a skull necklace."

"Good idea. She's coming for vengeance."

"She left you. You're the one who should be getting vengeance."

Angela shook her head. "I think Dad sent her away. She's after him…and everybody else on this reservation. Obviously they didn't care enough about her."

When they were done with the painting, both girls stepped back to admire their creation. The lightning burst out in jagged spears, while the buffalo and his wild-haired rider both looked absolutely insane. Insanely cool, that was.

"What do you think?" Angela asked, a big smile on her face.

Before Kiki could answer, a rough male voice interrupted, "I think you are in trouble, young lady."

Angela jerked around and came face-to-face with Harold Fox, one of the tribe's elders.

CHAPTER SIX

CALEB FELT AS if he was at his wits' end as he parked in front of his mother's house. He'd barely had a half hour of happiness thinking about his upcoming date with Grace before getting the call from Mom. Climbing out of the truck, he slammed the door to let off some steam. He'd known something was up when Angela had ridden off on that motorbike with Kiki. Rather than going home where she belonged, his daughter had gotten herself in trouble yet again, and while she was still grounded, no less.

His mother came out on the stoop to meet him. "Your face looks like it was hit by a thundercloud."

"Yeah, a real Summer Storm."

Mom actually smiled at that. "My granddaughter *does* have talent." She hugged him. "And the temperament of a true artist. She paints what she feels, and she's obviously feeling a lot of difficult emotions right now."

Hugging her in return, Caleb said, "Yes, but she's creating where she's not supposed to. First the community center at Green Meadows, now the rez's recreation center."

"I told her she needed permission."

"You knew about this?"

"She mentioned how she would like to make her mark at the rez when she was here the other day. I tried to advise her on how to get her work approved." Maddie shook her head. "She should have listened to me." His mother cupped his cheek as if in sympathy. "This is no end-of-the-world situation. Angela just painted a mural on the bulletin board. Harold Fox said it was a very vivid, if inappropriate, image."

Sighing, Caleb called, "Angela, come on out. We're going home!"

"Honey, she's not here. Harold insisted the girls paint over the work and restore the bulletin board with the signs and posters they removed. He said he would give back the keys to the motorbike when they finished."

Even though he was angry with Angela, Caleb wouldn't mind seeing the work for himself. It had to be related to the Green Meadows mural. Had to be about his daughter's emotional upheaval over her mother's continued absence. But a wild woman on a buffalo? He needed to find a way to talk to her about it.

"I'm going to head over to the center, then."

"Walk," Mom said. "It'll give you a few minutes to even out that temper of yours."

"All right," he groused, brushing his mother's forehead with a kiss before going after his daughter.

The recreation center was a five-minute walk that started down a street lined with tidy houses, several with big yards. Two goats frolicked in one of the fenced properties, and chickens squawked from another. A woman was out working on her early spring vegetable garden and a toddler who reminded him of his Angel at that age was helping.

Where had the years gone? He would give anything to go back in time a little, to when his daughter still thought he sprinkled the heavens with stars just for her. Now he couldn't even get her to respect his wishes.

Caleb turned the corner at the shopping area—the recreation center was on the other side of the village. He was halfway there when he saw a familiar-looking woman coming his way. His stomach immediately tightening, he stopped in his tracks.

It couldn't be…or could it?

He looked harder.

Long blue-black hair swirled around a traditionally attractive face that had matured since the last time he saw it. Broad cheekbones, straight nose, dark, fathomless eyes. Eyes he would know anywhere because they had once haunted his teenage dreams.

Eyes that widened when they set upon him. Still coming toward him, she murmured, "Caleb Blackthorne…"

"Lily Trejo." His voice was stiff. "What are you doing back here?"

"This is my home."

"You haven't been here in fifteen years, and your parents moved away more than a decade ago. What home do you mean?"

"The rez…or…well, that all depends." She moved closer, her lips turning up.

"On what?"

"On my being able to get a decent place to live. You can help with that." Lily zeroed in on him and placed a hand on his chest, gave him one of those flirty looks she had perfected as a teenager. "I need money for rent and food, Caleb. Or the least you can do is give me a place to stay."

Did she really think he was going to let

her back into his life? She was doing her best to charm him, but Caleb wasn't buying. That ship had sailed when she'd abandoned him and their baby and had never so much as called to find out how they were doing. Gripping her hand a bit harder than he meant to, he removed it from his chest. He wanted nothing to do with her personally. There was no soft place left in his heart for her anymore.

"My mother can help you find some place to stay and get you into a job program."

"I didn't say I was looking for work."

She tried moving closer again, but Caleb stepped back. "You can't think *I'm* going to give you any kind of assistance."

"It would only be fair so I can get a proper place to live for Angela and me. You had our daughter all these years. Now it's my turn."

"Angela? That's what this is about?" So this was why his daughter had gone off the deep end lately? Because of her mother's influence? Angela hadn't even told him she'd met Lily! "You're not taking her away from me!" He couldn't keep the edge out of his voice. "Angela isn't going anywhere with you."

Lily's expression grew cross. "She's a young woman now. She needs her mother's influence."

"Only if that influence is a good one."

"You mean like the influence of an outsider?"

"Excuse me?" He grew aware of people stopping in the street, staring at them.

"I've seen you with that woman."

Lily meant Grace. She must have seen them talking or something, since they hadn't even had their first date. "Who I see is none of your business."

"But our daughter *is* my business. I'm here for her now."

"I've been here for my daughter for fifteen years while you went off and—"

A shrieked "Dad!" got through to him.

Caleb rose from his cloud of anger to see his daughter standing in front of a knot of onlookers barely two yards away. How much had she heard?

"Angela—"

"Don't!" she yelled at him. "I knew you were responsible!"

"Angela," Lily said, using her sweetest tone. "I'm your—"

"I *know* who you are!" Their daughter shoved past them in the direction of his mother's house. "Right now, I hate you both, so leave me alone! I'm staying with Gran Maddie tonight!"

"Angela! Angel!" Caleb called in vain. Turning back to Lily, he said, "Now see what you've done. You left her easily enough. You said you didn't want any responsibility. You never even told her you loved her and that you were sorry to leave her!" Which he'd never stop holding against his child's mother. "Why couldn't you just stay away?"

He didn't miss Lily's hurt, though she quickly covered it with a neutral expression. She couldn't hide the tears in her eyes, though, as he turned and walked away from her the way she had from him and their baby all those many years ago.

ON SATURDAY MORNING, Grace found herself in the office again, since Dad had made an appearance, having driven out from Milwaukee to take a look at the landscaping proposal for Green Meadows. Grace had turned the landscaping blueprints and cost analysis over to him, then had retreated to her office. Distracted as usual from her growing stack of paperwork, she couldn't help smiling as she leaned back in her office chair and thought about that afternoon's date with Caleb Black-thorne.

Boating on the lake and a picnic at the nature center seemed like a fun way to end the week. He'd confirmed with a call the night before. She'd volunteered to bring the picnic and that morning, on the way into the office, had stopped at the Main Street Cheese Shoppe, where she'd asked Priscilla Ryan to pack a basket of goodies for her. She and Priscilla had developed a close friendship over the past year, though Priscilla spent most of her free time with her boyfriend, Sam Larson. Thinking about the handsome ex-rodeo rider, Grace couldn't blame her friend. She was looking forward to spending a little downtime with a man of her own one day.

Maybe Caleb Blackthorne…

A thrill ran through her at the now-familiar thought. She hadn't been able to stop wondering what it would be like to go on an actual date with him. They had so much in common, she looked forward to learning more about his ideas on conservation. And more personal things about him, as well. There was simply something about Caleb that was irresistible. A charisma that gave flight to a little fantasy on her part. The only negative was his daughter's obvious dislike for her. She hadn't forgotten the looks Angela had given her at the Pancake Day festival.

What could she do about that?

Hopefully time would soften the girl's attitude.

Assuming she and Caleb continued to see each other...

Grace sighed as she rose from her desk to meet with Dad in his office. He'd been more grouchy than usual with her lately, undoubtedly because she'd skipped the past couple of meetings he'd wanted her to attend in Milwaukee. She'd felt she was needed more here...and attending those meetings would only reinforce his determination to make her his successor in the company.

Grace did manage to pull herself together and put on a pleasant expression as she traded her office for her father's. Sitting behind his massive mahogany desk, where the landscaping cost analysis was spread out before him, he wore an expression of extreme disappointment when he met her gaze.

"Dad, what's up?"

"The numbers on the landscaping."

Uh-oh. "They are a little high because we're planning on using so many native plants."

Which were, admittedly, more expensive than the more popular plants one could buy from a big-box store.

"A little high? The cost analysis is twice what it should be."

"But totally worth the extra cost." Grace took a deep breath and placed her hands on the desk so she could meet his gaze directly. "This is a green community. It only makes sense to landscape the grounds so they meet the same standards."

"Who is going to know the difference?"

"I will. This is my baby, Dad. I want it to be perfect."

He scowled at her. "Or you can simply make it look good at a lower cost, an alternative you should be considering as the next CEO of this company."

There it was. Her father must sense her emotional upheaval about taking over for him. He'd never asked if she wanted the job. He'd simply assumed she would move up when he retired. And she couldn't tell him straight out that she didn't want to be a CEO, that she wanted to explore more green building, an idea that truly excited her. Her father had already suffered too much heartbreak in his life. She just couldn't admit she didn't want to be CEO, not when he counted on her so deeply, but she wasn't going to give up on Green Meadows, not without a fight.

She cleared her throat. "So let's be clear about this. Your only objection is the money."

"Profit is what makes a company a success."

"Walworth Builders *is* a success, Dad. You've devoted your life to it and it has done very well by you. By us." She tapped the papers on his desk. "How much of a difference will the cost of using native plants make in our lives? We have more than enough money."

His frown deepened. "The economy could make another downturn anytime."

"Then we'll deal with it the way you did before," she reasoned. "In the meantime, you have that new shopping center going up outside of Milwaukee. If you want to cut corners on landscaping, do it there, not here. Green Meadows is going to be a beautiful home to a lot of people. Let it be all that it can be."

"This is that important to you?"

"Yes, it is. And if there are extra costs, I'll find a way to deal with them. This is *my* project, Dad. Trust me to see it through."

He sighed but didn't let go of the frown. "Fine. If I can't trust the next CEO of Walworth Builders, who can I trust? When you're in my seat next year, you'll come to realize that *perfect* is more of a nice concept than a reality. But with that in mind, I won't interfere in your landscaping decisions."

"Thanks." Grace smiled, but her face felt stiff.

CEO...next year...

She had to keep reminding herself that as much as she wanted no part of that job, somehow she would have to make peace with the fact that it was hers.

CHAPTER SEVEN

BY THE TIME Caleb picked Grace up from the Main Street Cheese Shoppe, she was holding a woven picnic basket lined with a red-and-white-checked cloth.

"Looks mighty fancy for a picnic," he said.

"A nice presentation always makes good food taste even better."

He thought Grace looked pretty sweet herself in pale yellow pants and a matching cotton sweater. She'd pulled her long dark hair up into a ponytail. About as casual as he'd ever seen her. He liked it, made him feel more in tune with her somehow.

He took the basket from her and swung it in the back of his truck, laying it on top of the plaid blanket he'd appropriated from his daughter's sweat lodge. Helping Grace into the passenger seat wiped away thoughts of anything but the woman. As she brushed by him, her hair smelled real nice, like fresh lavender when a breeze blew through the yard.

Reluctantly letting her go, he rounded the truck and got in on the other side.

"So where do you keep your boat?" she asked as he pulled from the curb.

"I don't own. I rent from McClintock Boat, Bait and Tackle."

"Oh, John McClintock's place. I met him and Margaret Becker at the Cheese Shoppe," Grace said. "Priscilla told me they've been an item since Margaret's niece Kristen Lange Novak came back to work at Margaret's quilting shop a couple of summers ago."

"Proof that romance can happen at any age."

"So you're a romantic?" she asked.

"Try *hopeful*."

Grace laughed. "We have something else in common."

"See, it's working already." Caleb grinned.

He really liked Grace Huber. There was an easiness about her that made him feel good.

"It's a perfect day, don't you think, for an outing on the lake?" Grace said.

"Perfect," he agreed, swallowing hard.

Hopefully, some time spent in nature with charming company would distract him from his problems, at least for a few hours. Grace deserved his undivided attention, just as he deserved hers.

Within a few minutes, they'd arrived at Mc-Clintock's business and left the truck parked in the lot at the top of the slope.

When they went down to the landing, John McClintock greeted them personally. "Going out on the lake, are you? Good thing I saved this last boat for you." He winked at them. White-haired with bright blue eyes, the man was in his midseventies, retired and running a small, cherished business that kept him vital.

"Thanks, John. I appreciate it."

Margaret Becker was there, too. "Caleb. And Grace." Her eyebrows shot up as if in pleased surprise. "Good to see you both. Together."

Caleb grinned at her. "Sorry I haven't had that chance to call you about teaching those combined workshops yet."

"We still have a couple of weeks before we have to submit the proposal for a short-term project between summer and fall sessions. Maybe we could get together to talk about it next week."

"Sounds like a plan. I have an early morning class on Tuesday. Would you be free around ten thirty?"

"Perfect," Margaret said. "We can meet in the faculty break room."

That settled, they got down to the business of renting the sole boat tied to the dock.

"Stay out as long as you like," John said once they had climbed aboard. "If I'm closed when you bring it back, just make sure it's secure."

Caleb gave him a one-finger salute. "Will do."

Releasing the line and pushing away from the dock, he took over the oars and began rowing. The boat quickly shot toward the middle of the lake. Grace had draped herself backward, her face lifted up to the sun. She looked so pretty, relaxed as she was, that it made his gut tighten a bit.

Then she said, "So Margaret has some ideas for the two of you to combine your teaching areas in a class?"

"Apparently. Makes sense, especially for a late-summer workshop, perfect weather for going on excursions."

"So you would help them identify plants, and Margaret would then take over when they drew them?"

"I'm guessing that's her idea."

Grace nodded. "You'll give your students

a new appreciation of nature." She liked the fact that he was willing to try different things. They had that in common.

"I keep looking for ways to get my students invested in conservation."

"What? They aren't all enthusiastic?"

Caleb pulled at the oars and the boat flew across the calm water. "Most of them take my beginning class to fulfill their biological science requirement. They choose it rather than having to dissect small animals."

Grace shivered. "Oh, I wouldn't like that, either. But if I took your class it would be because I was truly interested."

"You would take a beginning class?" he asked.

Did that mean she was really thinking about it? Because she was considering staying in the area? The idea warmed Caleb toward her even more.

"Possibly. Assuming I'm still around."

He let the subject drop for a while, simply taking pleasure in the sun and the breeze blowing over them. Taking more pleasure in watching Grace, who seemed to absorb the experience as if it was her first time flying across a lake in a rowboat. He doubted that was true, because she was an outdoor person.

Liked hiking and birding, so no doubt any kind of boating was on her list, as well.

They skimmed the smooth waters and quickly reached the nature center. Caleb was glad to see that the small dock was free. They would have the picnic area to themselves. Alone with Grace Huber…he had to admit this was perfect. He tied up the boat and helped her out, then picked up the basket and blanket and led the way to a flat area that would give them a spectacular view of the lake and the houses lining the shore.

Spreading the blanket, he asked, "What about Phase 2 for Green Meadows? Do you think you'll go ahead with it?"

"Still under consideration." Grace sat and pulled the basket to her, then set out paper plates and plastic cutlery.

"What would be the downside?"

"Lack of sales." She spread out the largesse of goodies—sandwiches and small containers of potato and fruit salad, plus a couple of sample cheeses and crackers, along with cans of soda and packets of gourmet cookies. "Only half of what we've built so far is sold or rented. Things were going at a good clip until the past week or so. We need to be further along to make the time and monetary commitment." A shadow crossed her face. "The reason we don't need any adverse publicity."

Wondering if something negative had hit the press, he didn't want to ask and ruin the afternoon, so he sat across from her and kept his silence on the matter as he heaped his plate with a little of everything.

Tasting a cheese new to him, he said, "This is really a treat. You went to a lot of trouble."

"You can thank Priscilla for that. I gave her free rein, just told her to pick whatever she thought would be good."

They clinked sandwiches together as if in a toast and started eating. Caleb hadn't realized how hungry he was until he'd nearly wolfed down the first half. He guessed he hadn't been eating too well the past few days. But being with Grace gave him an appetite. Realizing she'd barely eaten half of what he had, he slowed down so she could catch up to him. And he decided to broach the topic he'd been avoiding.

"So are you really worried about adverse publicity?" he asked.

She shrugged. "Interest in the available units actually has slowed down this week. I'm hoping spring vacation just pulled potential buyers and renters in different directions with the kids out of school and all."

"Good point." Caleb took another bite of his sandwich and thought about the single problem he could see. "What about the guy from Spooky Tours? Has he been back?"

"Not yet. Not a tour per se. At least I haven't spotted that old bus of his. But I suspect we haven't heard the last of him, considering he's managed to have someone distribute fliers all over town."

He hadn't known that. His concerns had been far more personal the past week. Even when he tried his best, he couldn't keep Angela's unhappiness out of his thoughts. But he would make an even greater effort this afternoon for Grace's sake.

"So what if it doesn't happen?" he asked. "Phase 2?"

She shook her head. "Then I'll be done here in Sparrow Lake."

And here he was just getting to know Grace. "So you'll go on to your next project." The thought of her leaving saddened him.

"There is no next project." She frowned. "Not a *green* project that I can get behind."

"I thought that was your dream."

"Yes, mine, but not my father's. His dream

is to retire and leave Walworth Builders in my hands."

He could see that she didn't look happy at the thought. "I sense your lack of enthusiasm for that plan."

"I never wanted to be CEO. Not of anything."

"But you're considering it."

"I don't see that I have a choice," she admitted. "I'm the only Huber left to take over. Unfortunately Dad doesn't appreciate my slant on our work or my hopes for the company's future."

"You don't have to work for him, do you? Any number of green companies would be glad to have you." Being an environmentalist himself, Caleb appreciated Grace's dreams. "Living up to your father's aspirations instead of your own is very generous of you, but maybe misguided where your own desires are concerned."

Her voice took on a slight edge when she said, "Loyalty is never misguided."

"I'm just thinking it's making you unhappy."

"You don't understand the big picture."

Caleb realized that was true. And that maybe—if he wanted to get to know her better—he needed to understand what she meant. "So tell me about it."

"Dad has done everything for me since my brother died and Mom couldn't cope. She left us. I was a mess. Got into trouble. May have gotten into *serious* trouble if Dad hadn't saved me. I was going off the deep end, and he pulled me back."

The way he was trying to do with Angela, Caleb thought. No wonder Grace was so understanding and supportive of his daughter. She must identify with her.

"He sounds like a good father."

"A *great* dad. He made me see that my life wasn't over, and that what I did with it mattered."

"It *does* matter. But it should be something *you* want to do, not something he wants *for* you."

"It's kind of a moot point." She shrugged again, as if she had no control over the situation. "I'm an amateur at all this green stuff anyway. I mean, I've been reading a broad range of experts and I've been trying to incorporate the best ideas. I may be learning as fast as I can, but I don't know enough to be a true environmentalist. I'm just playing with the idea at Green Meadows."

"It seems to me you've done a great job there," he insisted. Obviously, she was learning fast.

"Thanks."

"And it would be a terrible waste of your drive and desire if you gave it up simply to fulfill someone else's dream."

"It's a complicated situation."

"But you need to do what's best *for you* even if your father doesn't agree. You have to take a stand."

Irritation crossed her features. "I'm sorry, but you just don't get it."

This time she sounded annoyed with him, making Caleb back off once again. "Apparently not," he muttered, diving into a second sandwich. The last thing in the world he wanted to do was create more strife in either of their lives. He just wanted a chance to enjoy being with her.

If that was even possible now.

The atmosphere between them had suddenly thickened. His fault for not minding his own business, he guessed. But he couldn't help himself when he saw what a strong love for the land Grace had. Environmentalism was his passion, and he'd finally met a woman he liked who shared it. He thought she had a real feel for successfully taking her father's company in a new direction.

Why couldn't she see that and follow her own heart?

IRONIC THAT CALEB was pushing her to defy her father when he was having the same problem with his own daughter. Angela wanted to be an artist and Caleb wanted his daughter to do something practical. In some ways, the two men were a lot alike. But both were devoted to their daughters, and that part she appreciated.

That both of them were telling her what to do now…not so much.

Her mood had been spoiled for a moment, and it was clear Caleb recognized that. His continuing to eat in silence bothered her. They'd had a lovely rapport going and she wanted it back. Talking about the potential for Phase 2 wouldn't hurt anything.

"Seeing your house gave me some ideas for Phase 2," she said.

"What kind of ideas?"

"Possibly building a half-dozen A-frames similar to yours in a heavily wooded area. That would appeal to a different type of resident than we have now."

"Sounds wonderful."

The return of Caleb's smile was wonderful, too, and warmed her inside.

Relaxing, Grace leaned in closer to him. "I'd just worry about how much of the wooded area I would have to clear."

"I'm the wrong guy to ask about that. I had my place built in a clearing that already existed, so I didn't have to remove any trees. I don't know much about planning construction myself, even if I know how to do the grunt work of building. I assume you have someone who could advise you."

"I do. Several someones, probably. It's just a little early in the game, since I don't even know if there will be a Phase 2."

As if warming to the topic—and to her—he edged a little closer. "If there is, and if you were to build a home for yourself, what would it be like? Would you want an A-frame?"

"I'm not sure. Maybe." Her pulse picked up a beat and she felt a bit breathless with him so close. "I know I would like to bring the outdoors inside with a big screened porch. And take the indoors outside with an outdoor kitchen and living area."

"Sounds like you've put some thought into it."

"A little dreaming here and there."

She took the last bite of her sandwich and as she swallowed, he reached out and rubbed a thumb against the side of her mouth.

Startled, she stared at him wide-eyed, and her heart thumped so hard she swore he could hear it.

"You had a little mustard there," he murmured.

"Oh. Thanks." She shrugged. "Messy eater."

He grinned and she couldn't help but laugh. The easiness with which they'd started their date had returned.

Deciding to turn the focus on him, she said, "So tell me about your classes. I really will consider taking one if I have the opportunity this summer."

"We're already past midterm, so most of the students are preparing final projects. Well, hopefully they are. The good ones will come through."

"And the others?"

"Some will undoubtedly fail." Sighing, he shook his head. "I wonder why they're there when they obviously don't want to be. Fortunately, I've only seen a couple of those this year."

"Maybe they're finally getting the idea that education is important to their future.

And maybe you've had a positive influence on them."

He grinned at that, the softening of his rough features sending a thrill shooting through Grace. She liked seeing him like this. Natural. Easy. One with her.

"Weekend after next," he said, "I'm taking students out on an overnight field trip to the Ojibwe Woods between Green Meadows and the Chippewa Sparrow Lake Reservation."

"You're taking your students on a camping trip?"

He chomped into a cookie and nodded. "With sleeping bags and a bonfire. And tents for those who prefer more privacy. It's just overnight, but it's a way for them to get a better feel for the land, to be part of it."

"That sounds like a lot of fun. Not that I would know personally." Though she had always wanted to camp while in her teens especially, she hadn't been part of a group that was that adventurous. "I've never been camping."

Caleb started at the admission. "And here I thought you were an outdoor girl."

"I pretty much am. I just never had the opportunity to go camping with anyone."

"We can fix that." To Grace's surprise, he

asked, "How would you like to come with my class?"

Warmth flowed through her at his invitation, so she didn't hesitate. "I would love to go camping with you!"

Caleb's return grin was infectious, and Grace found herself laughing out loud with him. She couldn't help but think he was a man after her own heart...

THE INFERNAL YAPPING of a dog in the complex sent Olive flying into bed with Nellie that night, as if for protection.

"Go back to sleep, girl," Nellie moaned, patting the fur ball that shuddered against her.

"Me-e-eow!"

The complaint issued in her face popped Nellie's eyes open. And the continued yapping made her sit up straight in bed. Alarmed, she grabbed her glasses from the nightstand, shoved them on and squinted at the clock. Twenty past midnight. What in the world was going on?

She patted Olive, who squirmed under the covers. Grudgingly, Nellie left the comfort of her bed, slid her feet into slippers and pulled on a wrap before stumbling into her living room and peeking out the bay window. The moon was bright enough that she saw her neighbor Fran Willowby outside with her poodle, Sampson, whose voice still cut through the night as he jerked at his leash.

Oh, dear, who could sleep through that?

Nellie opened the door as her neighbor tried to rein in the dog. "Fran, is everything okay?"

"No! Sampson, c'mon, please!"

The dog stopped barking but he trembled as he stood, legs spread wide, and stared toward the wooded area, the very same area that had spooked Nellie the week before when Olive had gotten outside.

Fran jerked on Sampson's leash. With a final bark, he went off guard and walked with her back toward the apartment complex.

"I'm so sorry, Nellie," Fran said in a low whisper. She glanced over her shoulder as if looking for trouble.

"What's going on?"

"Sampson woke me. He was super anxious. I figured he just needed to relieve himself, but when we got out here, he headed straight for the trees and I couldn't stop him."

Not that the poodle was particularly big, but apparently he was strong enough to jerk his elderly owner around.

Nellie swallowed hard. "But you didn't see anything, right?"

She noted how Fran's eyes widened. "Um, well, something…"

"What?"

"I swear I saw something spooky running through the trees."

"Just like I did last week," Nellie whispered.

"Well, I don't like it. I don't feel safe here."

Nellie got that. She'd never figured what exactly had been out there. She pushed her glasses at the bridge so they settled in place on her nose, but as hard as she stared at the wooded area, she saw exactly nothing. "Did whatever it was threaten you in some way?"

"Well, no, it didn't come anywhere near me, but it scared me anyhow. Scared Sampson, too." She patted her dog, who seemed to have regained his comfort zone. "I don't like this at all, Nellie. I didn't sign up to live with ghosts. Moving into this complex was a mistake. If this area is haunted, I'm getting out before the ghost gets me."

Nellie remembered having a moment like that, thinking the place really was inhabited by a ghost. But that was silly. "You don't have to move anywhere, Fran." And hopefully, she wouldn't go around telling others what she'd seen or they might decide to move, as well. "There's no such thing as a ghost! Those Spooky Tour fliers just put the idea in our minds."

"You don't know that!"

"Look, I was afraid, too, until I had time to think about it. We do have animals in these woods. Deer—"

"No! It wasn't a deer. I'm telling you, it was something floaty and spooky looking!"

A thrill shot through Nellie. Just as she would have described it, too. Something that changed in shape. Undefined. Phantasmal.

But it was definitely not a ghost, because there was no such thing.

So what could they both have seen?

CHAPTER EIGHT

By MONDAY MORNING, Grace had heard all
about the new ghost sighting at Green Meadows. Gossip apparently was rife in Sparrow
Lake. Probably a form of entertainment for
the citizens. Only Grace wasn't entertained.
Fearful that the ridiculous rumors were going
to hurt her pet project, she knew she needed
to do something about them, so she decided
to hear firsthand what had gone down from
Nellie Martin herself.

Halfway through the morning, she gladly
abandoned her latest stack of paperwork to
walk over to Nellie's Treasures. She'd been
meaning to get over to the consignment shop
anyway. She believed in supporting local
small businesses, and Nellie had been one
of the first to move into the Green Meadows rental building, so having a look at her
store was the least Grace could do. Maybe she
would find something fun to buy. Glancing
in the window, she loved the peek into what

appeared to be a pretty boudoir with a fainting couch and vanity, the couch draped with a flowery dress and scarf, the vanity with beautiful jewelry and gloves and a spring hat.

Nellie had just opened, so Grace was the first customer of the morning. On her way inside, she passed the rack next to the door that held advertisements and fliers for local businesses. Including a stack of fliers that set her on edge. She froze there for a moment and clenched her jaw.

"Grace, how nice to see you."

"Nellie!" She whirled around to face the shop owner.

Nellie's smile fell into a frown. "What's wrong?"

Grace sighed and turned back to the rack. "It's these fliers from Spooky Tours."

"Oh, can you grab them? I meant to throw them away, but my hands were full when I came in."

Relieved, Grace scooped them up and handed them over to Nellie, who took them from her and disappeared through a doorway for a moment. When she came back into the store proper, she brushed her hands together as if satisfied she'd gotten rid of something distasteful.

"I didn't even know someone dropped those awful fliers in my store until I noticed them this morning. They're making people imagine things."

A good intro to what was on Grace's mind. "I heard something about another ghost sighting last night."

"My neighbor Fran thought she saw something in the woods."

"Did she describe it?"

Nellie shrugged. "Nothing real specific. Basically she saw what I did last week. Just something moving through the trees. Something floaty. Sampson sure didn't like it. Her dog," Nellie clarified.

"But it could have been another animal, then, right?"

"I thought maybe it was a deer, but Fran said that it wasn't."

"She was probably upset, so it could have been anything."

"That's what I was thinking. But this morning, Lavinia Miller told me her boy Johnny came home late from basketball practice last night, sounds like right before Fran and Sampson went out for that walk. He saw something in the woods, too, something different. Swore it was black and white and big—a cow—like in that story the Spooky Tours man told everyone."

"If there was a cow out there, there would be hoofprints," Grace reasoned.

"Even if it was a ghost cow? Johnny also said there was a spooky whishing sound."

Grace nearly choked on that idea. "Do you really think that's likely?"

"Heavens, no. I just think people are getting some kind of weird thrill with these stories." Nellie waved a hand. "Enough of that nonsense. What can I do for you this morning?"

Grateful that Nellie wasn't trying to make the haunting seem real, Grace smiled at her. "I needed a little break from work and I've been wanting to visit your shop. It is lovely." She looked around at the muted blue-green walls and the dressing area with pale peach curtains. All around her were racks of clothing, and in the middle of the floor, a mannequin was dressed to the nines, as if about to step out of the place to go to a special event.

"Are you looking for something in particular?" Nellie asked.

"Well, on Friday evening, I was thinking of going to the Ladies Auxiliary fund-raiser social." She was trying to take Heather's advice to meet as many people as possible to gain support for Green Meadows.

"Oh, aren't they raising money for the new air-conditioning system for the church offices?"

"Right. And I have either casual or business clothing with me. I wasn't planning on making a trip back to my condo in Milwaukee just to pick up a dress. I thought something new—or old," she said, since this was a consignment shop, "might be fun."

Nellie sized her up. "Try this rack. I think one of these dresses would work for you."

Grace started at one end, Nellie at the other. The dresses were colorful and decorative and beautifully designed, if not Grace's normal style. She usually chose solid colors and simple lines for herself. Dresses that didn't make a statement. But maybe she should try something new...

"What about this one?" Nellie said. "It will bring out the blue in your eyes."

Nellie pulled out a dress with blue and lavender flowers on a white background. She held it out to Grace, who—despite the flounced skirt that was something she wouldn't normally consider—took the dress from her. It was very feminine, very soft and dreamy compared with her usual pick.

Even so, she couldn't say no. "Let me try it on and see how it feels."

"Exactly," Nellie chirped. "You're going to feel wonderful in it."

And indeed, Grace did feel wonderful as she slipped the dress over her head and checked herself out in a mirror. It fit her like a glove and emphasized her curves. The colors were gorgeous. The style was perfect for a social event and fund-raiser. When she turned, the skirt fluttered out just enough that it made her smile. She loved it.

And when she paid for it, she couldn't help but wonder if Caleb Blackthorne would have the opportunity to see her wearing it.

IN TOWN THAT AFTERNOON, Caleb was picking up some cleaning supplies from the local hardware store, when Grace walked in. After looking over the rack near the door with free local papers and advertisements, she picked up a stack of fliers and approached the counter, where owner Lloyd Kinney, old Bob Kinney's nephew, was rearranging a display of key rings.

"Afternoon, Lloyd."

"Grace."

"Filling in for your uncle?"

Who must be about a hundred years old, Caleb thought as he moved closer.

"He says his back is out. If you ask me, he needs to retire."

Grace showed him the stack of Spooky Tour fliers. "Can you do me a favor? Dump these? This guy is hurting business over at Green Meadows," she explained just as Caleb approached the counter and set down his purchases. Grace gave him a quick smile before telling Lloyd, "This Vincent Pryce guy is worrying people about the place being haunted."

"Haunted?" Shaking his graying head, Lloyd took the fliers from her. "Sure thing, Grace. No one even asked if they could leave these here." With that, he dropped them in the nearby trash container.

"Green Meadows is a great place," Caleb said, earning another smile from Grace.

"So I've heard. The wife just redid the kitchen and bath in our place, so we're not looking for anything new, but I'll pass on the word to anyone I can."

"Thanks," Grace said. "Very kind of you."

Lloyd started adding up Caleb's purchases

and bagging them, but Grace seemed reluctant to leave.

And reluctant to lose her company so quickly, Caleb asked, "So are you going all over town getting rid of the fliers?"

She sighed. "Something like that. Everyone is being really agreeable."

"Which probably means you have nothing to worry about." Caleb paid and picked up his bag. "Besides, you'll get a lot of people from neighboring towns, as well."

"Oh, dear, do I have to go around collecting more fliers?"

"The flier doesn't identify where the ghosts are, so unless people actually take his tour, they won't make the connection."

"That makes sense."

She seemed relieved as he opened the door for her.

"So where's your next stop?" he asked, as they left the hardware store together.

"Green Meadows. I'm going to look for hoofprints."

"What?"

She reiterated Nellie's story about some kid seeing a "ghost" cow walking on a path along the wooded area the night before. By the time she finished they had reached her car, and

Grace leaned a hip against the door as if she needed the support. Laughing, Caleb drew as close as he could get to her without actually touching her.

Only he would really like to touch her. And kiss her. He'd been thinking about kissing her a lot.

His pulse thudded unevenly as he said, "You really think you're going to find proof that this cow was real?"

"Probably not, but I figure it'll only take a few minutes to check it out. This situation with supposed ghost sightings has really been gnawing at me. Something is going on, and I aim to figure out what it is."

Amused despite her sober expression, Caleb asked, "Want some company?"

"If you don't have anything more pressing…sure."

Anything as an excuse to spend some time with her. She made him feel young and energized again. He'd taken on so much responsibility raising Angela alone that he'd forgotten how good it felt to have fun. Like anything was possible. "All right then. Meet you in the community center lot."

Caleb grinned to himself all the way there. Grace had a way of doing that to him—

picking up his spirits. It seemed like a silly venture to go looking for cow hoofprints, but what the heck. She was concerned, and he wanted to help relieve her stress. Considering how hard she was working to make Green Meadows a success—with her father, then this shyster tour operator bringing her down—she deserved to have someone on her side.

Once parked, they left the lot, though Grace took him to the wooded area on a more direct route than she had last time.

"The Millers live in the condo building," she said, pointing. And farther back from the road, so closer to the woods, he noted. The three-story building was surrounded by trees. That would likely inspire a dose of fantasy, especially in a kid who might have been looking for a ghost. He didn't say so, though, simply let Grace take the lead. He enjoyed watching her as she started down the sidewalk that skirted the natural area farther from the buildings. He loved the way the breeze played with her hair. They followed the path for a while. He wished she wasn't so upset. Her steps seemed heavy, her spine straight and stiff.

Caleb reached out and placed an easy hand

on her waist, just to give her some psychological support. Besides, he liked touching her. "No hoofprints," he said.

She stopped. "No, but what's that?" Frowning, she pointed to a disturbance in the dirt along the sidewalk. "Some kind of weird lines."

"Looks like something went off the sidewalk...then back. Maybe a laundry cart?"

She hesitated for a moment. "The laundry for the units is next to the community center. No one would need to be pushing a cart over here."

"Wheelbarrow?"

"I don't see why one would be needed. At least in this location. Not until the landscaping is started. Workmen would take the scraps out the other direction."

She continued looking around with an intensity he couldn't miss. But when Grace found nothing else to catch her attention, they walked on until the sidewalk ended and the path changed from cement to a thick mulch.

"I guess there's really nothing to see, after all," Caleb said.

"Let's go a little farther."

Wanting her company for as long as he could have it, Caleb gave her no argument. He slid his hand a little farther around her waist and pulled her closer. She felt good pressed against his side. And she must have felt the same about being next to him, because he physically felt her relax a bit. She even threw him something of a smile.

"Thanks for indulging me."

"I have to admit my curiosity is aroused, too."

She slowed to a halt. "This is getting kind of silly, isn't it?"

Caleb gave her a sober expression. "You didn't hear that from me." And then he looked at the ground just beyond where they stood. "Wait a minute. What's that?"

Grace took a step forward, stooped and traced a finger along the impression in the mulch. "Looks like a pretty big paw print."

"Hmm." It was indeed very large. "A wolf?"

"Wolf!" She jerked and stiffened before he drew her even closer. He could see the hairs standing up on her lower arm. "You're kidding, right? There aren't any wolves around here."

She actually seemed scared.

Which gave Caleb the opportunity to take Grace in his arms as if for protection.

Keeping a straight face when he wanted to grin at her, he said, "Well, um, yeah there could be wolves around here. Despite the sanctioned wolf hunts now allowed in Wisconsin, they've been expanding their territory down from the north." He added, "Don't worry. They're a danger to rabbits, not people, but if we see one, I promise I'll protect you."

He held her a little closer.

She gave him a searching look. "Are you putting me on?"

Caleb chuckled. "Maybe a little. Wolves generally stay away from people. I took a wolf ecology workshop while studying for my degree. Though I can't say for certain that it's a wolf print, I can reassure you that it's not a hoofprint from a ghost cow."

Grace gave a sigh that dissolved into a soft laugh. "I know. I'm probably being ridiculously obsessive about this. I just wish I could figure out what's going on."

Letting her go, he laughed, too. "We could do some factual research about the original farm. If there were really murders or hauntings, some of that was bound to hit the local newspapers of the time. Maybe we can find out if these rumors have any basis. I've gotten curious."

"Do you think the Sparrow Lake Library keeps that kind of information from a century ago? Priscilla's mother still works there part time."

"Maybe not the local library. But the college library could have a history of the area. It would be far more comprehensive than the town library for sure. If they don't have the old newspapers online, they would probably still have them on some sort of microform."

"Hmm. Checking that out sounds like an idea. If we do find the history, I'll have whatever facts there are to make potential clients feel more comfortable."

"Let's do it, then." That would give him more face time with Grace. "I'm done teaching tomorrow at three. Can you be free then?"

"I'll make certain that I am."

They made plans on the way back to their vehicles. Grace would meet him at his classroom and they would spend the rest of the afternoon together.

Caleb walked Grace to her car and then hesitated a moment.

"Thanks for coming with me," she said.

A strand of hair played over her cheek. Using one finger, he brushed it aside and looked deep into her beautiful eyes. "I know investigating the area was an uncomfortable situation for you, so I'm glad I was with you. Truthfully, I enjoyed it. Enjoyed you."

"Me, too."

Her lips curving in a soft smile were too tempting to resist. He had to try them. Leaning in close, he stole a quick kiss. A soft brush of his lips across hers. A taste of what was to come if they kept spending time together.

Then they stared at each other for a moment, both grinning until Caleb said, "I'd better get going."

"Me, too. See you tomorrow."

"Right."

Climbing into his truck, Caleb could hardly believe how much he was looking forward to spending a spring afternoon in a library.

GRACE ARRIVED IN the Sparrow Lake Community College science building the next day with a bounce in her step. She was going to gather factual information that she could use to fight the crazy rumors going around. A ghost cow, indeed! Digging up the real story of the old farmstead with Caleb was a plus. She couldn't wait to see him again.

Checking the calendar on her smartphone for the number of Caleb's classroom, Grace took the nearest stairs to the second floor. His room was halfway down the hall and students were quickly rushing out the door. As she drew closer, she could hear voices coming from the room—more specifically, Caleb's calm, firm voice.

"No, you can't turn in your observation journal entry next week. It was due today," explained Caleb.

"I have to find another plot of woods. The one you told me to visit isn't there anymore."

"Not there? It was there when I drove by it yesterday morning."

"Well, maybe someone went in and chopped all the trees down, at least the decidiferous ones."

"I think you mean deciduous," said Caleb. "No, those trees were there, too."

"Maybe they burned."

"We would have heard the fire trucks from town."

Grace peeked around the corner to see Caleb facing a tall skinny kid dressed in a baggy sports T-shirt.

"Well, I don't know what else to tell you, Prof," the kid was going on.

"I'm sure you don't." Caleb's dry tone and

impassive expression hid what was probably irritation.

"It wasn't my fault."

Caleb picked up his briefcase. "Don't worry, you won't flunk because of an observation journal, Jeffrey, but I suggest you come to class from now on and keep up with the other assignments."

"I have to pass this class. Otherwise, I can't play basketball."

Caleb looked toward the door and saw Grace, an expression of relief suffusing his face. "I suggest you work as hard at your classes as you do at basketball practice."

"Yeah, right," the kid grumbled as he exited the classroom ahead of Caleb, turned left at the hallway and loped off.

Grace grinned. "Wow, that was something. Does he really think you'd believe a section of woods disappeared?" She couldn't imagine giving that kind of an excuse in college.

"I have no idea. We get some kids who don't know what they want to do in life, and their parents push them to keep going to school. Which is good…school, that is. Except for the ones who refuse to work at it. Or are more interested in basketball and hanging out with their buds." He closed the classroom door behind them. "Now you and I can get down to some real work." He pointed toward the stairs. "This way."

They quickly left the science building, one of five similar buildings spread over a couple of acres of land just outside town. Caleb seemed to be at home here, and Grace thought that was exactly as it should be. Work should be welcoming and satisfying and make a person happy. Today Caleb Blackthorne looked as happy as she was feeling.

"It's a beautiful place to spend your days," she said. "You're awfully lucky."

"I had a little to do with the environment. Several years ago, when I was first hired, and the last of the buildings was under construction, I was on the coordination committee, so I can take some pride in how well the campus all came together."

"That's the way I feel about Green Meadows," she admitted.

"Which means you've found your place. You simply can't give up your dream because your father wants something else for you," he reminded her.

Grace clenched her jaw rather than answer. Her father told her she had to do one thing, now Caleb told her she had to do something else. Two men telling her what to do. Right. She needed that, especially since she was firmly in the middle, wanting to fulfill her dream, but also wanting to make her father happy. Some days she almost convinced herself she could figure out how to do both, but realistically, she knew it came down to making a choice. And she already knew what that choice had to be. Dad had done everything for her to give her a great life. Could she do any less for him?

They reached the library, which was located in the middle of the campus. When they entered, Caleb approached a raised desk in the center of the room where an attractive woman sat, a single thick streak of gray through her otherwise dark hair. "Hey, Lorraine, I could use your help today."

The woman beamed at him. "Whatever you need, Caleb."

"We're looking for information on the old Whitman farm."

"Whitman. Hmm. What kind of information?"

"We want to find out what happened to the owners. There's a rumor going around about murders and hauntings and such."

Lorraine's eyebrows shot up. "I've been

hearing something like that about the new community." She turned her attention to Grace.

"Yep, Green Meadows is my project. I'm Grace Huber."

They shook hands.

"Nice to meet you, Grace."

Caleb said, "Green Meadows is a terrific place. You're the perfect person to spread the word. Some of the college's full-time faculty might be interested in living there."

Lorraine nodded. "I'm sure."

"Or if you know anyone else who wants to take a look at a condo or town house, let Grace know," Caleb continued.

He was being rather pushy, Grace thought. She needed more sales but announcing the availability of the dwellings to everyone they spoke to was not the way she wanted to do it. Not wanting to sound desperate, she preferred making acquaintances, then sending out mailers.

"And don't worry about those rumors about hauntings," he added.

"Hmm." The librarian looked thoughtful. "Hauntings."

Wondering why he had to bring that up, Grace joked, "Our friendly ghost tour operator is making up stories to get more customers. I hope he won't discourage anybody."

The librarian laughed. "I hardly think so." Then she got back to the task at hand. "What exactly are you looking for?"

"We need records that start at the end of World War I," Grace said. "Not sure how many years we need to check."

"Give me a few minutes."

Lorraine disappeared into the bowels of the library. Grace wandered over to a directory and map both of the campus and of the building, which also housed offices, the computer lab, the media production center and the cafeteria. Everything a student could possibly need outside the classroom. A large area of the library was devoted to research computers, and she could see that most were in use by students.

A few minutes later, Lorraine returned with a stack of boxes. "This is the *Sparrow Lake Journal* collection. Each microfiche holds a year of newspaper accounts. I brought all years from 1818 through 1925."

"That should do it," Grace said.

"Thanks, Lorraine." Taking the stack from her, Caleb led the way to a bank of computers hooked up to other equipment.

Grace was glad to see that, at the moment, they had free access.

"The microfiche and microfilm readers actually feed into the computers," Caleb said. "And if the original materials aren't the best, they can be manipulated so they are more readable. You can even save a file and make notes on it, then scan and email it to yourself if you want."

"Wow. I guess I'm a little behind on technology."

"You probably didn't have reason to go searching through old records before."

"True."

"It's easy enough. I'll get you started."

Grace sat. Caleb stood behind her and helped her hook up the microfiche that covered the *Sparrow Lake Journal* in 1918. He was so close and kept brushing her arm or hand with his, leaving her wildly distracted every time they made contact. It was a relief that once he set her up, Caleb seated himself at the station next to hers. Maybe now she could concentrate.

Going through the microfiche via the computer was fast work. Though the armistice hadn't been signed until November 11, Grace started in January and quickly scanned the weekly front pages, which covered the war and had pieces on local heroes who gave up their lives for their country. Nothing about anyone named Whitman, though. When she got to the end of the year, she glanced over at Caleb, who seemed to be going through 1919 at a more deliberate pace. He was doing more than simply taking a look at front pages. He was scanning through the entire journal, though in those days, the local paper was only six pages, so it didn't take him all that long, either.

When Caleb realized she was watching him, he said, "Oh, you're done. I'll set you up with 1920."

"Perhaps you could simply tell me what to do so I don't have to bother you every time."

But he was the one bothering her. He gave her instructions as she asked, but he stood so close behind her that his breath feathered the hair around her ear. A thrill shot through Grace so that she lost her grip on the microfiche, and the next thing she knew, Caleb grabbed for her hand…and covered it with his own. Her pulse surged. Surely he could feel it. Surely he could tell he took away her breath.

But when he said, "Here, let me show you

how to do it," she wondered if he even had a clue.

She concentrated on the process Caleb demonstrated for her. She really tried her best, but when he was done, she wasn't certain that she'd absorbed enough details to manage it herself.

Even so, she smiled up at him and murmured, "Thanks."

"No problem."

Yes, there was a problem. Caleb Blackthorne was a problem. Ack! No, to be honest, *he* wasn't the problem. *She* was. He was doing just peachy. While he was on an even keel, her attraction to the man was getting her more and more flustered.

She had to get her emotions under control.

He obviously liked her or he wouldn't have asked her to go camping with his class. But that was still more than a week away. Too bad he hadn't asked her out for the coming weekend…although she could ask him.

She had to stop thinking about him or she would never get anything done. Caleb was back in his own seat, setting up a new microfiche. Forcing herself to focus on the *Journal* on her computer screen, she went through 1920, a week at a time, checking every page.

And then, in the third week of December, she found the story: Couple Dies Due To Early Snowstorm.

Glancing over the article, she said, "Maynard Whitman did die in the farmhouse in 1920."

The next thing she knew, Caleb was behind her reading aloud. "Mr. Whitman died from a head wound. It appeared he took an accidental fall in the kitchen and hit his head on the edge of the table. His wife, Arlene, was found on the road. She died of exposure, and authorities conjectured she was trying to go for help for her husband."

He was close enough that his voice vibrated through Grace, distracting her yet again. What would it feel like if he put his arms around her…touched his lips to her ear…

"Well, that's a totally different story from the one Mr. Pryce is selling."

Grace practically choked at the reminder of their purpose for being there. "So no one thought it was murder."

That did relieve her somewhat. She could counter the tour operator's claims. What was stressing her out at the moment was…well, Caleb! Grace forced her attention back to the screen as he continued to read.

"The Whitmans are survived by their only son, Frank, institutionalized in the state hospital after returning broken by the Great War."

"Poor man," Grace murmured.

"Institutionalized. Not running around with weapons looking for more Germans. And no murdered ghost cow, either."

"Well, that's a relief to know."

"And now you have proof."

He helped her scan the article and send it to herself. Rather, he pretty much handled it all—he was definitely a take-charge type of man—and Grace spent the time just staring at him. He was also something to see, especially up close.

When he finished, they took all the microfiche back to Lorraine.

"Did you find what you were looking for?" the librarian asked.

"Thankfully, yes," Grace said. "For Green Meadows. Not for the poor couple and their son."

Caleb told her, "Both Whitman and his wife died in the winter of 1920, but there was no murder involved."

"Glad I could help you clear that up. I've seen those fliers around." The librarian shook her head, then said, "You know, my youngest sister has been talking about moving back to Sparrow Lake from Indianapolis. She'll be in town next week, actually. I was thinking about taking her over to Green Meadows. I know she lives in a new condo complex now, so I bet she would like your community."

"That's great," said Caleb, though the woman had been addressing Grace. He looked at Grace. "Have a card?"

She was already digging in her purse.

Caleb said, "Give Grace a call if you would like a personal tour of the place."

"Thanks."

Grace smiled but told Caleb as they left the place, "You know I can do my own sales work, don't you?"

"Sure, but I didn't think you'd mind some help."

"I don't mind. It's…"

"What?"

She really didn't want to complain when she knew he meant the best. "Nothing. Thanks."

"You're welcome. Amazing, you cleared up the mystery *and* have a potential new client all in one sweep," Caleb said, as they crossed to the parking lot. "That's a positive outcome."

"This couldn't have turned out better for me. Thanks for thinking of using the school library."

"I enjoyed the challenge. And spending some time with you. The highlight of my day."

"Mine, too," Grace admitted.

When they stopped at her car, he asked, "I was just wondering if you were free Friday night."

"Friday?" Her pulse jumped and she had to swallow hard to sound normal. "Actually, I was planning on going to the fund-raiser social being given by the First Presbyterian Ladies Auxiliary."

"Oh." The corners of his mouth turned down. "Well, maybe another time."

"Unless…um…you would consider going with me. I have to warn you, though. Heather recommended I use the event to make more contacts for Green Meadows, so I'll be meeting and greeting."

"As well you should. You need to get to know everyone." His mouth relaxed into a natural smile. "Get those new sales going and you won't be able to leave Sparrow Lake."

Caleb sounded as if he wanted her to stay.

"Then you wouldn't mind going with me?" she asked.

"I would love to be your escort."

And she would love for Caleb to see her in the new dress she'd just bought from Nellie's Treasures. "It's a date, then."

The final positive touch on an all-around good day.

CHAPTER NINE

"WHAT ARE YOU getting all dressed up for any-way?" Angela asked as Caleb walked into the living area buttoning the sleeves of his new-est and best shirt, the blue one Angela had given him for Christmas.

"I told you I was going to the fund-raiser."

"Without me."

"I didn't know you wanted my company. You haven't exactly been paying me any mind lately," he reminded her. "Besides, your grandmother wants to spend some quality time with her granddaughter."

"Gran Maddie already saw me this week."

True. But Angela had always liked being around her grandmother. Caleb eyed his daughter with suspicion. She'd barely started speaking to him again, so he didn't believe she was eager for his company. There was something else twirling around in her teen-age mind. Her eyebrows were pulled together in a huge frown and she was glaring at him.

"So you want me to tell your grandmother you don't want to see her again?" he asked.

"I didn't say that!"

Thinking she looked ready to pop, Caleb asked, "What *are* you saying?"

Silent for a moment, her expression darkening, she said, "You're going out with *her*, aren't you?"

And there it was.

Caleb knew that Angela meant Grace, and of course she was correct, but he'd avoided getting into details of his evening out so as to avoid the argument he'd sensed brewing since he'd arrived home from school.

He was trying to figure out how best to handle the situation when Angela asked, "What's going on with you and Grace Huber, anyway?"

"We're friends."

He might like to be more, but for the moment, that was a good start. Plus, it was an accurate enough description for his daughter.

"No," Angela argued, "if you're going out with her tonight—a *Friday* night!—then you're *dating* her. How could you do that now? You need to think about *me*, Dad."

As if she hadn't been the only thing he'd thought about for the past fifteen years.

He tried to lighten her mood.

"You want to come along on the date?" He raised an eyebrow as he met her sullen expression.

"No! I don't want you to date her at all! What about my mother?"

A question that shot tension straight through him. Angela might be talking to him again, but he knew they weren't through with this particular topic. Not after the fight with Lily that his daughter had witnessed.

He kept his voice even. "Lily? What about her? What does she have to do with anything?"

"She's back and you're keeping me from seeing her."

"I don't even know where she's staying."

Truthfully, he'd been looking over his shoulder the past few days, wondering when Lily was going to pop up again. Also, truthfully, he didn't want his daughter seeing her mother right now, not with Lily threatening to take Angela away from him. She could legally assert her rights as a biological mother even though she'd never done a thing for her child. And what if Angela wanted to live with Lily and not him? The idea made his gut go tight.

Angela crossed her arms over her chest and challenged him. "You don't want my mother in my life. Just admit it."

But he would never say that, not to her. "I don't want Lily in *my* life. And please note that she hasn't done anything positive to connect with you." Which he had to admit had been a relief under the circumstances. "That's not my fault."

"Well, I don't want Grace Huber in *my* life," Angela told him.

"I'm sorry, sweetheart, but I do want to get to know her better." Caleb fought the stress suddenly multiplying in him. He didn't want to argue, didn't want to give Angela a reason to feel justified. "I like Grace. She's a good person. Whether or not you realize it, she could have pressed charges against you when you painted that mural in Green Meadows, but she didn't even consider it. She was more concerned about *you*. That's why she came here, to make sure that you were okay." The initial reason he'd been drawn to her.

"If you take up with her, where does that leave me?"

The touch of panic in Angela's voice made his chest squeeze tight. He couldn't love his daughter more, and there was no way he would leave her out of any equation, not even if Grace turned out to be far more important to him than a good friend. Which of course was likely, considering he couldn't stop thinking about holding her and kissing her.

But to reassure his worried daughter, he put an arm around her and pulled her close enough that he could kiss her forehead. "Why are you getting so worked up over my having a date? I've gone out with several other women and it never seemed to bother you before. Grace and I are not at any place where you need to be concerned. I'm just getting to know her." He tried joking to lighten the atmosphere. "I swear I haven't offered to pay her father six horses for her." But Angela's down-turned mouth told him she didn't appreciate his humor. "I simply enjoy being with Grace. We're interested in the same things. That's not anything to worry about."

But obviously Angela *was* worried, because she struggled out of his arms, yelling, "If you loved me, you would try rebuilding a relationship with my mother, not with some stranger!"

"A relationship?"

He wasn't even receptive to being friends with Lily. But was that a mistake on his part?

If so, he didn't want it affecting his daughter's future.

Car lights flickered through the front windows then went dim as the engine cut off. His mother was here to pick up Angela.

Swallowing hard at his daughter's unhappiness, Caleb knew he was going to have to rethink the Lily situation.

HAVING SPENT MORE than an hour getting ready for her date with Caleb, Grace felt her nerves escalating until the moment she heard the knock at her front door.

He was here!

She took a deep breath to calm herself and called, "Coming!" as she quickly moved to let him in.

After opening the door, she simply stood there for a moment, staring. Wearing trousers and a cobalt blue shirt open at the throat, Caleb was more formally dressed than she'd ever seen him. His long black hair was tied back from his clean-shaven but clearly rugged face. High forehead. Broad cheekbones. Straight blade of a nose. He was breathtakingly handsome. His dark eyes swept over her and his full mouth curled into a warm smile.

"Wow," he murmured.

"Wow yourself."

The words were out of her mouth before she could think about them. His smile deepened to a grin. As did hers.

"Are you ready to go?"

She felt as if she'd been ready for this all day. All week.

"I am. Just let me get my purse."

Which gave her a minute to steady her nerves. She fetched the small navy cross-body bag from the sofa. She wished she'd thought to buy a purse and shoes with a little more delicacy to go with the pretty dress, but the bag and a pair of navy work pumps would have to do for tonight. And from the way Caleb was staring at her, he didn't seem to notice. Or care.

They left Grace's apartment and walked down the single flight of stairs. Her rental was a half block off Main Street and located over a stationery shop, a three-minute walk from her office. Very convenient, but there were days when she wished she'd taken a condo unit in Green Meadows, just to enjoy the beautiful surroundings. If Phase 2 got the green light, perhaps she would consider moving.

"First Presbyterian is on the other side of

town, so I'll drive," Caleb said. Once they were settled in his truck and he pulled away from the curb, he asked, "So what kinds of things will they do to raise money tonight?"

"Other than the entrance fee, I'm not sure. I would think there will be things to buy. Or some kind of auction."

"Hmm. I wonder what they would auction off in this small town."

"Things people donate, I guess."

"Grass seed or a bag of feed? How about a car?" He laughed.

"I doubt if they could fit a car in a church basement," Grace said seriously, then noticed his grin. "You're joking."

Caleb smiled. "Just trying to keep things light."

"You have a good sense of humor."

"Thanks. Glad you appreciate it."

As they drove on, at his urging, they tried to think of other amusing things one could buy at a small-town auction.

"Special crocheted socks," suggested Grace with a giggle.

"The kind with separated toes," added Caleb. He glanced at a house bordered by statues. "Extra lawn ornaments?"

"Homemade cookies."

"Actually, that sounds pretty good," said Caleb.

The ride across town took less than five minutes. The church lot was already half full when they arrived. Grace checked her watch. The doors had opened about ten minutes before.

She said, "It looks like they're going to have a good crowd tonight."

"The locals usually turn out in support of each other when there's some kind of fund-raiser. Or anything, really, that brings residents together. People from surrounding towns, too. Most get tired of doing the same thing all the time. And we don't have a lot of entertainment venues in this neck of the woods. No movie theaters. No arcades. No nightclubs. We have to drive to Kenosha or Milwaukee to have a real night out."

Things that Grace wouldn't miss if she decided to stay in Sparrow Lake. She took advantage of city entertainment occasionally, but she didn't mind the drive to Milwaukee to do so. Thinking that Dad would have a lot of negative things to say about the idea of her living here made her sober a bit. She forced the thought away. She wasn't going to let anything ruin her evening with Caleb.

Since she'd invited him, she meant to pay their entry fees into the social, but he wouldn't let her. He took over, saying, "My town, my treat."

"Does that mean I have to take you to Milwaukee if I want to return the favor?"

They entered the church gym. High tables were set in one area and a bunch of people were already gathered around, standing while eating and drinking. Behind them were more traditional tables with low chairs, but that area was still mostly empty. People milled about, some looking over items carefully placed on display tables at the other end of the room. Items for auction? She didn't see any bags of feed or power tools. No crocheted socks with individual toes, either, though there seemed to be a couple of beautifully made afghans and a lovely quilt. There weren't many people she knew well, either. Which was good since the original objective of the evening for her was to meet new townies who would support Green Meadows.

The woman Caleb paid said, "We're having a big raffle to help raise money. One dollar per ticket. All the items are set over there."

So no auction, Grace thought. "I'll take

twenty," she said, and handed the woman her money.

"Twenty for me also." Caleb set down another bill.

The woman beamed at them as she gave them their raffle tickets. "Just fill these out and drop them in this," she said, indicating a large glass bowl that already had a bunch of raffle stubs. "And thank you both!"

Caleb slipped an arm around Grace's waist. "Let's get some refreshments. Then I can introduce you to some of these folks, and you can give them your business card. Actually, you could give me a bunch of cards and I can hand them out for you."

"You don't need to do that." She preferred finding out who people were and then sending them a brochure unless they specifically asked for a card. "I didn't mean for you to work tonight." Or to work in that way herself.

"How about if I want to? The more business you get, the more likely you are to stick around for a while."

Pleased that he wanted her to stay, she nevertheless discouraged him. "Well, thanks, but I have ideas as to how to approach them." More indirectly.

"You should feel free to use other people's ideas, too."

He seemed to forget she was the person with the sales experience. She didn't say so, however.

He went on, "If you really want to return the favor of the entry fee, you could always make me dinner sometime. I would appreciate a nice home-cooked meal that I didn't have to make myself."

Grace laughed. "If you survived my cooking. Not one of my best skills. I keep mealtime simple." And when in the city, she ordered out. A lot.

"Then I'll have to teach you some tricks. We can start on the campout next weekend."

"Ah, so cooking is part of your skill set. I always hoped to meet a man who knew his way around the kitchen." At the refreshment table, they took small plates and gathered together a few appetizers. "So your mother taught you to cook?"

"Actually, Mom is a great cook, but she was usually too busy working to do much other than on the weekends." Caleb stopped at one of the high tables. "Is this okay?"

"Sure. Easier to meet people as they walk

by from the refreshment table," she whispered. "So how did you learn to cook?"

"When I got tired of hot dogs and burgers, I started experimenting on my own out of sheer desperation. Bought a couple of books. Tuned in to the cooking channel. I'm no chef, but Angela doesn't complain…at least not about my cooking."

She heard the note of discouragement in his tone. And his expression darkened, as well. He must still be having problems with his daughter.

Trying to lighten his sudden mood shift, she asked, "Is there anything you *can't* do?"

He grinned at her. "Don't ask me to sing. It'll attract all the coyotes in the area."

Grace snorted loudly, garnering the attention of the people nearest them. She didn't care. "More like a howl, huh?"

"Not exactly a howl. I sound like a dying goose."

Grace shook with laughter. Caleb had an original take on things. "I don't think I've ever heard a dying goose."

"If you do, you'll never forget it."

"But coyotes like that sound?"

"All predators exploit situations. Dead goose is dinner *du jour* to them." He changed the subject. "Speaking of situations and food, we need something to drink with the appetizers. Iced tea? Lemonade?"

"Tea would be great. With lemon if they have it."

"I'll be right back."

"Okay."

Grace dug around in her purse and found her business cards, then slipped a few into a front pocket of her bag where she could more easily get to them. Caleb seemed bound and determined on her handing them out, no matter what. If he got too pushy, though, she was going to have words with him. Not liking to feel negative, she started filling out the raffle tickets.

"Hey, you made it," came a familiar voice.

Grace turned around to see Heather coming her way. "I always try to take good advice from a friend. Are you alone tonight?"

"No. Rick is getting us some drinks."

"Caleb, too."

Heather appeared pleasantly surprised. "Did you just meet up here or—"

"Nope. An actual date."

"Good for you. When the boys get back with those drinks, we can sit together."

Grace said, "I was thinking that standing

at one of these tables would make it easier to meet townspeople I don't know."

"Then stand it is." Heather's eyebrows arched. "Here comes a couple you might not have met before."

Heather waved them over. It turned out the couple owned a car dealership in Racine but preferred to live in a small town. They were good contacts as they might know people looking to move their families out of the city into a kid-friendly town.

As they were talking, Grace realized Caleb was standing off to the side, a glass in each hand. He winked at her and approached.

"Did you give them your card?" he asked Grace, not really allowing her time to work her own magic on the couple.

Annoyed and a little taken aback, she found it difficult to concentrate.

Of course, Caleb Blackthorne was a distraction in and of himself. And she had to admit, though sometimes a bit aggressive about helping her, he was the best distraction she'd encountered in…well…forever.

AT THE REZ, Gran Maddie and Angela started watching a scary movie together. After less than an hour, Gran fell fast asleep in her recliner. Angela knew her grandmother didn't like horror films and would tune out by either working around the house while the movie was on or dozing. She smiled, appreciating her own cleverness. She knew how to deal with things. Now she could do what she wanted.

She glanced at the nearest clock. 10:00 p.m. Dad wouldn't be home yet. He was out with that woman! Thinking about Grace, she again wondered how he could do this to her. All these years, he'd lied about keeping her from her mother. As far as she was concerned, he still was keeping them apart. Then, despite her feelings on the matter, he'd gone out with Grace Huber.

She simply couldn't stand it!

When her cell phone vibrated, she realized Kiki was calling, probably to check on her.

She stepped out into the kitchen and answered, keeping her voice low. "Hey. I was just about to call you."

"I could come over and keep you company if I can sneak out."

Angela glanced toward the living room area and Gran Maddie, who was snoring gently. "No, don't. I don't want you getting into trouble because of me again."

"I'm not worried."

"Thanks," Angela said. "You really are the best. But not tonight. I'll find something to do to take my mind off Dad's date. Don't worry, I'll be okay."

They talked awhile longer. Rather Angela let Kiki do most of the talking as her emotions continued to whirl and grow. No doubt about it, she was filled with confusion and anger.

Within five minutes of hanging up with her friend, and against her father's orders to stay put until he picked her up, Angela sneaked out of Gran Maddie's house to go do something to make herself feel better.

"THE NEXT ITEM is a haircut and blow-dry at Ginger's Luscious Locks," Emily Auerbach, the mayor's wife, announced. "And the winner is—" a nervous woman, her hand shook as she pulled a slip from the fish bowl "—Priscilla Ryan."

Though the mayor's wife wore a sour expression that seemed to define her, everyone else clapped as Priscilla accepted the envelope.

Grace was smiling. She'd been smiling the whole evening, and Caleb wanted to kiss her again. Seriously kiss her. No brush of the lips, but a kiss that would make her toes curl. Anticipation built in him.

Grace had met a lot of new people tonight, had given out a lot of her business cards, which had made Caleb nearly as happy as she seemed to be. Just before the raffle drawings had begun, they'd retired to one of the tables where they could sit. Heather and Rick had joined some other friends, so he was alone with Grace. They were close enough that he'd slung his arm over the back of her chair, leaving his hand on her shoulder, and him wishing he could hold her more fully in his arms.

A few more raffle wins were called out, and Caleb was getting anxious to leave. To be alone with Grace.

Even as he thought it, he could see Angela's disapproving scowl in his mind, but he pushed the unpleasant image away. The girl just needed some time. Once Angela calmed down, surely she would be open to getting on with a woman as nice as Grace was.

Holding her hand on the table, he squeezed it. Squeezing his in return, she gave him an intimate smile that warmed his insides. It had been far too long since a woman had made him feel like this.

Connected.

So right.

Longing for more.

"And the final raffle prize is a private trail ride for two from Sam Larson at the Larson Dude Ranch," Emily announced.

Caleb moved closer to Grace and whispered, "Do you mind if we leave after this?"

She turned her head so they were almost nose to nose. "Fine with me," she whispered in return, her sweet breath brushing his cheek.

And lips…

"And the winner is…Grace Huber."

"That's you!"

"Oh, my gosh!" Grace rose and headed for the mayor's wife, glancing back once at Caleb, a big grin lighting up her face. After taking the envelope, she headed straight back for him. He was already on his feet. Waving her prize, she said, "Here's how I'll return the favor. By taking you for that private trail ride."

He grinned. "Deal."

While their intention was to leave right then, it took at least ten minutes to get to the door, what with everyone stopping them to tell Grace how nice it had been to meet her.

Even so, Caleb's grin never faltered. Everyone liked Grace. Especially him.

"That was fun," Grace said as he finally helped her into the truck. "Even if it was part work."

"It was fun. And I loved watching you work." He just loved watching *her*.

"You did quite a bit of work for me yourself."

"I've been goal-driven since I was left with a baby to take care of. I had to be." Then, getting into the driver's seat, he asked, "Do you want to go right home?"

"What did you have in mind?"

"Someplace quiet where we could talk for a while." Where he could be alone with her. He wasn't ready for the evening to end just yet.

"Sure. Coffee?"

He shook his head. "Water."

"You want to go somewhere to drink water?"

"No, to listen to it."

"Ah, the lake," she said. "I'm game."

A few minutes later, they'd parked and were walking hand in hand down to the public pathway that circled the Sparrow Lake shore. Luckily, a nearby bench was free.

"We can sit there," he said, "so you don't get grass stains on your dress."

They quickly settled in, Caleb again putting his arm around her, this time pulling her a little closer.

They could hear the soft lapping of small waves against the shore. The streetlights lit glowing paths across the water. Above, there was a sharp sliver of moon and thousands of twinkling stars. Nearby, a night bird called softly.

Grace made a sound of contentment. "Mmm, I'm really glad Heather told me about the social."

"And I'm really glad you invited me."

"There's such a feeling of belonging at town events... I've never experienced that before."

"Nowhere? Not even in college?"

"I went to the University of Chicago, close enough that Dad expected me home on weekends. So no, not even in college. I just worked hard. And pretty much alone. After the first year, I didn't even have a roommate," she admitted. "The girl I roomed with had her own agenda, which didn't include me, so I got my own apartment."

"Sounds lonely," Caleb said. "The one thing about growing up on the rez, I was never lonely. There was always someone keeping track of me, which annoyed me at the time, and I eventually rebelled. But now I see it as a blessing. It takes a village and all that. It makes me wonder if I cheated my daughter of having that by moving off the rez."

"But she still goes there sometimes, doesn't she?"

He nodded. "To see Mom, mostly. She's kind of lost her connection with her old friends. Which is probably why she took up with Kiki."

"Is that really such a bad thing?"

"Kiki's influence isn't good."

"So you've said. Maybe they're both just finding themselves."

"Hopefully Angela will do that soon, but I don't know that Kiki ever will."

"Maybe you should find out more about her," Grace suggested.

"Maybe."

For a moment, they sat still, listening to the night sounds. Then Caleb dipped his head and found her sweet lips, kissing her the way he'd been imagining he would do all night. Slowly. Thoroughly. Deeply. Grace sighed and turned into him more fully so he could take her in his arms. Again, the way he'd been imagining.

She was soft and warm and welcoming.

A breeze skipped from the lake over them, attuning Caleb even more to his surroundings. He loved the outdoors, especially with Grace pressed against him. Their lips parted and they separated just enough that they could look into each other's eyes. Moonlight became Grace, and unable to think of a better way to end this evening, he kissed her again.

A buzzing sound pestered him. Two sounds. Both of their cell phones were ringing. They pulled apart, Grace with a little giggle.

"Okay," she said. "We got calls at the same time? That's odd."

"Yeah…maybe we'd better see who it is." Though Caleb was pretty sure he knew who was doing her best to ruin his evening.

A glance at his cell screen confirmed that. But it wasn't Angela herself. "Sparrow Lake Police."

"Me, too."

His gut in a sudden knot, Caleb moved away from the bench as he answered. "Blackthorne here."

"This is Alex Novak."

A sick feeling filled Caleb as he asked the police chief, "What's going on?"

"I hate to tell you, Caleb. Angela was just

brought to the station from Green Meadows by one of my officers."

Green Meadows…undoubtedly the reason he and Grace both got calls. He glanced her way, but she was listening to the person at the other end.

"What did Angela do this time?" he asked.

"She shattered a window on one of the town houses."

"How? Some kind of crazy accident?" He could hope.

"Sorry, Caleb," Alex said. "She used a brick to break it."

All the breath left him for a moment.

He looked at Grace, still on her cell, and simultaneously, they said, "I'll be right there."

CHAPTER TEN

THEY DROVE TO the police station in silence, Caleb feeling like a bomb ready to explode. His chest was so tight he could hardly breathe.

Grace must have gotten the same information he had, so thankfully he didn't have to explain anything to her. It was Angela who would have to do the explaining to them both. Again. If she would.

She'd thrown a brick through a window? This was far more serious than painting a mural on the community center wall. She'd destroyed property! What had she been thinking? And what had Mom been doing? Who knew? As long as there was an adult on the premises, Angela should have been okay. How could either he or Angela's grandmother suspect that a girl who was well behaved in the past would suddenly become an irresponsible vandal?

It was a little after eleven now. He'd planned to pick up his daughter by eleven thirty. Maybe

he should have gone right home after the social, shouldn't have wanted to spend more time
with Grace. Just having a few minutes alone
had been incentive enough for his daughter
to have gone looking for trouble! Well, she'd
certainly found it this time, he thought, as he
parked in front of the police station. Both from
the police and from him.

Before he could get out, Grace reached
over and put her hand on his. "I can only
imagine how upset you are, but it's going to
be all right."

"All right? How?"

"I don't know yet. But we'll figure it out."

We. Grace was including herself. She
wanted to help him help his daughter. Not
knowing what to say, Caleb simply nodded
his thanks and opened his door. Grace didn't
wait for him to go around to her side. She
got out and, by the time he stepped up to the
curb, joined him. As they walked to the station door, she slipped her hand in his and
gave him an encouraging squeeze. His throat
went as tight as his chest, and he couldn't
say a word. He simply squeezed back and
glanced her way and thought he'd never seen
any woman look more beautiful to him than
Grace Huber did at that moment.

Police Chief Alex Novak was waiting for them in the reception area. He indicated they should follow him into his office, where he circled the desk. "Have a seat." He nodded at the two chairs opposite him.

Sitting, Caleb said, "Alex, I can't tell you how sorry I am about this."

"You're not the one who needs to be sorry."

"Whose window did Angela break?" Caleb asked. He would seek out that person in the morning and apologize and tell him or her that he would take care of having the window replaced immediately.

"Actually," Alex began, "the window was in one of the empty Green Meadows town houses that hasn't been sold yet, which makes you the property owner," he told Grace. "A neighbor was walking his dog nearby, and he heard the crash. He had a flashlight on him and pinned Angela with the beam as she was trying to sneak away. He somehow made her wait there while he called 911 and got a squad on the way." He cleared his throat. "I'm sorry to say Angela committed a Class A misdemeanor by breaking that window." He looked to Grace. "That was actually her second such misdemeanor involving Green Meadows property. The neighbor recognized her as the one who painted a mural on the community center wall. I heard about that after the fact, but I was informed that you refused to bring action against her."

"I didn't think what Angela did warranted having her arrested then," Grace said. "And I don't now. She's at that volatile age where her emotions rule her. She's not a bad kid. She needs understanding, not punishment for something she doesn't know how to deal with right now."

Her voice trembled just enough that Caleb recognized that she was once more identifying with his daughter. This time he sought her hand and surrounded it with his. She gave him a quick glance. Her smile appeared strained.

Alex tapped a pen against his desktop. "So as the property owner, you won't bring charges against her?" he asked Grace.

"No, I won't."

"Your father may have something to say about that," Alex countered.

"I'll talk to Dad about it. He'll agree with me."

But she didn't sound all that certain that he would. Even so, Caleb murmured, "Thank you," and felt the pressure in his chest relax just a little.

"This may be a mistake," Alex said. "Angela is going down a slippery path. She needs to learn she can't just do whatever she wants because she's upset about something."

"I would rather we find a different way to deal with her outbursts," Grace insisted. "Perhaps having her do some kind of community service…"

Alex shook his head. "That's impossible to enforce without the court being involved."

"*I'll* enforce it," Caleb said. "If I have to, I'll stand over her and watch her while she works."

"Works at what?" Alex asked. "What kind of community service do you have in mind? And how will it relate to the crime?"

Caleb looked to Grace. From her expression, she didn't have any more idea of what kind of community service would do the trick than he did.

He said, "How about if you give us a couple of days to figure it out. We'll get back to you when we do."

"All right." Alex stood. "I'll get Angela out of lockup and meet you up front."

Caleb got to his feet. He felt a little shaky

until he met Grace's encouraging gaze. She nodded and they walked to the entryway.

"I probably should just walk home," Grace said. "That would give you some much-needed privacy to talk to your daughter about this."

"No. You are not walking anywhere."

"But Angela won't like—"

"I don't care." He insisted, "I'm taking you home. Angela needs to learn to think about other people. And to take responsibility for her own actions."

At which point he saw Alex with his hand around Angela's upper arm as he led her to them. She kept her head down, and he could see her jaw was tight as if she was gritting her teeth. So she wouldn't cry? Caleb wanted both to shout at her and to take her in his arms and plead with her to be his sweet Angel again. Instead, he met her closed expression with one of disapproval when she finally looked up at him.

"Thank you, Alex." Caleb fought his twin desires as he stared Angela down, growling, "Let's go."

Not saying a word, she gave Grace a sour expression, then flounced out of the station to the truck. Opening the door, she nodded at Grace. "Where is *she* going to sit?"

"Not in the back of the truck, where I should put you," Caleb said. "You get to sit in the middle between us."

Which he knew she would hate. Angela clenched her jaw and got in, but he couldn't miss the hot anger in her eyes as she slid across the seat. No way did she want to be next to Grace. Well, that was just too bad.

He helped Grace get in with a murmured, "Sorry about this," before going around to the driver's side. He'd barely secured his seat belt before demanding, "What on earth is going on with you, Angela?" He started the engine. "I've done my best to raise you to be a decent human being. Do you really think it's all right to do whatever you want to whomever you want?"

"She deserved it!"

"Grace deserved to have you destroy her property because we went to a fund-raiser together?"

"Not *her.*"

Not Grace? "Then who are you talking about?"

"My mother. She's living in that town house."

Grace started. "Wait. That town house is

empty. It hasn't been sold. You mean...she just moved herself in? How do you know that?"

"I've known for days because I followed her."

Caleb clenched his jaw. "When?"

"The night you went to bed early. I wasn't sleepy and I'd seen her on the property before, so I went looking for her. I spotted her coming home from the rez and followed her through the woods."

At night when he hadn't even known his daughter had left the house? "I'm going to want full details later."

It came to Caleb that while Angela wanted Lily in her life, she was still angry that her mother had abandoned her.

"Huh," Grace said, almost to herself. "I have a feeling I know why residents have been imagining they've been seeing a ghost at night."

"Lily trying to stay hidden in the woods while sneaking back to the town house," Caleb said.

Grace asked Angela, "Did you tell the police who was staying there?"

"No, and I'm not going to. It's none of the police's business."

Though it was Grace's business, so Caleb said, "Do you want to press charges against Lily?"

"She's an adult and should know better," Grace answered. "If there's proof."

"I'm not saying anything!" Angela cried. "Nothing seemed to be damaged."

"How do you know?" Caleb asked. "You didn't go in the town house, did you?"

Angela just sat there, stewing in silence. Caleb wondered if he should blame himself for the mess.

How to handle things, though? He didn't even want to be friends with Lily. It hit him that community service might be a type of punishment with merit, but it wasn't enough to quiet Angela's emotional turmoil about her mother. Only one thing could do that. He hoped.

For his daughter's sake, he would do something he never envisioned doing. He would reach out to Lily Trejo and try to make peace with her. He would try to negotiate a truce between mother and daughter so they could form some kind of relationship that would satisfy Angela.

His daughter's happiness was the most important thing in the world to him. He would do anything for her, even this.

THE NEXT MORNING, wearing an apologetic smile, Carol stopped Grace at the reception desk when she walked into the office. "Mr. Huber asked to see you the moment you came in the door."

So Dad had already heard about the broken window. From whom? He wasn't even in town the night before. He'd been in Milwaukee overseeing the shopping center.

"Okay, thanks, Carol."

Grace knocked at his door once, then opened it. Wearing a particularly grumpy expression, her father waved her in.

She said, "I have a lot to do this morning—"

"It can wait. First, you have some explaining to do."

She wore her most innocent expression. "About?"

"You know very well what this is about, Grace Huber. That wild teenager has been at it again, this time breaking a window in one of our town houses. And you told the police chief you wouldn't bring charges against her."

"Angela is going through a tough time, and—"

"And you're dating her father."

News traveled fast in a small town, but where had Dad heard it?

"Yes, I am dating Caleb Blackthorne," she said, "but I would be concerned about Angela even if I wasn't."

"Because she's a little criminal?"

"Because she's going through an emotionally difficult time in her life. Dealing with her as a person and having her do some kind of community service at Green Meadows will be more effective than making her go through the system."

"Community service? You want to give the little troublemaker *another* pass?"

"I want to show her that people care about her."

"Just because she's not getting that from her father doesn't mean—"

"How could you say that? Caleb is a wonderful father to Angela. His situation reminds me of *us* when I was that age. Angela has been acting out for several weeks now, and poor Caleb has been going out of his mind trying to figure out what exactly happened—"

though he obviously knew now "—and how to get her back on the straight and narrow."

Dad's brow furrowed. "How *did* she get off the right path?"

She told him about Angela's mother abandoning her. And about her returning. "Last night we learned that Angela threw that brick at the town house window because her mother has been staying there at night."

"Now we have a squatter? They both should be arrested!"

"They both need help," she countered. "The mother has no resources. She's probably desperate. And, we can't arrest a squatter without real proof anyhow. The police went inside the town house and found nothing but a bottle of water and a blanket. No damage. I didn't make an official complaint."

"What do you think you are, a social worker?"

"Actually, Caleb's mother is a social worker, and he's hoping Maddie can help her. As for me, I'm just paying it forward, Dad."

"You didn't destroy property."

"No, I just stole it," she reminded him. "And you made me go back to the store and return the bracelet and the sweater and apologize."

"Has the Blackthorne girl apologized?"

"Not yet." But she wasn't through with the past yet. "And then there was that rave that guy took me to. You came and found me and got me out without my being arrested."

"This is different," her father argued. "You were being self-destructive. She's destroying other people's property. *Our* property! You must press charges this time!"

Grace hated it when her father tried to force her to his will, which had been happening more and more lately. Probably because he sensed her yearning to break from the family company.

She jumped to her feet. "I'm not pressing charges against Angela Blackthorne! Nor against her mother." In fact, if she did, Angela would never forgive her and she and Caleb wouldn't stand a chance at being a couple.

"Fine, there's nothing stopping *me* from pressing charges, both against the girl and her mother!"

It was one of those rare moments when she was so angry she actually saw red. "You do that, Dad, and I'm done!"

"Done with what?"

"With Walworth Builders!"

And with that threat, she stormed out of

the room. Trembling inside, she hoped Carol didn't notice as she whipped by the receptionist's desk to go into her own office, where she had a good cry. How could she have lost her temper like that? Her father had done everything for her. Why hadn't she figured out some way to talk him down?

Her threatening to quit Walworth Builders had probably stabbed him in the heart.

She already regretted her words.

Even if she'd spoken the truth about the one thing she truly wanted to do.

CHAPTER ELEVEN

"Are you calm?" Mom asked Caleb the next morning.

"I'm okay."

He was ready to face the inevitable. Had been for a while. The night before he and Maddie had decided that a meeting between mother and daughter simply had to take place. As he expected, the cops hadn't caught Lily after the broken window incident, though they'd seen someone running away from the town house. If Mom hadn't had friends on the rez, the woman might have returned there undetected. As it was, Mom had cornered Lily before she'd had the chance to make another move.

And now Lily was waiting to talk to them all in Maddie's living room.

While Angela sat, morose, at the kitchen table.

"Well, we can't deal with this too soon, considering we aren't able to trust you, Angela," said Maddie, disappointment in her voice.

His daughter remained seated, scowling, but she croaked, "I'm sorry, Gran." At least she apologized to someone.

"Come on, Angel," he said, motioning toward the living room.

"Don't call me that."

Angela flounced past him.

All seated, they made an uncomfortable-looking group. Maddie had traded her usual easy smile for a stern expression, Lily was pale and downcast, while Angela pouted as she stole glances at the woman seated on the couch.

Finally Lily raised her eyes to her daughter. "I'm sorry we had to meet this way, honey."

Angela merely grunted. "How did you want to meet?"

"I thought I would be in a better position." Lily smiled tremulously. "As it is, I haven't been able to find a job. Or a permanent bed to sleep in…yet."

Right. Caleb remembered how Lily had tried to hit him up for cash. She'd said specifically she wasn't looking for a job.

His expression must have communicated itself to his mother, who reached across her chair arm to touch his shoulder. "Just let them talk, Caleb."

Angela and Lily both gave him angry stares.

Then the girl turned back to her mother. "I know Dad told you to stay away from me."

"I'm afraid he wants me to have nothing to do with you." Lily sighed. "But I'm your mother."

"My mother? What mother goes off and leaves her child for fifteen years?" Angela asked, a tremor in her voice.

"There were so many problems. We were so young. We'd had a terrible fight."

"We did not have a fight," Caleb insisted. "You just took off."

Lily dismissed him with a shake of her head. "We had so many fights you probably don't even remember."

Angela blurted, "I don't care about the fights. Why would you leave your own baby? That was a horrible thing for a mother to do!"

Tears welled in Lily's eyes, reminding Caleb once again that the woman was not without feeling.

Lily sniffled and Mom handed her a box of tissues. "The important thing is I'm here now and I—I want to contribute to your life."

"And how do you think you're going to do that?" Caleb asked.

"I know you think I can't do anything without a job or a place to stay."

Mom spoke up quickly. "If you need housing, I can probably find you a spare room for the time being, Lily. There are people who knew your folks who still live on the rez. We might even be able to find you a job of some sort."

"And who says I want to have a relationship with this woman?" Angela looked at Caleb and her grandmother, then turned to Lily. "I think that's the first thing you ought to think about."

"You care," Lily said. "You broke a window trying to get my attention."

"Maybe I did it to tell you to go away."

"You can at least agree to see your mother a few times," Mom told Angela gently. "We inherit a lot from our parents—physical traits, psychological inclinations—whether we want to or not. You need to find out about them."

Lily was pulling herself together. "When I get settled, you can stay with me."

"I don't want to stay with you."

Thank goodness for small favors. If a fifteen-year-old didn't want to stay with one parent, the law would surely listen to her, Caleb thought.

"You need to get to know me." Lily sniffed and wiped her eyes.

Mom started negotiating. "How about if you meet with Angela once a week for now. Here, in my house. That way, she's in a neutral environment." She looked at her granddaughter. "Wouldn't that be okay, Angela? Your mother does have a point. And, legally, she does have some rights."

Caleb said, "I think that could work."

He doubted he'd be able to trust Lily Trejo anytime soon. Angela's gaze slid from her grandmother to him, then to her estranged mother. "I guess we can talk." She sounded reluctant. "You've been hanging around here for a while. You haven't been deliberately avoiding me, have you?"

"Of course not. I just wanted to get settled. Is that what you've been thinking, honey? I'm so sorry!" Lily leaned forward to hold out a hand to Angela.

But Angela scooted back in her chair, away from her mother. "We can do what Gran says, I guess."

Caleb tried to assure himself he wouldn't regret the decision.

GRACE STILL FELT badly about the fight she'd
had with her father by the time the weekend
rolled around. They hadn't made up, though
he'd called to tell her he was going to Milwaukee for a couple of days for the business. He'd
sounded neutral and hadn't mentioned pressing charges with the police. Alex Novak was
waiting for Grace to get back to him about
appropriate community service for the teenager. Not that he had an official position here
since she wasn't pressing charges. But she felt
she owed him that much.

Grace had a couple of ideas ready to run
past Caleb when he picked her up early Saturday morning. The back of his truck was
loaded with camping gear, and in the middle sat a couple of students. Grace exited her
apartment with the duffel bag and backpack
she'd just recently bought. Her regular lug-
gage was in no way appropriate for a camping trip.

Caleb eyed the large duffel bag. "It's only
one night."

"I know. I just couldn't decide what to
bring, so I probably packed too much."

"Any food in here?" asked the skinny
young guy to whom Caleb handed the duffel.

"I'm afraid not," Grace said with a smile.

"Unless you count the bag of trail mix for later." She held out a hand. "I'm Grace Huber."

"I'm Jimmy." The skinny guy shook her hand with a grin. He had curly blond hair and an abstract blue tattoo on his forearm.

"And I'm Graham," said a quiet-looking student who wore glasses.

"Nice to meet you both." Grace then got into the truck when Caleb opened the door.

The students' stares followed her, making Grace wonder if something was wrong with her outfit, designer blue jeans paired with the oldest T-shirt she owned and her walking shoes.

"Take a picture, why don't you?" Caleb called to the students before climbing up into the driver's seat and fastening his seat belt. He grumbled, "Sorry about the leers."

"They were leering?"

"You're a good-looking woman, Grace. And you're with me. Students always like to gossip about their professors."

Grace smiled at the compliment. She also loved being "with" Caleb.

They took the main highway out of town, rolling green hills with small stretches of timber on either side. High above a meadow,

Grace noticed a red-tailed hawk soaring on the wind.

"I'm looking forward to this," she said with a sigh. "The peace of nature."

"We hope it'll be peaceful. Only six students of fifteen chose to participate—the rest will meet us there. Everybody pretty much knows what they're supposed to be doing."

She was so looking forward to seeing Caleb, Grace hadn't thought much about the students. "You said they're working on extra credit projects, right?"

"Yeah. Graham is doing a study of indigenous plants versus those that were introduced by Europeans. Jimmy is looking at the impact humans have had on some of the fauna in the forest preserve."

"Sounds interesting."

"I particularly like the initiative of three of the students who are going to meet us there. They're planning to take water samples from several key areas, then test them in a lab for pollutants."

"Sounds complicated."

"They've taken biology and chemistry already, so I think they can handle it."

"And you're there for questions and guidance?"

"As well as supervision," Caleb admitted. "About that peace you're hoping for—these are college students but a couple of reckless eighteen- to twenty-year-olds are fully capable of sabotaging the experience for everyone else."

"Surely no one would do that."

"Some kids like to party wherever and whenever. They get carried away."

"I suppose so. In a way then, we're chaperones."

Caleb gave her a sly grin. "You're there to inspire and support the professor."

She smiled back, raising her brows. "I'll do the best I can."

He seemed to be in a good mood, considering he must have been dealing with his daughter. Thinking about the teenager again, Grace said, "I've come up with a couple of ways Angela can do some meaningful community service."

"What did you have in mind?"

"She could help Heather Scofield with the landscaping at Green Meadows."

He was thoughtful. "I like that she would be helping improve the place she tried to destroy. But is there something else? Angela has never shown any interest in gardening. Mom has an herb garden and tried to get Angela to help her with it. Mom said she wandered off after about ten minutes."

"There are lots of tasks in landscaping besides actually putting plants in the earth," she told him, "but I've also got another idea." One that might appeal to the girl enough to make a change in her attitude. "We have a community center that could use some decorating, like a mural on the inside wall."

"A mural? She already did one of those," he reminded her.

"One that was inappropriate, yes. But Angela is so talented. I saw the paintings you have in your home. Maybe she could design and execute a nature scene."

"Hmm. Paint a mural?" He glanced at Grace. "You know, that might be very appropriate. If you really need a mural, that is."

"We definitely could use one. I like using creative, individualistic details to beautify the place."

"Will that really be punishment, though? She might enjoy it."

"She doesn't have to hate what she's doing, does she? It will take a lot of work and give her time to think about things."

He seemed to consider the idea for a minute. "And it's constructive, using her creativity for a positive, rather than a negative, purpose."

"Exactly what I was thinking."

They slowed to take an exit onto another highway. This one was blacktop and a bit beaten up in places. The trees grew closer to the sides of the road.

"I'll ask Angela for some ideas on Sunday when I get home," Caleb went on. "A mural could keep her busy. That and the meetings we've set up with Lily."

"Meetings?"

"I don't want Angela living with Lily, but she could spend some time with her."

"That sounds reasonable."

Grace hoped something good would come out of interaction between mother and daughter. If her own mother had been willing to communicate and relate to her as a teenager, she was certain that would have helped her get through the emotional turmoil that had put her on the wrong course.

The campout was at a site in a state park about twenty miles from Sparrow Lake. Driving through the entrance some time later, Caleb reached in his jeans pocket for a crumpled hand-drawn map.

"We're at campsite 32."

"Want me to keep a lookout for it?" Grace asked.

"Not sure that it'll be marked that clearly. I know we have to turn to the right."

They drove for a while longer through thickening stands of trees, the truck's tires crunching on gravel. Finally they arrived at a clearing where the other students were waiting. As they pulled up under a tree to park, Grace noticed a building on the other side of the road.

"Do we have plumbing?"

"Sinks and flushing toilets over there. Students appreciate having a few amenities."

Graham and Jimmy leaped out of the back when the truck stopped, then started taking out the gear: a couple of tents, sleeping bags, a box of what seemed to be cookware.

"Let's get everything set up before taking our first hike," said Caleb.

He introduced Grace to a burly, bearded young man named Steve, and three young women: Lindsey, Beth and Sheridan, a girl with red hair and bright pink fingernails.

They put up three tents, one that Beth had brought for herself and her two friends, a pup tent for Graham, and Caleb's small green tent, which he insisted on giving to Grace.

"That way you'll have some privacy," he told her. "I'll roll out my sleeping bag near the fire along with Jimmy and Steve."

"What if it rains?"

"It's not supposed to rain this weekend, but, if it does, the rest of us may have to jump in the vehicles."

Caleb had brought a large cooler, which he told Jimmy and Graham to put back in the truck. He instructed the rest of the students, "Keep the food in your car trunk unless you've got trail mix or sandwiches to bring along on the hike. We'll eat lunch wherever we find ourselves today. Meanwhile, we don't want critters getting into our stuff while we're gone." He explained to Grace, "You can hang food in bags from tree branches. But we don't need to go to that much trouble for an overnight."

Grace hadn't brought anything but a couple of bottles of water and the aforementioned trail mix, since Caleb had insisted he was providing the meals. When he handed out sandwiches, she took one for herself. Then she prepared for the hike, doing some stretches and making sure her shoelaces were tied securely.

Soon they set off on a narrow, rocky path

that wound between towering trees. Dappled sunlight fell through the canopy overhead and the sound of the wind made music through the thick leaf cover. Grace stared up at a patch of sky overhead and took in a deep breath of fresh soil and crisp vegetation.

"You can almost taste the beauty of the woods, can't you?" asked Caleb from behind her.

"I was just thinking that."

"The Japanese have done a study that proves walking through a forest lowers blood pressure and decreases the heart rate. They call it *shinrin-ryoho* or 'forest therapy.'" He laughed. "Pardon my pronunciation. I never learned Japanese."

Grace turned back to him with a grin. "Neither did I, so I wouldn't know whether you pronounced the term correctly or not."

They slowed to make their footing through a maze of huge roots surrounding a big oak tree. On the other side, Caleb stopped.

"Hey, everybody, stop and take a look." He pointed at some plants growing in dappled shade. "Especially Graham. What do you see here?"

The student quickly pulled out a plant ID

book and shuffled through the pages. "I'm not sure."

Caleb bent to pull a leaf off one of the plants. He crushed it in his palm. "What does this smell like?"

"Garlic," said Graham. "Garlic mustard plant?"

Caleb nodded. "Right."

"Yum," muttered Jimmy. "Wish I had a hot dog right now."

"I'm not trying to whet your appetite," Caleb said with a laugh. "Though garlic mustard can indeed be used in cooking. Why is it here, Graham?"

"An invasive species introduced from Europe," said the student, reading from his book. "Once it takes root, seeds can also hitch rides on the fur of animals."

"And it's a rapidly spreading woodland weed," said Caleb. "Once it takes over, it crowds out indigenous plants." He unfolded a larger map he had in his backpack. "Take out the maps you were supposed to bring. We have to mark this and report it to the park authorities."

"Why don't we just pull them out?" asked Jimmy.

"It's not legal," Caleb explained. "I might

teach environmental science, but I'm a regular citizen, not an expert hired by the state. I can't take it upon myself to remove or add species to the park."

After they'd marked the area on their maps, the group went on, Caleb leading the students in a discussion on endangered, as well as invasive, flora and fauna.

"There's a spring up ahead with a swath of grassland around it. A long time ago you'd probably find prairie white orchids growing there."

"Orchids grow in Wisconsin?" asked Grace.

"They used to, in wet areas. You won't find prairie whites any more except in a few places in the southeastern part of the state. Other invasive species crowded them out."

"I guess that happens everywhere."

"But we can do something about it if we're ecologically aware."

Grace realized she had lots to learn, having mainly investigated green building until now. She decided she would ask Caleb for a reading list before she went home.

The group stopped near the spring for lunch.

"This is such a peaceful place," Grace said, joining Caleb under a large tree a few yards

from the group of students. Dandelions edged
the shade cast by the tree, a ring of gold in
the sunlight.

"They're even talking more quietly than
they would in a classroom." Caleb nodded
toward the students. "It's the wilderness influence. People feel better when they have
something larger than themselves surrounding them."

"I'm glad you think so." His view was a
positive one and she knew it was another reason she found him attractive. She pointed at
the dandelions. "Those are really pretty, but
I'm sure they're just a weed, right?"

"Another invasive species." Finishing his
sandwich with a couple of bites, he leaned
back to pluck a few of the yellow flower
heads here. "At least we can make a healing
tea out of the roots and leaves."

She leaned forward to take the dandelion
from his hand, their fingers brushing, then
held it close to his chin with a flirty smile.
"And we can also find out if the person likes
butter."

He laughed, the look he gave her warming her insides and making her wish they
were alone in the glade. "An old folktale."

He leaned closer but was interrupted by a call from one of the students.

"Hey, Professor Blackthorne, come look at this."

Caleb gave Grace a look as if to say "later" and rose to join the students, who were foraging around.

The spell broken, Grace gathered up the sandwich wrappings and stuck them in her backpack. By the spring, the girls were doing water testing with Caleb supervising.

A few minutes later, the group decided to split up, a couple of the students saying they would follow the spring to its source. Before they left, the music of a cell phone jangled the air.

"Hey, who brought a phone?" Caleb looked around.

That was soon obvious as Sheridan pulled hers out to answer it. After a few remarks, she quickly slid the phone back in her pocket. "Sorry, Professor Blackthorne. I had to change a hair appointment."

Caleb scowled. "Hair appointment?"

"It was an emergency."

"Emergency or not," Caleb told the students, "turn your cell phones off, at least for this weekend. You can't experience the woods if you're waiting for a text or a call."

Grace and Caleb returned to the camp with only Jimmy in tow. The others had wandered off in other directions.

"They won't get lost, will they?" Grace asked. She'd heard that this campground was one of the largest in the state.

Caleb shook his head. "They have maps. And I told them to bring compasses."

Something scrambled through the branches overhead and Grace looked up. A squirrel? But whatever it was had quickly hidden itself.

"Can't you just imagine this place as primordial forest?" asked Caleb. He reached for her hand. "Just us and the wilderness."

She enjoyed his touch, his fingers firm and calloused, then nearly jumped out of her skin when Jimmy suddenly came up behind them. "Yeah, just me and you and Professor Blackthorne in the wilderness. Big trees and scary animals all around."

Grace let go of Caleb's hand.

"If there are any scary animals around here, you'd better go find them," Caleb joked. "They'll be a part of your study."

Jimmy looked puzzled. "Yeah, I guess so."

Then he asked, "But there aren't really any bears or wolves around here, are there?"

"Not many. That's something you can note. What happened to them, the top of the food chain?" Caleb urged, "Go on. See you for supper."

Laughing, Jimmy shuffled off.

Caleb and Grace returned to the campsite together and sat companionably on a log near the fire pit built in the center. Caleb slid an arm around her shoulders. "I'm glad you could come."

"Me, too."

"I can't believe you've never been camping before."

"Neither can I. And I don't want this to be the last time, either."

"I know plenty of great places you would enjoy."

Especially with you, she thought. She gazed into his eyes, dark and fathomless. His breath feathered her cheek. They leaned closer, lips brushing, then meeting for a sweet kiss. Grace touched his cheek and the kiss deepened…

…until a loud beep jerked them apart.

An old sedan had emerged on the road through the trees and come to a stop at the edge of the camping site.

"What…?" breathed Caleb. He stood up. "Mom." He strode to the car. "Something's wrong."

Grace just remained on the log, staring. The woman in the driver's seat must have been close to sixty, gray streaking her black hair. Angela sat on the passenger side.

Caleb's mother rolled down her window. "You said there were no cell phones this weekend, so I just drove here, hoping we could find you. The park ranger told me a class had booked this area."

"You could have called my cell phone," said Caleb, concern in his voice. "Since it seems to be a real emergency. What's wrong?"

"It's not that bad, but I have to drive up north. Una's broken her hip."

"Aunt Una. How?"

"An unfortunate accident. She fell down some steps. There's no one else and I'd like to take care of her, instead of a stranger. I could be gone for as long as a week. Given the circumstances, I thought it best to deliver Angela to you."

"Sure."

Caleb motioned for Grace to come over so he could introduce her. "Grace, this is my mother, Maddie. Mom, this is Grace."

Maddie was pleasant-looking, with a kind face and intelligent eyes. Her voice was pleasant, as well. "Grace, it's wonderful to meet you." She reached for the door handle. "I guess I should at least get out of the car."

"That's okay." Grace figured time was of the essence or the woman wouldn't have driven to the campground. "Sounds like you have somewhere you need to go." She motioned to the tents. "And we don't really have many amenities. No chairs. No refreshments."

Maddie nodded. "We'll have to sit down and talk the next time we meet."

Angela had gotten out on the other side. "'Bye, Gran," she said before slamming the door.

The girl carried a sleeping bag and a backpack. "Where do these go, Dad? In your tent?"

She started for the green one but stopped short when Caleb told her, "Grace is using that tonight."

"That's okay," Grace put in swiftly. "We can share. There's enough room for two of us girls in there."

The look Angela threw her way could have frozen her solid if the coldness were due to natural phenomena. The girl ignored her offer. "Where are you sleeping, Dad?"

"In a sleeping bag by the fire."

"I'll roll mine out there, too."

CHAPTER TWELVE

"How about finding some firewood?" Caleb asked Angela. "You're good at that."

And many other tasks of camping. The two of them had enjoyed outings in the woods since his daughter was small. Maybe this would be a chance to re-create some of that goodwill they used to share. It was worth a shot.

When Angela set off into the woods with no complaint, he told Grace, "We can get the food ready and the cookware." Then he broached the topic of Angela's surprise appearance. "Things didn't turn out the way we expected this weekend, I guess."

She smiled. "Don't be concerned. It'll work out."

He hoped so. Meanwhile, he'd try to keep himself in check. No searching gazes with Grace. No handholding. Not that he'd been planning on romancing her during a campout with a class. But he was finding it difficult to keep his distance.

Grace eyed the surrounding trees. "What about sticks for roasting hot dogs and marsh-mallows?"

"Save the branches." He opened the front door of the truck and reached under the seat for the foldable metal forks he'd stuck there. "I brought a dozen of these."

She nodded. "Using reusable sticks for roasting food is ecological."

"It was nice of you to offer to share the tent with Angela." He was glad Grace didn't seem fazed by the change in plans.

"I probably wouldn't have wanted to get so up close and personal with my father's girl-friend when I was a teenager."

"Did he have a girlfriend?"

She looked thoughtful. "At least once. He didn't talk about her much." Then she laughed, her blue eyes crinkling in that way he appreciated. "He probably wasn't serious or he would have introduced me. I don't know what I would have thought. It's interesting to see the other side of things, isn't it?"

She could always put herself in another's shoes. Empathy. Another of her qualities that he liked.

A few minutes later, his daughter entered

the camp with an armload of wood. Her expression was neutral.

"Go ahead and build the fire, too," he told Angela.

"Uh-huh."

She built it like a pro and the wood was crackling by the time the students had returned for the evening meal. Caleb introduced them to his daughter and everyone seemed pleasant and didn't question why their professor now had two extra guests for the campout.

Furthermore, from the way the students were talking, it sounded as if they had gotten a lot of good work done. Graham had found another patch of garlic mustard and had marked it on the map. The next part of his project was to notify the authorities about it. Beth and Lindsey and Sheridan had collected water from the spring and the creek. They planned to get another sample the next day from a small lake on the other side of the grounds. Now everybody pitched in to set up a grill over the fire for burgers and corn. Steve had made a big pot of chili to heat up. Jimmy volunteered to roast hot dogs for anyone who wanted them.

Caleb filled up plates for both Grace and Angela, as well as for himself. He handed one to Angela, then came back and seated himself on the log next to Grace.

"Yum," she said, folding the bun over her burger. "There's something about food cooked over an open fire that just can't be beat."

"I totally agree."

After the main course, they toasted marshmallows for s'mores. The sun having sunk beyond the trees, the woods were dark.

"Guess you really like 'em burnt, huh?" Steve remarked when Jimmy's marshmallow went up in flames.

Jimmy grunted and rose to shake off what was now a burning ember at the end of his stick. He looked around. "Wow, we aren't alone."

Caleb glanced about. More than a dozen sets of small golden eyes glowed back at the group of humans from the surrounding brush and trees. He felt Grace edge a little closer to him on the log.

"Just raccoons," he stated.

Jimmy peered into the bushes. "Do you think they like marshmallows?"

"They like anything edible." Caleb chuckled. "Don't feed them or you'll be inviting an invasion."

"Aw, but they're probably hungry," said Lindsey, captivated by the small furry creatures.

"You'll encourage them to bug other campers," Caleb told her. "And make them even more dependent on humans."

Jimmy reached in his backpack. "I need to take some photos of this, don't I, Prof? This is a perfect example of how animal behavior has been changed by humans. I bet lots of campers actually do feed them."

"Which is the reason there are so many," agreed Caleb. "That and the lack of predators. I mean coyotes run some of them down, but they don't have to worry about wolves or cougars."

Jimmy turned on the camera's flash and snapped photos while everyone watched. The raccoons didn't seem frightened at all. In fact, some of them showed themselves at the edge of the clearing, black masks, fluffy pelts and big striped tails making them look like mischievous, roly-poly "bad guys" from old movies.

"Ooh," Sheridan breathed. "There used to be wolves and cougars in this forest, huh? Predators that could eat raccoons! I wouldn't want any big creatures looking us over in the dark."

Caleb grunted. "We aren't on many of their menus."

"But what if there were still cougars in southern Wisconsin? Or bears?" said Steve. "And what if one went crazy or something?"

That launched the group into telling scary stories that featured bears, wolves, mountain lions, even a moose attack, all probably seen on Animal Planet. Caleb patted Grace's hand, though he didn't think she was scared. She reached for his to give it a squeeze. He noticed his eagle-eyed daughter giving them a dirty look. He wondered what it was going to take to get her used to the idea of his liking this woman.

"I saw a video of a place in India where a tiger killed two fishermen who were rowing up a river," said Beth. "People started having to wear masks on the back of their heads to stop the attacks."

Steve snorted. "There aren't any tigers in Wisconsin!"

"Thank goodness," Beth shot back. "I wonder if the same mask technique would work with cougars."

"Hey, let's be conscious of what we're

doing here," Caleb cut in, having heard enough. "Remember you're just telling stories. People like drama and being scared, yet safe. We've demonized a lot of predators that way through the centuries. If you see big teeth, you think they're for you. They're not. Big predators prefer moose or deer."

"Or raccoons," said Steve, laughing. He looked around. "Hey, anybody know a good ghost story?"

"Well, it's not really about ghosts but there's the one about two teenagers who were parked in the woods," began Jimmy. "At the same time, there was a convict on the loose and he only had one hand."

"But he had a hook," Graham went on. "While the teenagers were sitting there, they heard a scraping sound and took off."

"Then the next day, they found a hook hanging from the car handle," finished Sheridan. "Who hasn't heard that old story? It's a cliché."

"You mean urban legend," said Jimmy. "When it's been around long enough, it's legendary."

Steve shrugged. "Whatever. We've all heard it."

The discussion centered on scary stories

then, all of which ended up being retellings of horror movies.

"Gee, I guess we just don't know many original ghost or monster stories," Jimmy finally said.

"Don't look at me," said Grace.

Angela leaned forward. "I know one."

Caleb suddenly had an uneasy feeling.

"You do?" Sheridan asked.

"It's bloody and real scary."

"Great." Steve leaned forward eagerly. "Tell us."

"Well, there was this old farmhouse near Sparrow Lake," Angela began, "and a weird old couple lived there and they had cows."

Though they weren't touching, Caleb was certain he could feel Grace stiffen. "Angela!"

She glared at him, her face like a thundercloud.

Caleb frowned right back at her. "Don't be telling that story. You're just spreading rumors." And he knew it would annoy Grace.

"Rumors are okay," said Steve.

If Caleb simply commanded the group not to talk about it, he knew it would only pique their interest. "That farmhouse drivel is just a story manufactured by some Wisconsin ghost tour. Actually, an elaboration of something fairly mundane. It's stupid—who's afraid of a ghost cow?"

"Oh, right, I think I saw something about that on a flier," said Jimmy. "They're all over town."

"I have a better idea," Caleb said, deciding to tell an old story that Maddie had used to scare him when he was getting out of hand. "Ever heard of the wendigo, the half beast of the North Woods?"

"Now, that's an old legend, right?" Steve quickly jumped in. "I mean, really old, like Native American or something."

"Ojibwa." Then Caleb put the spotlight back on his daughter. "You want to tell it, Angela?" They'd both heard Maddie's rendition through the years, about the wendigo stalking and carrying off unlucky wanderers in the woods.

But leave it to Angela to be peevish and uncooperative. "I don't want to tell that one. You can tell it yourself."

Caleb wanted to sigh with frustration but instead launched into the story about a monster that had stalked a village and the young hunter who refused to believe he couldn't defeat it with his spear or bow and arrow.

"He wouldn't listen to the tribe's elders and

he roamed the woods alone at night. Finally, he disappeared and all they found was a moccasin that was torn to pieces and scattered along the creek bank. So whenever the moon is low and the wind sings through the trees, keep close to camp or the wendigo might run you down."

"Pretty good," said Steve when Caleb had finished. "Though it could use more gory details."

"Yuck, that's what I hate about horror movies," muttered Sheridan. "Gory details."

"It's getting late," Caleb told them. "We have an early morning tomorrow. Probably should turn in."

A couple of students had already been yawning. Steve and Jimmy sorted through a pile on one side of the fire, looking for sleeping bags. Grace headed for her tent and ducked inside to grab a towel and washcloth. Then she headed for the park building, its single light glimmering through the trees.

Caleb flicked on his flashlight and followed her down the path.

"I'll be happy to escort you."

"Thanks, I wouldn't want the wendigo to get me." Her voice was filled with warm humor.

"Don't worry, I'll make sure it doesn't," he said, thinking they might even steal a little alone time in the dark. That would be a nice nightcap.

He found a chance as he caught up with Grace in a shady area just out of sight of the camp. He wrapped her in a bear hug.

"Oof!" she said, hands against his chest, but she sounded amused.

"How about a kiss for your protector?" he whispered, covering her lips with his own.

"Sure *you're* not the wendigo?" she mumbled, winding her arms about his neck.

ANGELA ROLLED HER sleeping bag out on top of the tarp her dad had brought, feeling thoroughly disgusted. She grabbed her toothbrush out of her backpack and headed toward the restroom only to see her dad nudge that woman off the path, into the shadows. Then he enveloped her in his arms and kissed her!

She couldn't believe her father had brought Grace Huber along on a class camping trip. Or that he was flaunting her in front of his students. That he was kissing her! What if someone else saw them? Bad enough she did. Her dad was too old for this kind of stuff.

Yuck! She loudly cleared her throat.

They immediately pulled apart and her dad said, "Angela?"

"Good night!" she announced smugly, passing the pair without a glance back, knowing she'd thoroughly interrupted the moment.

Inside the restroom, Angela quickly took care of her teeth and rushed back out of the building, passing Grace in the doorway. Her expression seemed uncomfortable. Good.

Angela stomped back to camp and had made herself comfy in the sleeping bag when a vibration buzzed on her hip. The phone! She slid it out to take a look and saw it was Kiki.

"Hi." She glanced about but no one was paying attention to her. Still, she quickly dived under the covers and kept her voice low. "I'm up north at Birdwing State Park. Yeah, with Dad for his ecology class campout. And that Huber woman is here with him. And I saw them kissing!"

"Blea-ah! Want me to come to the rescue?" asked Kiki.

"I don't think you can find us. And Dad would be mad."

"Why? He shouldn't be the only one who can bring a guest. Where are you?"

"Campsite 32. It's too far, though. Don't bother."

"It shouldn't be that far on Viper's scooter. I'll look at a map."

Eyes on the path to the park building, Angela had been watching carefully for her Dad's return. He suddenly appeared, only yards away, Grace beside him.

"I've asked everyone not to use their phones. So please turn yours off."

Punching the phone off, she carefully tucked it under the pillow she'd made out of a towel and hunkered down, her back toward the space where she assumed Dad would put his sleeping bag. She heard him get it ready and climb inside. Then things got quiet. The fire was dying down and she wasn't at all sleepy. What was she going to do with herself?

GRACE CRAWLED INTO the tent and switched off her flashlight. Before getting into her sleeping bag, she unzipped the mesh and stuck her head out of the door flap to appreciate a scene of incredible beauty. Tall trees surrounded the campsite and the dying fire bathed the scene in a dim orange glow. Wind rushed through the trees. High above, a half-moon slid west across the sky. Humans had been gazing at that moon since ancient times and listening to the sounds of nature. Modern society should listen a bit more, she thought, grateful that Caleb had brought her along on the campout. She needed to immerse herself in the outdoors more often. She felt like a new person.

And she so enjoyed being with Caleb. Even if she had to share him with his class and now his sulky daughter. The girl was so angry all the time. Grace would love to make friends with her. Instead, she found herself constantly fending off the teenager's hostility.

She closed the tent flap then and scrunched down into her sleeping bag. Hiking through all the fresh air had made her feel deliciously bone-tired. The sound of moving leaves in the wind lulled her better than any lullaby. Soon her eyelids drifted shut...

...only to pop wide open again at the sound of a bloodcurdling shriek! Grace sat straight up in the tent, her heart pounding.

"Hey, stop it!" came Jimmy's voice.

"What's going on?" mumbled someone else.

Poking her head out of the tent again, Grace caught sight of two furry bodies, raccoons, dragging a large plastic bag toward the trees, spilling food as they went. Two other raccoons ran in to pick up the spoils, faced off, and one of them let out another loud shriek.

The camp stirred, everyone awake.

"What's going on?" shouted Caleb.

Things quieted down quickly and Jimmy said sheepishly, "I guess they got into a fight over my cheese puffs. I didn't know raccoons could scream like that."

"Cheese puffs? What are you doing with cheese puffs?" grumbled Steve. "We're supposed to be sleeping."

"And the food should be in the vehicles," chided Caleb.

"But I always take food to bed with me," said Jimmy. "I get hungry at night."

"You had an open bag of cheese puffs in your sleeping bag?" Caleb sounded disbelieving.

"I didn't have the snack *in* my sleeping bag. Nearby. I didn't think they'd come that close."

Caleb said nothing else but he was up and moving around. "Okay, anyone else got any food? Otherwise, let's get back to sleep."

"Cheese puffs!" Steve laughed and most of the others joined him.

Caleb came by the tent to see Grace. "I guess you're okay?"

"Just fine." She chuckled, relieved that they

were only invaded by raccoons. Getting back into her sleeping bag, she pulled the cover up to her chin. She glanced at her glow-in-the-dark watch and noted it was around 1:00 a.m.

Soon it was quiet and very, very dark.

She quickly fell asleep.

She dreamed of trees. Lots of trees. And leaves. And branches. And the wind.

Then the trees started moving, branches fell and covered her, even her mouth.

"Yeeek!"

THE SCREAM BROUGHT the camp out of their sleeping bags again. Heart beating fast, Caleb rolled to his feet, thinking he saw a shadowy figure run toward the trees. Someone was in the camp? An attacker? He wasn't sure whether to go after the intruder or help the victim.

Who *was* the victim? In the dark, he could barely make out anyone. He scrabbled to get his flashlight, but when he located it, the beam showed nothing but trees. And rumpled campers.

Steve staggered to his feet. "Professor Blackthorne? Raccoons again?"

"I don't think so. That scream sounded human."

He could still make out muffled cries and they were coming from the direction of Grace's tent.

"Grace!" Caleb ran toward a struggling mass on the ground where the standing green tent used to be. Arms and legs thrashed beneath the canvas.

"Hey, the tent fell down!" Steve was by Caleb's side.

Holding his flashlight under his chin, Caleb searched for the mesh beneath the front flap and opened it. Grace popped out, her hair standing on end.

"Whew! Wow, that was a scare!"

"Are you okay?" He helped her up.

She was trembling, and without thinking, he gave her a tight hug.

"I think so." She told him, "I was dreaming about trees and branches falling. Then, all at once, they fell on me. What happened?"

"That's what I want to know." He'd put up the tent himself and knew it had been secure.

Moving the beam of the flashlight around, he saw the problem.

As did Steve. "Someone tore a couple of the stakes up! Right out of the ground!"

All the campers were awake and on their

feet by now. But they hadn't made the jumble of footprints surrounding the tent.

"Somebody's been up to no good," said Caleb.

"A stalker?" asked one of the girls.

"Nah." Caleb didn't want to frighten them. "Probably just high school kids playing a prank." He slid the beam of the flashlight around, noticing Angela's empty sleeping bag. His heart sank. "And I think I know who. Go back to sleep."

"How can we sleep now?" said Sheridan, but she and the other two girls returned to their tent.

Steve muttered but went back to his sleeping bag and Graham crawled into his tent. Jimmy had gone to one of the vehicles, probably to get something to eat.

Caleb asked Grace to hold the flashlight while they put the tent up again. He repositioned it slightly so the stakes could be driven into new holes.

When they had finished, she told him, "Thanks."

"You're welcome. Sorry about this."

"Angela?"

"I'm afraid so." He looked over his shoul-

der. "She may have run off through the woods.
I'm going to look for her."

"I'm so sorry for all the trouble."

He bit back anger at his wayward daughter.
"You shouldn't be sorry. It's not your fault."

"She may never accept me. We have to
consider that."

He knew that, unfortunately, but he said,
"You're not the real problem."

They parted when Grace crawled back
under the tent. Caleb glanced toward the east
where he thought he could catch a glimmer
of a lightening sky. It would soon be dawn.

Using the flashlight, he followed the footprints into thick foliage until they ended at
the road. He crossed it and headed for the
park building, where he caught sight of Angela sitting on the concrete step.

"I can't believe it." He strode toward her
with purpose. "You can't behave yourself no
matter what." At least she hadn't taken off
completely.

She didn't say anything, merely hung her
head.

He stood over her. "Are you ashamed of
yourself? Finally? You ruined the campout."

She sounded as if she'd been crying when

she said, "I didn't ruin it. The students can do their projects."

"Well, you ruined the experience for Grace." And would probably make him look like an idiot to his students, once they found out his daughter had sabotaged the tent.

"You ruined things yourself. You shouldn't have brought that woman."

"Grace is a decent person if you'd ever take the time to find out. My entire life does not revolve around you."

"It doesn't even include me."

"Angela!" He felt genuinely hurt. "I can't believe you'd even say that. I've worked so hard to make a life for you, to make sure that you got what a child needs."

She didn't reply, merely gazed at her shoes.

"What do you want, to be arrested or something?"

"Arrested?"

"One of the students might call the rangers tomorrow morning about an intruder in the camp. I'm going to have to tell them it was you."

"It wasn't me, Dad."

"Don't lie to me."

"I'm not lying. I didn't touch that tent."

"Then who did?" Even as he said it, he already knew.

"I told her not to do it. I knew it would just make even more trouble. She wouldn't listen!"

Kiki.

"That's enough from her, too." He quickly made up his mind. "Wandering around in the middle of the night. Pulling pranks. She's not even of age. I'm going to have a talk with her foster parents."

"Dad! They'll put her in the state juvenile facility!"

"Yes, they probably will. Maybe that would be better for her. Give her some structure and discipline."

"Dad, please! She's my best friend."

He sighed. What was he going to do?

CHAPTER THIRTEEN

NELLIE HAD BECOME something of a night owl as she got older, especially on the weekends when the consignment shop was open only Saturday afternoon. She got a kick out of fixing a big bowl of popcorn and allowing herself the luxury of eating it in bed while she and Olive watched one of the classic movie channels.

It was around midnight on Saturday when she decided there was a movie she wanted to see starring Gary Cooper. She'd always loved that actor. After putting a bag of popcorn in the microwave, she poured herself a drink of water. She nearly spit it out when she heard the most unholy screams coming from the direction of the community's parking lot.

"What in the world?" She grabbed her robe and, doing a fancy dance with her feet to keep Olive inside, exited the condo.

Lights were turning on in other units. A couple of people joined her on the trek out back.

"Someone's been attacked!" cried Sandra Higgins, a neighbor from the other side of the little plaza dividing the buildings.

"Sounds like it," agreed Nellie, though she wasn't the sort to come to hasty conclusions. However, she was suddenly sorry she hadn't brought her broom as a weapon.

Several residents had gathered together in a little group around a figure sprawled on the concrete. It was Mr. Cassidy, the quiet man who lived in a corner apartment. Nellie couldn't tell for sure, but it looked as if he had a big gash on his head.

"Did you see it?" Cassidy panted as the others helped him get up. He didn't seem to be badly hurt.

"See what?" said Nellie, looking around. "The trespasser? Is she back? I thought the police took care of that."

"It ran right over me! It was big and black and white!"

"It?" repeated Nellie.

"The ghost cow!" exclaimed one woman. "It really is haunting the place."

"There are no ghosts!" Nellie insisted, though her voice quavered. Big and black and white?

Mr. Cassidy groaned and picked up his

glasses, which had fallen on the concrete. "I couldn't see so well without these, but, well, it sure *felt* like a cow. Galloped right up behind me and knocked me flat."

For once, Nellie was speechless.

ON MONDAY MORNING, Grace felt great physically. Despite being startled awake twice during the night of the camping trip and having a tent fall on her, she'd had no trouble going back to sleep. Chalk it up to the power of nature and its bone-deep peacefulness.

She'd slept fairly well last night, too, even though she'd headed for bed questioning her relationship with Caleb. She was beginning to wonder how serious they were going to get and whether going forward was such a good idea when his daughter objected so strenuously. That thought was the only darkness shadowing the beautiful sunny day she could see outside her office window.

With a brisk knock on the door, Carol poked her worried face in. "There are a couple of people from Green Meadows here to see you. Are you available?"

"Sure," Grace said with surprise, not having expected anyone.

The receptionist opened the door farther to admit Nellie Martin and Ed Cassidy, another resident of the community. Like Nellie, Ed had purchased one of the smaller apartments and lived alone. Today, he wore a large gauze bandage on his forehead.

"What can I do for you?" Grace asked, motioning for them to take a seat in the comfortable chairs across from her desk.

"Well, um…" Ed began, then cleared his throat.

"It seems we're still having 'ghost' problems," Nellie said bluntly.

Grace was nonplussed. "What? Is the trespasser back?"

"It wasn't human," Ed broke in. "Ran right over me in the parking lot."

"Not human?"

"I said it was a 'ghost' problem but it's got to be a human or an animal," said Nellie, correcting her companion. "I told Ed we should talk to you. I think somebody is trying to mess around with us out there. We have to do something about it."

"First things first." Grace needed focus. "Exactly what happened? When?"

"On Saturday night I went out to the

parking lot to get something out of my car," explained Ed. "I heard some kind of noise—scraping or some such—and then a big animal came up from behind me and knocked me flat. Could have given me a concussion."

Grace stared at the bandage. "Did you go to the emergency room?"

"It wasn't that bad a bump. I got more of a scare, really."

"What on earth?" Grace remained puzzled. "Was it a robbery attempt, I wonder?"

"No one stole anything. I said it was some kind of animal," said Ed. "I couldn't see the details." He pointed to his wire-rim glasses. "It knocked them off. But I could tell it was big and black and white. It had terrible breath, too. All hot and foul like."

Grace tried to figure out from his description what had attacked him but, for the life of her, could come up with nothing. Big and black and white? "Could a local farmer have had some livestock escape? It might have been an accident, not a deliberate prank."

"Or some teenager decided to take another swipe at us," said Nellie. "So far, we've had painted walls and broken windows. Now this."

Grace objected, "On Saturday night, the teenager who was responsible for those other acts was on a camping trip."

Nellie shrugged. "I'm just saying, it seems like another prank."

"Well, I'll look into it right away," Grace promised. Though what she was going to do, she had no idea.

"I guess we should tell the police," said Nellie. "But I thought we needed to talk to you first, since I heard you were already working with those teenagers."

"I'm putting together some community service for one of them."

Grace didn't know about Kiki. Caleb said Angela's friend had visited the campground in the wee hours of the morning. Would the girl have had enough time to visit Green Meadows' parking lot beforehand? If so, she would have been on a scooter.

Grace asked, "You didn't hear the sound of a motor, like one from a scooter, before or after you were hit, did you?"

"No, no motor. Just a scraping sound and thudding feet."

Feet? "Hooves? Could it have been a horse?"

"Big as a horse," was all Cassidy said.

Grace didn't think Kiki had access to a horse and she couldn't have ridden it all the way to Birdwing Park. Not to mention Angela had claimed she drove the scooter up there.

"Exactly what time did you say this happened?" was Grace's final question as Nellie and Cassidy got ready to leave.

"I was about to watch a midnight movie when I heard the commotion," Nellie told her.

"Midnight." Then Grace added, "Don't worry about talking to the police. I'll contact them."

"This has to stop," Nellie repeated, getting up.

"It certainly does."

Grace watched the pair leave, then turned to gaze out the window again, thoroughly perplexed.

BY MIDAFTERNOON, GRACE had talked to Alex Novak, who suggested she install security cameras. She wrote down the number of someone local who could do the work but decided to deal with that tomorrow.

Meanwhile, Alex had also asked about the community service so she needed to call Caleb to see if Angela had come up with any ideas for the mural she'd suggested. She was about to make the call when she saw her father enter the offices, a grumpy look on his face. But then, when didn't he look grumpy?

Henry Huber gave Carol a nod, put his briefcase down and came right on in to talk to his daughter. That was unusual, since he normally summoned her to his own desk.

"And how have things been going with you?" He made himself comfortable in a chair.

"I had a good weekend. Camping. How's Milwaukee?"

"I got a lot accomplished. Green Meadows been nice and quiet?"

"Uh…"

He raised his brows.

"Except for something or someone running down a resident in the parking lot." She may as well tell him. Otherwise, he would hear it somewhere else.

"Now the parking lot?" His face darkened. "One of your precious teenagers again?"

"Not Angela Blackthorne, the girl who broke the window. She was on the same camping trip as me."

"You went camping with her? Is that a new way to counsel troubled teens?"

"No, Dad. The campout was an extra-credit project for Caleb's environmental issues class. Angela just happened to come along." She went on, "Her friend Kiki, the other culprit in the pranks at Green Meadows, showed up later on, so it can't have been her that knocked Mr. Cassidy down in the parking lot, either." At least she didn't think so. Alex Novak wasn't so sure.

"Was this Cassidy hurt?"

"Just a scratch."

"This is outrageous, don't you think?"

"All these incidents? Yes."

"Are you sure it's not the teenagers?"

"Fairly certain. Ed Cassidy said some kind of big animal knocked him down. With foul breath. Neither of the teenagers has a cow or horse at their disposal."

"Cow? Cows and horses are vegetarians. They have sweet breath."

"They do? When did you smell a cow's breath?"

"Your great-grandparents had a farm. You know that."

She nodded. "I guess I do." That was long before her time.

Her father gave a short laugh, though nothing was funny. "I don't know about ghost cows, of course. Sure it wasn't a Newfound-land?"

She pictured a large dog in her mind. Which reminded her of something.

"But that's not why I came in here to talk to you." Her father interrupted her thoughts, reaching behind him to close her office door. "We had a spat the last time we spoke. I wanted you to know I'm okay about it."

Good. Although he should really ask her how *she* felt about it. She knew he wouldn't.

"I've decided to give you free rein with Green Meadows."

"Uh, thanks."

"It's your baby," he told her decisively. "You need a project to learn from, before moving on to higher responsibilities."

Which she was more and more *not* looking forward to.

"All these minor decisions about costs, problems like vandalism. They're the kind of snags that teach you how to deal with larger issues, such as whether or not to sell shares or how to settle hostilities between board members."

She said nothing. She was used to her father dealing with arguments by implying they were her fault but that he would forgive her.

Then he just pushed on with his own agenda. Frankly, today she wasn't in the mood to dispute anything with him.

"I'm so happy you can give me so much insight." She tried to keep the sarcasm from her tone.

"That's what a father is for." He rose. "Guess I'll go and make some calls. I'm sure you have plenty on your plate today already."

"I surely do."

At least he hadn't contacted the police chief himself about the broken window last week as he'd threatened to do. He would have told her. And Alex would have mentioned it.

After taking a few deep breaths, she phoned Caleb's cell.

"Hi, Grace."

She loved the way he said her name, with such warm intonation.

"Have you recovered from the weekend?"

"Actually I found it rather peaceful in spite of falling tents." She got to the point. "Have you talked to Angela about the mural?"

"She already has some ideas sketched out. Want to come by later and discuss them?"

"I'd love to." She had thought about supplies. "She'll need paint for a big mural and brushes, right?"

"I'll pay for them. I can order supplies from the art store near the campus. Faculty get a discount there."

He didn't have to provide anything but she knew he would insist. "Is there a special paint for murals?"

"A type of acrylic. Paint that's made for stone or walls. The girls weren't using that before when they vandalized Green Meadows."

"Is there a particular palette of colors?"

"Colors depend on the subject of the painting. I believe an artist can pretty much mix any tone or shade with the basics. But you should have some input. You know what would look nice with your decor out there."

"I want it to be a personal expression. Real art."

"That still gives you a lot of leeway. Why don't you drop by the store and take a look at the paint? Pick up a color chart. We'll discuss it and decide how much she needs when we talk about the mural this evening."

"Sounds like fun." And she'd have another chance to see him again.

"So you can drop by, say, at six or so?"

"Six is fine. But I don't want to interrupt your dinner."

"You won't interrupt. In fact, I'm setting out a plate for you."

He was cooking dinner. How sweet. "Can I bring something?"

"You don't have to bring anything but yourself."

"I insist."

"Well, okay. How about dessert? I've never been good at baking."

"All right. See you then."

"I'll be counting the minutes."

She could hear the smile in his voice. They had such an easy rapport. Surely something would work out with Angela if they just put their minds to it.

GRACE LOCATED THE art store, a small purple-painted storefront that catered to the college's needs. Half the place featured stationery and office supplies and the other half artist materials. Tables and shelves were packed with paints, inks, pencils and so many different kinds of papers and canvases, Grace hardly knew where to look. She headed for the counter up front, where the clerk was talking to another customer, a woman with the longest, most beautiful blue-black hair she'd ever seen.

"She already has a lot of stuff," the customer was saying. "I just thought I'd see if I could find her something different, a little gift."

"What kind of art does she do? Printmaking? Painting? Sculpture?"

"I think mainly painting and drawing." The woman fingered a tin box of colors on the counter. "Wow, forty dollars for a set of pastel pencils. I didn't know they were so expensive."

"We stock the best professional quality here, not just for craft. The art students and instructors buy their supplies at our store." The clerk, an older woman with gray hair, indicated a smaller cardboard box. "You could get her a regular set of colored pencils. Or some markers."

"Hmm." The woman didn't seem sold on the idea.

When Grace came up to the counter, she saw that the other customer was Native American and her face was as beautiful as her hair. She widened her dark eyes slightly at Grace's arrival but returned her smile.

"I guess I'll think about it," the woman told the clerk. "Maybe I'll ask Angela what kind of present she'd prefer."

Grace couldn't help repeating the name, "Angela?"

"My daughter."

"Angela Blackthorne?"

"You know her?"

Grace realized she was speaking to Lily, Angela's mother. "I'm, uh, friends with her dad, Caleb."

Lily nodded. "Right, she's living with him. For the moment. I'm staying at the rez myself."

After illegally helping herself to one of the Green Meadows town houses. Should Grace mention that? She thought better of it. No proof was found and Angela wasn't going to come forward.

"I thought I'd get my Angel a special gift," mused Lily.

"Uh, that's nice."

"I'm going to give it to her during our next mother-and-daughter time." Lily laughed throatily. "Or I guess you could say *family* time. I'm so happy to be reunited with them."

Grace merely stood there, feeling very uncomfortable. She hardly paid attention to Lily leaving, with a promise to the clerk to come back another time. When the woman then turned to Grace, asking her what she wanted, it took her a moment or two to remember.

CHAPTER FOURTEEN

GRACE ARRIVED AT Caleb's house a little late. Disconcerted by her encounter with Angela's mother, she had to take some time to just sit in her car and chill out. Lily had indicated Angela was living with her father only "for now," which didn't mesh with what Caleb had said. More important, Lily had said she was getting back with "her family." Did that mean Angela or did it mean Angela *and* Caleb? Grace couldn't help fearing it was the latter.

Did Lily know who she was? Grace wondered. There was something about her tone that made her think the woman had been trying to upset her on purpose.

Whatever, Grace told herself, she needed to remember she had no hold on Caleb. They had made no agreement to be exclusive in dating. Just in case, for the future, perhaps she should keep a little distance between herself and the man she found herself liking so much.

That thought sent her mood spiraling downward.

At the moment, she needed to pull herself together. She had to go through with the plans she had agreed to for Angela's sake. Picking up the color chart for the special mural paint, she got out and walked up to the A-frame's door.

Caleb opened it before she had the chance to knock. He grinned. "Hi, there. You look good, as usual."

"Thanks."

So did he, with his well-worn jeans, T-shirt and bare feet. He took hold of her shoulders and leaned forward to kiss her but she offered her cheek. An action that made him look at her oddly.

They sat down at the kitchen table with Angela. She merely nodded when Grace said hello and helped herself to spaghetti from a heaping bowl. There was also salad and some crusty garlic bread.

"Do you like my special tomato sauce?" Caleb asked Grace after they'd started eating.

"It's delicious. It tastes like there's a bit of heat in it."

"I add cayenne pepper for some zing." He passed the salad. "More?"

"No, thanks." She was managing to eat, since she was hungry, but she didn't feel completely at ease.

He put more salad on her plate anyway. He peered at her curiously. "Is everything okay?"

Pushing aside the extra salad she hadn't wanted, Grace was a little annoyed that he hadn't taken her at her word.

She decided she might as well tell him about the attack in the parking lot on Saturday night. She ended with, "So Mr. Cassidy was knocked flat by some kind of animal."

"Weird." Caleb looked surprised.

"The ghost cow," Angela intoned with a little smile.

"How can you be so sure?" said Grace.

"What else could it be?"

"At least we know it wasn't you." Caleb considered a moment. "But how about Kiki?"

"She was up in the park with us, as you know."

"As you *told* me."

Angela's eyes flashed. "It's the truth, Dad."

"The incident took place around midnight," said Grace. "I don't think Kiki could have been in our parking lot with her scooter. No one heard a motor of any kind."

Since they were finished eating, Caleb

picked up the dishes and stacked them in the sink, motioning for Grace to stay seated. "No help needed. You're our guest." He turned and leaned back against the counter. "Something has to be done about Kiki. I've called her number repeatedly but she's not picking up. I guess we'll have to contact her foster home."

"No!" cried Angela. "I told you. They'll put her in juvenile!"

"I hope that's not necessary," said Grace, attempting to calm her. "I'm not going to press charges against her."

"If those awful people, her foster parents, hear anything about her, they'll try to put her away," said Angela. "She was just playing a prank at the campsite. You weren't hurt."

"Thank goodness." And, luckily, Grace wasn't the sort who would hold a grudge about it. "Doesn't Kiki have any other relatives? An aunt or uncle or cousin?"

"She has a grandmother. Somewhere."

"A grandmother," Grace repeated.

"Her mom's mother. Kiki said they were living with her grandmother in Chicago, but her mom got mad and told her mother they were leaving and would never come back."

"Chicago." Grace echoed. "I wonder how hard it would be to find her."

"Do you know her name?" Caleb asked.

"Elizabeth Hartl."

They were all silent for a minute or two.

Then Caleb switched topics. "Dessert?"

Grace suddenly realized she'd completely forgotten to buy anything. "Uh-oh, I was going to bring cupcakes."

"No problem," said Caleb. "I'm too full for much of anything."

"So am I. It's just that I promised." And it had completely slipped her mind.

Caleb said, "Seriously, we have cookies that my mother made last week. Chocolate chip. We can have them later."

She agreed reluctantly.

Caleb wiped the surface of the big round table with a towel. "Let's look at the sketches for the mural. Bring them out, Angela."

Angela left and returned with a large drawing pad.

"I haven't seen them myself," Caleb told Grace, leaning over to center a large sketch on the table, a drawing executed mainly in shades of green. He narrowed his eyes. "A forest? Looks kind of dark."

Grace didn't like the sketch at all but she decided it would be best to let Caleb be the critic. She leaned forward to point to a couple of red spots peering out of the leaves. "And what's this?"

Angela cleared her throat. "Ghost eyes."

Caleb reacted immediately. "Angela! You're just trying to be unpleasant."

"You said they wanted authentic expression."

Caleb scowled. "You're deliberately baiting us. What's the matter with you?"

The girl's face was stony. "Obviously, a lot, at least according to you."

Grace wasn't sure what to say. She wanted to be diplomatic. Finally, she settled on, "You've done such beautiful pictures of nature." She indicated a painting on the kitchen wall. "Like that landscape. Something along those lines would be nicer for Green Meadows."

"What else have you got?" Caleb demanded of his daughter.

"Well, there's this one." Angela took another sheet from the pad, a drawing of an old Gothic-looking house.

Grace sighed in disappointment. "The haunted farmhouse."

Suddenly Caleb stood, startling both women. "That's it, Angela. Either come up with something appropriate or I'm going to ask Grace to go ahead and press charges!"

"Dad!" Angela sounded tearful. "Do you want me to have a record?"

"No, I don't, but you deserve one." Caleb didn't bother to hide his disappointment. "Why can't you behave like the decent human being I raised you to be? I know you're mad about your mother but I don't deserve to suffer for that. And neither does Grace. She's gone out of her way to treat you more kindly than you deserve."

"Only because she wants to impress *you*!" Angela sniffled.

"I haven't been trying to impress your father," Grace said quietly, "I've been easy on you because I've been in your position."

Angela gazed at her disbelievingly. "Your life can't be anything like mine."

"When I was a little younger than you, my mother went off and left me, too. It still hurts me to think about it." It was time Grace shared more with the troubled young girl. "I had a twin brother, who was killed. My mother couldn't deal with it and left my father and me to fend for ourselves. I felt rejected and angry and acted out."

Angela focused on Grace. "Acted out? What did you do?"

"Oh, I hung out with kids my father hated. Snuck out at night. Partied. Got involved in a little vandalism." Though she'd been sneakier than Angela. It seemed as if the girl wanted to get caught.

"You can see why she understands this situation." Caleb pulled out a chair to sit back down at the table. "And I was a wild kid myself. You're not alone in your experience, Angela."

"You're lucky you have a parent in your corner," Grace said. "Your dad does everything he can for you, just like mine did."

Angela was silent for a couple of minutes, fingering the drawing pad. She gave a big sigh, then said, "Okay, let me think about the mural." She started to head out of the kitchen but stopped. "How big is the wall anyway? Is it a square or a rectangle?"

Grace thought she detected a difference in attitude. "A rectangle. But I haven't measured it. We need to do that."

"The size will affect the final composition," Angela said.

"Does this mean you're going to work on a *real* landscape?" Caleb asked.

"My art is always based on reality but I'm going to work up a sketch that is more natural." The teenager made her way across the adjoining family room and turned down a hallway, calling back, "I have homework to do, so I'll have the new sketch done in a couple of days."

Caleb raised his brows at Grace. "We can take that as progress, right?"

"I hope so."

Now if only she could get a better handle on how much energy to put into their problematic relationship.

Since it was relatively early, not yet quite dusk, Caleb suggested that he and Grace drive over to Green Meadows to check out the wall for the mural. Angela was doing homework but he still didn't trust her, so he told her they would be back in a few minutes.

In reality, he intended to spend a bit more time alone with Grace. He wasn't sure why but there seemed to be a distance between them tonight. Maybe she was just in a bad mood but, if so, he wanted to find out what had caused it.

"Have a hectic day?" he asked as he drove.

"Somewhat."

"Who complained about the attack at Green Meadows Saturday?"

"A resident named Mr. Cassidy. Nellie brought him in to talk to me. I think there were other people awakened by the incident, though."

"Well, it can't have been Lily who knocked him over. She's living on the rez now."

"I know."

"Did I tell you that?" He couldn't remember.

"She said that she was living there. I saw her this afternoon at the art store."

"Today?" He was surprised. "I wonder what she was doing there."

"She said she was looking for a gift for Angela."

"Really? You talked with her?"

"Just for a moment. I overheard her mention your daughter's name and I asked her if she meant Angela Blackthorne."

"Though where she'd get the money for a gift, I don't know. Did she say something that upset you?"

"We've, uh, never agreed to be exclusive, Caleb."

He frowned. "What do you mean by that?"

"Lily said she was glad to be back with her

family. I assume she meant not only Angela, but you, as well."

She was jealous! He couldn't believe it. "I'm flattered, Grace, if that means you're concerned about Lily and me getting back together, but there is no such possibility."

Her face turned pink. "I shouldn't even have brought it up. I have no hold on you."

She definitely had a hold on him. "You have every right to bring it up. But, for your information, I only date one woman at a time and, at the moment, that woman is you."

In fact, she might just be the woman he wanted to be with forever, but he wasn't going to admit that right now. It could scare her. Not to mention they had a few obstacles to deal with, number one being his daughter.

She still looked uncomfortable.

"Did Lily imply that she and I were getting back together?"

"Not in exact words." Grace sighed and gazed out the passenger window. "Look, I'm sorry. This is awkward."

They had reached Green Meadows, so he pulled in to park.

He turned off the truck and slid an arm across the back of the seat. "Look, I don't know what her motives are, Grace, but Lily

Trejo isn't on the up-and-up, as you know from her squatting in your empty town house. She knows who you are. She might try to take advantage of you."

"Why would she want to do that?"

"Because of your connection to me. She doesn't love me anymore, if she ever did, but I believe she's jealous of anything that might make me happy. Don't let her get to you. She's turned Angela inside out. You've been so understanding about her from the day we met. You have no idea how much I appreciate that," he said, meaning it from his heart.

"I guess you have to remember Angela has a mother who wants to see her. Maybe something good will come of it."

"Maybe. I'll just have to ride it out." He looked at her. "Meanwhile, being with you is the only positive here. I don't want to lose you."

"You won't."

"Things might get even messier. I hope you'll stick with me."

"If you're honest about your intentions, you won't be able to get rid of me."

"I'll take that as a yes." And he drew her closer to kiss her.

Her lips were soft and she wound her arms

around his neck. For a moment, the day's problems and irritations melted away.

GRACE FELT MUCH better after she had talked with Caleb. The subject matter had been uncomfortable but he'd handled it well, making her feel as if there was real promise in their relationship. She appreciated being with a mature and thoughtful man.

When they inspected the wall she had in mind, inside the community center, Caleb was enthusiastic. He took out his tape measure. "A nice rectangle that's perfect for a landscape. Ten feet by what, eight feet? Do you want the mural to reach the ceiling?"

"I think it would be better to limit it to eight by five feet, actually. It can be framed by the wall around it."

"Whichever, it'll be the largest piece Angela has ever done."

"She could bring in a friend to help."

He gave her a warning glance. "Not Kiki. I'd like to see her with kids who are less problematic. I need life to be simple."

"I completely understand." She hesitated a second, then said, "Maybe if we could find Kiki's grandmother, someone who cares about the girl, it would put her on a better path."

"If we knew how to find her." He considered a moment. "Maybe Mom would have some ideas of how to go about it. I'll ask her."

Grace looked at her watch. "About ready to call it a night?"

"I guess so. I enjoy being with you so much, I forget the passing of time."

She grinned. "That's a great thing to tell a woman." After the fears she'd had at the beginning of the evening.

"I aim to please."

It was completely dark when they returned to the truck. Caleb opened the door for Grace and got in himself. He nosed the vehicle down the driveway and stopped before entering the highway to allow a car to pass. On the other side and a few yards to the south was a turn-off for a country road bordered by thick brush and trees. Grace glanced at that area when Caleb pulled out and immediately stiffened. Two glowing red orbs stared out at them amid the leaves.

"Stop!"

Caleb braked to nearly a stop. "What? A deer?"

"No, go back. I saw something on the side of that gravel road."

"You saw something?" He quickly did a U-turn, after checking both directions for oncoming cars. Then he turned down the country road.

"There." Grace pointed. Only one of the red orbs showed as the beam of the headlights swept over the foliage. Then the other winked in the darkness. She felt gooseflesh rise on her arms. "Red eyes."

Now Caleb saw it, too. "Red eyes?"

"The ghost cow?"

"They're not moving." He waited a minute. "But something is flapping." He parked the truck on the edge of the road and reached over her to remove a flashlight from the glove compartment. "We're going to investigate."

She wasn't dressed for walking over uneven ground. Her high heels sunk into the gravelly dirt, and thick weeds scratched her legs. As they made their way through low-hanging branches and leaves that slapped them in their faces, Caleb put an arm around her waist to steady her.

"Careful," he said, then flashed the beam of the flashlight on a nearby fence post, separated from the overgrown roadside by a small ditch.

Grace started when something fluttered in the wind, something dark with spots. Then they saw the glowing red orbs. But it was no ghost cow they faced. It looked and sounded like plastic. A garbage bag fastened or caught on the post?

"And reflectors," Caleb finished her thought. "Stay here. Hold on to that tree so you don't fall."

He jumped over the ditch and approached the fence post, leaving Grace in the dark. The garbage bag crackled in the breeze, followed by a ripping sound.

"Got it," said Caleb, grunting. "Now for this. I'm gonna tear out these reflectors. But I need a tool." He rummaged in his pocket, coming up with something—probably a pocketknife.

When he finished, they returned to the road and the truck.

Caleb held a large torn piece of black plastic in the beam of the truck's headlight. It was splotched with what looked like white paint. "I didn't get all of it but somebody tore up a garbage bag and attached it to the post. Look at the nail holes." He reached in his pocket and took out a three-inch translucent red disk. "This is the type of reflector farmers can buy to put on equipment."

"It glows in headlights."

"And there were two of them nailed close enough to look like eyes."

"Someone had to have done this deliberately."

"They sure did. With a hammer."

"Why? To look like a ghost cow?"

"Seems like it." Caleb mused, "Green Meadows is haunted all right, but not by a ghost. Someone is playing pranks."

"Angela?"

"I hope not. But I'm going to ask her," he said. "Have you seen this before?"

"No, but it was kind of hidden in the brush."

"You spotted it tonight."

"And I've been out here after dark. I'm in and out a lot of the time to check on things."

"I don't think Angela would have had time to do it, at least in the past few days," he said. "It would more likely be Kiki."

Grace was angry that the girl kept pulling pranks. "If you think it could be her, I'd like to talk to her."

"We'll have to deal with the foster family."

Grace hoped that was a good idea. If the girl's situation went from bad to worse, Kiki might never have a chance at a decent life.

CHAPTER FIFTEEN

"THIS IS IT." Caleb parked in front of a modest two-story house at the edge of town. After he'd picked Grace up at her office, it had taken him merely minutes to find the house where Kiki lived.

Grace still wasn't certain Kiki was the one responsible for the glowing-eyes contraption they'd found by the side of the road. She'd already eliminated Kiki from contention for the parking lot incident, if not the tent falling on her at the park. The girl couldn't have been in two places at the same time. But still they needed to talk to her.

Caleb glanced at his watch. "School is out by now, though that doesn't mean we'll find Kiki here. She seems to get around."

The blare of a TV could be heard as they climbed the steps to the front porch and knocked. A woman wearing a big frown answered the door. "Who are you?"

"Caleb Blackthorne. And this is Grace Huber."

"Sarah Watson."

"We'd like to talk to you for a few minutes," Caleb began.

"About what? One of the little maniacs do something again?"

"Maybe," Grace answered, not liking the woman's accusatory tone.

"Kiki is a friend of my daughter's."

"Come right in." The woman opened the door wider. "Kiki's not here right now, though."

They entered a hall that passed by what Grace assumed to be the living room, and then headed for the kitchen. Off the kitchen an addition had been built with strikingly different flooring, cheap laminate in comparison with the kitchen's linoleum. The large space held the TV that was blasting away, a couch and chair set that had seen better days, and two unsmiling teenage girls, who were now staring at the visitors.

Rather than introduce the teenagers, the woman said, "Kiki's just like her no-good mother. She'll end up in jail, too." Then she turned to Caleb. "You might want to be more careful about who you let your daughter be friends with." She headed for the stairs. "You can check her room."

Caleb and Grace followed.

On the landing, Sarah opened a door, revealing a medium-sized bedroom with bunk beds against one wall and two single cots parallel with another. The bedspreads were the same cheap-looking blue plaid and the walls were bare except for a small drawing of a bird tacked above the cot. Sarah Watson reached over and tore it from the wall. A wave of sadness washed through Grace at the gesture.

"I told Kiki to keep her little drawings in her notebooks." Sarah sounded disgusted.

Grace asked, "Why can't they have artwork or pictures on the walls? Or a bulletin board?"

"I want things clean and neat. These girls' lives are so messy, it can spill over into how they function day to day. I'm not a counselor. We provide a roof over their heads and two square meals a day. Otherwise, they'd be living in the streets." Sarah tore up the drawing and threw it in a wastebasket by the door. Then she said, "If you want to search for whatever the little thief stole, she has a couple of boxes under the bed."

"We're not looking for stolen items," Caleb

said. "We're just wondering if Kiki has been involved in some pranks around town."

"What kind of pranks?"

"Knocking someone down in a private parking lot," offered Grace.

"Or putting up some kind of scare cow off a country road," said Caleb. "On public property."

Sarah Watson frowned. "Scarecrow?"

"Scare *cow*," corrected Grace, enjoying the even more puzzled look that spread across the woman's face.

"We know that Kiki was in the Birdsong campground on Saturday in the middle of the night, scaring campers," said Caleb. "Don't you give these kids a curfew?"

Sarah sighed deeply. "Yes, they have a curfew." She gestured to the window. "But Kiki doesn't pay much attention to it. She climbs out the window and gets down somehow, usually when I'm asleep. Sorry, but the county doesn't pay me enough to watch them every minute." She looked back at them. "Do you want to make an official complaint? Go to the police. She'll be sent off to an institution a little sooner is all. Probably for the best."

Grace just gave Caleb a look as they finished up the conversation and left, heading for the car. They had lots to talk about.

"WE ARE NOT taking this to the police," Grace announced vehemently as they drove away.

After the visit to the foster home, Caleb could see why she'd reached that opinion but he still had doubts about how to handle the situation. "Not all young people are like you or me, Grace. Sometimes professionals are needed."

"Professionals? Such as guards and wardens?"

"I mean social workers or counselors."

"A kid doesn't get much of that in an institution."

"But you can't just let Kiki go around creating havoc." Caleb gripped the steering wheel harder. "She might really hurt someone one of these days."

"I won't be responsible for putting her in a detention center."

"If not you or me, it could be someone else who does it, then."

"Surely she's not that bad." She turned to him. "You've seen her with your daughter. She's not a serious criminal."

"Still, you can't personally save every troubled teenager in the world. You need to know when to back off. Maybe it's time we talk to Alex Novak."

"*Turn her in?* You sound like my father!"

He didn't know where that was coming from. "Is that bad?"

She made a disgusted noise.

Her irritation bothered him. "I thought your dad was in your corner when you were growing up?"

"He was always supportive of me, but that doesn't mean he would stand up for anyone else."

"Kiki has a grandmother."

"I only wish I knew where we could find her. Or if she might take the girl."

He had reached the downtown area of Sparrow Lake and turned onto the street that passed the police station.

"Police can trace people," Caleb said. "Heather Scofield once told me that Alex Novak has a heart for troubled youth." He pulled into the station's parking lot.

Grace looked around and started. "What are we doing here? I don't want to talk to the police! At least not yet."

"Then what do you suggest we do about

Kiki? Let her keeping pulling pranks?" It wouldn't hurt to talk to the police.

"No, Caleb," she said in a tone he'd never heard before. "*No*. Please drive me home."

She was actually upset, he realized.

He was about to apologize when a Sparrow Lake police car drove up and parked next to them. Alex Novak got out and opened the passenger door. A freckled kid of around twelve or so tumbled out and then a huge black-and-white Great Dane that must have been at least a yard tall at the shoulder. The dog trailed a long leash.

His window was down so Caleb could hear Alex tell the kid, "Wait here."

Then the police chief popped the squad car's trunk to remove a skateboard. Seeing Caleb and Grace, he nodded.

"Where'd you find that creature?" Caleb asked. "It's as big as some ponies."

Alex laughed and nodded toward the boy. "This is Randy Beaman." He waved to the dog. "And this is Atlas. They've been terrorizing the slow and the elderly around these parts."

"I've seen that dog," mused Grace. She raised her voice. "Has Randy been having Atlas pull him on the skateboard?"

"Wherever there's concrete. Anytime, day or night." Alex turned to Randy, motioning him to go inside the station. "We're going to have to call your folks, son. You can't use the town sidewalks for your personal speedway." Before following the boy, the police chief asked, "Did you have some problem, Caleb?"

"Not right now."

He and Grace sat for a moment, silent.

Then Grace said, "Well, I think I know who and what 'attacked' Mr. Cassidy in the parking lot."

Caleb added, "I think I know who left the big footprint beside the Green Meadows walking path."

She nodded. "And the wheel marks."

He started the engine and pulled the truck out.

The tense atmosphere having eased, he and Grace made small talk as they drove away.

"Do you want to have some supper at The Busy Corner?" he asked.

"No, thanks. I need to get home and catch up on a little work."

When he reached her building, she said, "You don't need to get out and open my door for me."

Why not? Before he could ask, she leaned across to give him a chaste kiss on the mouth. He objected, "Hey, that's not a real goodnight kiss."

"It is for this night."

"You're still angry. I said I was sorry for driving to the police station." He told her, "And I am. I care about what you think and want."

She relaxed a bit, her expression seeming to soften. "Okay. I accept your apology." She even laughed. "You could try being a little less pushy sometimes."

"I know, I know. Just push back."

And he reached for her again, this time for a longer, deeper kiss. He enveloped her in his arms, wishing they could stay like that forever. But there were things to do and places to be.

Finally, she pushed him back gently. "See you," she said, then jumped out of the vehicle.

"See you," he said as well, hoping that would be sooner rather than later.

IT TOOK GRACE a full day to forget her irritation with Caleb. Sometimes he just seemed to run over her wishes, not respecting them.

Which reminded her of the not-so-great part of her relationship with her father.

While sorting through papers on the table in her apartment, she'd found the envelope with the certificate for the dude ranch that she'd won at the fund-raiser social. There was a time limit, so she'd called Caleb and they made a date to go a few days later.

When Caleb picked her up, she noticed his baseball cap. "Nice cowboy hat."

"Isn't it?" He laughed. "I would have worn my ten-gallon Stetson but it's in storage."

He seemed to be relaxed and in good humor.

They made small talk while driving the short distance to the ranch. A fancy wrought iron gate with running horses announced "Larson Dude Ranch" where they turned in. Sam Larson was waiting for them.

"Hi there." Sam shook hands with both. "Ms. Huber."

"Grace, please."

Then he turned to Caleb. "Professor Blackthorne, I've heard about your environmental classes from Heather Scofield."

"Caleb. Nice to meet you," Caleb told him.

Sam, an attractive man with the look of an authentic cowboy about him, showed them around and let them choose their mounts. There were several horses in the corral. A young man stood inside the door of a nearby tack shed, examining a saddle.

"I like the paint," Caleb said. "How about you, Grace?" Before she could answer, he told Sam, "Something nice and gentle."

Paying no attention to Caleb, Grace pointed out a frisky, bright-eyed chestnut mare with a white streak marking her face. "I'd like that one."

"Saddle up Cloud and Lightning, Logan," Sam ordered the young man. "I'll take Marengo, as usual." He turned to the couple. "I don't know what kind of ride you want— beginning, intermediate, expert?"

"How about intermediate?" said Caleb. "That'll probably suit us."

Grace didn't know how much experience Caleb had but it may have been a while since he was on horseback.

As if he knew what she was thinking, Caleb said, "I rode a lot on the rez growing up. I don't do it as much now."

Sam and Logan tacked up the horses and Grace was the first to mount.

"Take hold of the mane, not the saddle horn," Caleb said from behind her.

"I know."

Caleb was being his usual take-charge self. Though she appreciated his warm hands on her waist as he helped her mount Lightning.

As soon as everyone was ready, Sam swung up on his own horse and led the way through a gate, then along a stretch of fence. They soon entered a beautiful, wide-open pasture.

"Notice the grasses are longer than usual out here?" Sam said. "We're letting it go back natural, only keeping the trail clear." He added, "Constant hooves on it helps keep it free of growth anyway."

"Looks great," said Caleb. "I see you have some original prairie species."

"I guess you would know," said Sam.

"We're going to create some prairie areas at Green Meadows," Grace said.

"I've seen the place when I drive by," Sam commented. "It's looking great."

"Didn't notice any ghost cows?" asked Caleb.

Sam looked puzzled. "Ghost what?"

"I guess you missed the ghost tour fliers claiming the land around Green Meadows is haunted," said Grace. She chuckled. "By a ghost cow."

Sam admitted, "Logan said some guy from

a haunted Wisconsin tour stopped out here and wanted to leave fliers. He didn't. Not sure why Logan refused."

"Well, I appreciate that he did," Grace said. "Green Meadows doesn't need bad publicity. We already have someone pulling pranks out there, trying to prove something."

"Pranks?" Sam turned back to glance at her. "Such as what?"

"Somebody built a contraption with reflectors for eyes and a white-splattered garbage bag for a body on the side of the road near the community's entrance."

"Kids?" suggested Sam.

"There's one kid we're checking into," Caleb told him.

Sam snorted and shook his head. "A fake cow might startle some people but I doubt anyone would take it seriously."

"I don't know," Grace said. "Some residents are starting to believe there might be a ghost." She had heard rumblings when she visited the community that morning. "Even though the figure people saw sneaking around at night turned out to be a squatter, and the animal that knocked down a resident in the parking lot proved to be a very large, friendly black-and-white Great Dane towing his owner on a skateboard." She'd checked with Randy Beaman and he'd shamefacedly admitted he'd accidentally run someone down at Green Meadows and was sorry about it.

"Whoa, you've had a lot going on," Sam observed. "At least it wasn't deliberate sabotage—except for the cow contraption, maybe. I was having all kinds of problems with the ranch when I first opened up. Seems I had an enemy."

"Really?" This was news to Grace.

"An old enemy. It's unbelievable how low some people will stoop to get even."

Caleb, who rode behind Grace, brought his horse up beside her. "Do you have any old enemies?"

"Not that I'm aware. I don't even have any new enemies." Unless she counted Lily. But she didn't want to think of Caleb's ex that way.

Sam called back, "When we get to the top of this hill, past that tree, how about we loosen the reins and let 'em gallop?"

Grace was about to say that sounded great when Caleb asked, "Will you be okay going fast?"

"I'll be fine." His concern was unnecessary.

"Lean forward when the horse takes off."

"I will…and I'll post when we trot, don't worry."

Grace put her heels to her horse when they reached the designated tree and felt the wind lift her hair as Lightning leaped forward. The mare's gallop was effortless and steady. Caleb's horse easily kept up, but Sam reined in Marengo after about half a mile. He turned and signaled for everyone to stop.

"I thought you'd enjoy the view. This is the highest point on the farm."

Hills undulated around them and the sky stretched blue and bright from horizon to horizon. In the distance, above some trees, Sparrow Lake's water tower was visible.

Grace took a deep breath. "I love open land and fresh air."

"Me, too," admitted Sam. "I could never be cooped up in a cubicle or some meeting room every day."

Neither could Grace. She wasn't sure how she was going to adjust if she had to move back to Milwaukee. There were plenty of running trails and the shores of Lake Michigan but she wasn't certain that would be enough.

After they'd ridden for another half hour, Sam asked, "Race you both back to the barn?"

"Whoa, I don't know if…Grace wants to do that," said Caleb.

"You don't have to protect me." Grace had had enough. "I've been riding since I was a child. I even had my own horse when I was a teenager."

"Oh." Caleb sounded a little sheepish. "Why didn't you just say so in the first place? You sit on a horse very well. I guess I should have known."

It was an exhilarating gallop back to the barn. Grace won, though she figured both men had held back a little. After dismounting, she thanked Sam and told him she wanted to come back, soon.

Caleb also seemed pleased but when they got into the truck, he said, "Why didn't you tell me about your experience? I felt silly after trying to give you tips on riding."

"Why didn't you ask?"

"I don't know. I guess I just expect you to share. I have the feeling that you don't always say what you're thinking."

"You could be right. I grew up with a parent who had plenty to say most of the time. When I didn't agree, I usually just kept things to myself. It was more peaceful that way."

"You might be better off speaking your mind more frequently."

"And you might be better off not telling me to speak my mind." But she laughed.

"Message received!" Caleb grinned. "As I said before, I'm used to telling students what to do and to raising a daughter on my own. I guess I can get a little officious."

And that might be one of the reasons Angela had become rebellious. Though Grace didn't say so and wondered if she should. She decided it was probably too much of a sore point right now.

"How's Angela doing anyway?"

"She's been busy with school and working on the mural design. Plus she's meeting her mother at her grandmother's place."

"Has she seen Kiki?"

He shrugged. "No time for that unless it's at school. They may have talked on the phone."

"I wonder what kind of student Kiki is."

"Amazingly, I've heard from Angela that she's passing."

"Well, that's one good thing at least."

Grace hoped there were more good things about the girl. Kiki'd had a terrible start in life with her father dying and mother going to jail. Grace wouldn't be surprised if the teenager was an emotional wreck.

She prayed that they could find Kiki's grandmother and that the woman would want to do right by her granddaughter. She was happy when Caleb brought up doing that internet search again. Obviously, she knew he had serious reservations about his daughter's friend, but he was still willing to help her.

A fact that made her like Caleb Blackthorne even more.

CHAPTER SIXTEEN

THE NEXT MORNING, Grace arrived at her office to find Carol wearing a glum expression.

Uh-oh. "Dad around?" Grace asked, figuring he might be making problems.

"Mr. Huber is still in Milwaukee."

"Good," she said, then covered her relief with, "Er...are you doing okay?"

"Well, the kids have driven me nuts lately... but that's not what I need to tell you." Carol had a newspaper spread out on her desk. "There's an article about Green Meadows in the *Kenosha Journal.*"

Grace picked up the paper.

"It's in the lifestyle section."

"Lifestyle? Instead of real estate?" Grace skimmed the page, stopping abruptly at the heading Haunted Green Community in Sparrow Lake.

"Oh, no!"

Accompanied by a large photo of the complex, the article went on for several columns about the history of the Whitman farmhouse, ghostly run-ins between current residents and some type of spook. The story included the parking lot incident and reports of glowing eyes in roadside foliage, along with quotes from Mr. Vincent Pryce, professional ghost hunter.

"Who is giving this ridiculous information to a reporter?" Grace asked as much to herself as to Carol. She dropped the paper back on the desk.

"Who knows? News spreads fast around here. Maybe the reporter got a lead from someone."

"Or maybe someone contacted the reporter just to make trouble."

"I saw that Spooky Tours bus drive through town last weekend," said Carol. "It was loaded with tourists. I was going to tell you about it, but I forgot. The good thing about the article is that the final paragraphs are on the community itself. Nice description."

"Really?" Grace picked up the paper again and read the end of the article more closely. "It is a good description...solar panels, sustainable materials, walking paths through the woods, harmony with nature." She sighed.

"Well, I guess, if nothing else, we got some free PR."

"Might as well look on the bright side. You can't sue them, right?"

"Probably not, but I can complain."

Which led to several frustrating phone calls to the *Kenosha Journal*, a couple of which went to voice mail. The only person Grace found was a receptionist who told her that the reporter wasn't available except by private cell number.

Grace gave up then and decided she might as well buckle down to some work for the moment. That didn't stop her from trying to figure out who had fed the reporter information and why.

MEETING WITH HER mother made Angela nervous, though she told herself Lily should be uncomfortable, not her.

But Lily looked very composed seated across from Angela at Gran Maddie's big dining table. Maddie herself was outside fussing with her herb garden, trying to give the pair a little privacy.

"So you got the afternoon off from school?" Lily asked.

"We only have a couple of weeks to go. I

had English today and the teacher excused us so we could work on our final research paper in the library."

"But you aren't in the library."

"I will be later. I only plan to be here for an hour or so."

"You want to limit our time?" Lily sounded disappointed. "I would think you have a lot of questions to ask me."

"Like what?"

"Maybe things like what I've been doing. Where I've been. I've lived in at least six states, been to all kinds of powwows. Sometimes I perform as a dancer."

"Oh? What kind of dance do you do?"

"Jingle dancing. For healing. Ever tried that yourself?"

"No, but I know something about it." Angela had seen dancers at the rez in the traditional single-color dress ornamented with rows of small metal cones. "Those outfits look heavy."

Lily smiled. "They're not that bad. It can be difficult to sit down in them, though."

"And impossible to sneak up on anyone."

Now Lily laughed. "I like your sense of humor."

Her mother was very beautiful, Angela had

to admit. She wished she'd taken more after her than her dad. The strong chin she'd inherited from him made her face look square.

"Do you have any boyfriends?"

"Uh, not right now."

"Really? When I was your age, I had at least a dozen guys after me." Lily smiled. "It's your personality that intrigues a man, you know, not just your looks. You have to know how to handle them."

"I'm not in a hurry."

And Angela wasn't ready to discuss her most personal feelings with a woman she barely knew and still did not trust. She only talked about love with her best friend, Kiki. Besides, a dozen guys interested in Lily when she was fifteen? Wasn't that when she'd been with Dad? When she'd been *pregnant*? Was that why she'd run away, because she hadn't loved Dad?

"Your father says you're an artist. Are you going to create art for a living?"

Angela shrugged. "I don't think that's possible from what Dad says."

"Oh? He's still crushing dreams, huh?"

"I wouldn't say crushing them." Angela felt protective of her father to a stranger, which her mother literally was. "He wants me to do something practical enough to earn a living."

"He was all about practical with me, too. That's why we didn't get along a lot of the time. I'm a dreamer. You ought to move to Santa Fe, New Mexico. I know a lot of people there. People who could give you a leg up in the art world."

"Really?" Angela couldn't help feeling intrigued.

"Sure." Lily folded her hands and leaned on the table, looking intently at her daughter. "I have a friend who makes a fine living selling his work in New Mexico. He's from Wisconsin originally. He would be a good mentor for you."

"Hmm, I'm not sure. I might want to just do my art as a hobby and go to school for something else."

Lily laughed. "Oh, honey, you are so innocent. You do what you want to. Follow your dreams. You know what's best for you."

Angela had always thought so. Until now. She didn't like how Lily talked about dreams so easily, as if they didn't actually mean anything. "Well, whatever I do, I want to go to college and then be successful at it, like my dad."

"But that's all overrated, honey. It's what people like your dad want you to believe. It just kills your soul."

"Dad worked hard to get where he is. He had jobs in construction and forestry, all kinds of stuff, before he got his degree."

"Uh-huh. Whatever." Lily rolled her eyes. "You could hang back a bit and do just as well, or better. You need to use your brains for something else besides stupid books."

Angela didn't agree, but she didn't know enough to argue her point.

"I'll see if I can get hold of my artist friend. We could meet," Lily said. "Meanwhile, we have to get my living situation straightened out."

"Did you find a job?" Angela knew Gran Maddie had given Lily some contact information.

"Not yet. I think I'll look for a place to stay, first. A two-bedroom would be best, don't you think? A room for me and a room for you. Honey, I'd like you to live with me. We've had too many years apart."

"I didn't agree to live with you."

"But with some money, some child support from your father, we could make it. You need to have fun. Your dad is a wet blanket. He just keeps you down."

"I love Dad."

"Well, of course you do. And he loves you." Lily's voice softened. "But I love you, too. And I'll help you make your dreams come true, Angela. If you want to be an artist, just go out in the world and create art. I don't believe in putting the practical ahead of a person's desires. That's backward."

An hour later, Angela left her grandmother's house with very mixed feelings. She needed to talk to someone else, and neither Gran Maddie nor her father would do.

AT THE LIBRARY, Angela found a couple of resources to finish her English paper. She was almost done copying some quotes when Kiki appeared and slid into a chair beside her.

The other girl looked upset. She wasn't even wearing her usual heavy makeup. "I can't believe it! Your dad and that Huber woman visited my foster home and got Mrs. Watson all freaked out. She told me to get my stuff ready to move because they're going to the police about the campground prank. It wasn't that bad, was it?"

Angela felt a thrill of fear. "Why didn't you call me?"

"I haven't been in one place long enough to recharge my phone."

"What are you going to do? Don't run away." Angela would be devastated if she lost her best friend.

"I don't want to run. I'm nearly done with this school year. I have to finish."

"I'll talk to my dad." Even if she had to beg.

"Maybe I should talk to him. We were just fooling around. It didn't hurt anybody." Then Kiki added, "He even told old Watson that I made a scarecrow or something. I don't know anything about it."

"Oh, that." Angela reassured her, "They found some contraption that was meant to scare people near Green Meadows. I told Dad I would have known if you did that. And you didn't."

Huddling together, they talked about Kiki hiding out somewhere…at least until the school semester was over. And then Angela told Kiki about her visit with her mother.

When Kiki heard the details, she remarked, "Wow, sounds like she knows a lot."

"She thinks I could get my art into galleries

in Santa Fe. I bet we can get your art sold, too. She has a friend she wants to introduce me to. He makes a living with his art. She says my dad doesn't believe in making dreams come true. He's all about the practical and that's why they didn't get along." Angela frowned. "Maybe I'm more like her than him."

"Maybe," Kiki agreed. "Your dad has done a lot, though, Angela. I kind of admire him. He has a house and a profession. What's your mother doing with her life?"

"Well, she can do a jingle dance."

Kiki's eyebrows shot up quickly. "A what?"

"A Native American dance that's supposed to promote healing."

They stayed in the library for a while longer, laughing and catching up. Soon Angela had convinced her friend that things would be all right, even if she had to hide Kiki in another sweat lodge in the backyard. If they built one before, they could do it again.

CALEB STOPPED IN to see Grace in her office at the end of the afternoon. She was sorting through a file in the reception area as her secretary got ready to leave. She looked as beautiful as usual, wearing a crisp apple-green outfit with her typical high heels.

She looked up, her face brightening. "Caleb! And how's your day been?"

"A mix of good news and bad." And it promised to be getting better just being near Grace, something he wanted to do more and more often.

"How about giving me the good news first?"

"We found listings for two Elizabeth Hartls, women who probably would be around the age of Kiki's grandmother."

"We?"

"I got my mother involved. She has a lot of connections through her social work." He took a piece of paper, a printout, from his pocket. Being that she'd pressed him into investigating the grandmother's whereabouts, he was doubly pleased to show this to her. "One of these Elizabeth Hartls lives in Chicago. The other one is in Nebraska."

Her face lit up as she scanned the information. "Now we have to contact them."

"Yeah, I already tried. I left a message for the woman in Nebraska. The phone in Chicago just rang and rang."

"No voice mail, huh?"

"It may no longer be her number."

She appeared thoughtful. "And what's your bad news?"

He sighed. "Lily contacted me and wants child support."

"I thought you said Angela doesn't want to live with her."

"The last time I talked to her, she didn't. Lily claims she's changed our daughter's mind."

"She's persistent. I'll give her that."

"I'm afraid she'll move out of state and take Angela with her."

"She can't do that, can she?"

"I don't know. I'm thinking I'm going to have to get a lawyer involved."

Grace pushed him gently down onto one of the comfortable chairs in the reception area. Then she stepped behind to massage his neck and shoulders. "That's a worry, isn't it?"

Just her touch made things better. "That feels great."

"If worse comes to worse, my dad and I know a lot of good lawyers."

"I figured you did." Though that wasn't the reason he'd told her about the problem. It seemed important to tell her everything. And hear everything from her in return. Though he was beginning to think he wanted to share more than just talk. "How was your day?"

"I've had bad news and good, too."

He leaned back into the massage. "Tell me."

"I started the day with an article from the *Kenosha Journal*." She stopped kneading his neck muscles with a gentle pat. Then she went to the desk and picked up a newspaper. "Take a look at this."

He frowned. "Haunted Green Community! Oh, great! Where did they get this information?"

"I wondered about that, too." She sat down across from him and laughed.

He couldn't help feeling surprised. "You find this amusing?"

"Well, keep reading. By the end of the article, there's a wonderful description of the green community and hints about the perks of living there. We had two calls this afternoon from people who read the article and want to look at condos or townhomes."

"They want to live where there are ghosts?"

"They probably don't believe in them. They said they hadn't heard about the community until now—thanks to the article being in lifestyle instead of real estate." She smiled, her blue eyes bright. "The reporter did us a favor."

Caleb realized the enormity of that favor. It might make Phase 2 a reality, which would give Grace a reason to stay indefinitely. He grinned at her. "This is great news!"

She nodded. "Sometimes you actually can make lemonade from lemons."

He reached over to take her hands in his. "Sometimes you can."

SPRING WEATHER WAS getting warmer. Enjoying being outside for a change, Nellie sat on one of the benches in the courtyard of the condo complex and chatted with her neighbor Fran. Darkness had fallen and the automatic lights had come up along the walkways and what would be a fountain of some sort once the landscaping was done.

Still, both women wore light sweaters.

"This is why I moved here," Fran told her. "The feeling of community."

"You can get that in a town, too," said Nellie. "But you have to put more work into it. Here, we live closer and have places to hang out that are only footsteps away."

"You've had community for years through that quilting collective you belong to."

"It's not a collective, just a bunch of women with similar interests. And I volunteer at the Seniors Soup Kitchen, as well as run my store. I know a lot of people."

"You're busy."

"Too busy, I think, at times. I'm going to have to slow down one of these days." Nellie adjusted her large glasses. "Did you see that?"

"See what?"

Nellie stared in the direction of open space between two buildings, leaning forward. "Over there. I saw a blob of white."

"Oh, no!" Fran started to get agitated. "The ghost?"

"There is no ghost," Nellie said firmly. "No matter what the newspapers say. That reporter was just trying to attract attention…and get his article published." She settled back. "Probably just the wind blowing a bunch of leaves or something."

"Mr. Cassidy said the 'haunting of Green Meadows' went viral on the computer. What does that mean?"

Nellie frowned. "That ridiculous ghost rumor must have been repeated on the internet in various news pages or blogs. Whatever. I'll have to look it up on my computer at the store." She didn't keep one of the confounded things at home, though she knew how to use one.

"Who told the reporter all the details? It must have been a resident."

"Everyone denies it," said Nellie. All the residents she knew at the complex had read the latest *Kenosha Journal*. She slapped at an insect that flew too close to her face. "Dratted mosquitoes are out." A given in Wisconsin with all the lakes and streams. "I'll have to spray myself with insect repellent the next time I plan to spend some time out here."

"Let's go inside," said Fran. "I need to get the dog ready for his evening walk."

Both women rose and headed in opposite directions. Nellie had unlocked her apartment door and slipped inside when she heard Fran's scream and Sampson's outraged barking. Heart beating fast, adrenaline flowing, she grabbed her broom and ran back outside as fast as she could.

"Help!" Fran was sprawled on the stoop and a large white figure was moving away from her into the shadows, with an irate poodle clamped to its leg.

A yeti? Bigfoot? A polar bear? Nellie could hardly believe her eyes. But she wasn't about to let whatever it was get away with terrorizing them. She picked up her broom and swung as hard as she could. The broomstick connected and someone or something made a pained sound.

"O-o-omp!"

"Come here, you!" Nellie yelled, striking again.

"A-a-gh!"

And with a desperate shake, the white creature took off, dragging the poodle.

"Sampson!" cried Fran. "Don't let him take my dog!"

Brandishing the broom, Nellie followed, not thinking about the uneven ground, stopping only when she reached the end of the building.

To her relief, Sampson came running to her. "Hey, boy."

Then she peered around the building, out toward the walking paths, but saw absolutely nothing. Not even a bunch of leaves blowing in the wind.

CHAPTER SEVENTEEN

ANGELA WAS ON her way to Gran Maddie's house when an old beat-up pickup slowed and pulled over to the curb. To her surprise, Lily sat in the driver's seat and leaned across to roll down the passenger window.

"Get in. I'll give you a ride."

Hesitating, Angela asked, "Where did you get this truck anyway?"

"It belongs to a friend," Lily told her, "and speaking of friends, I got hold of that artist I was telling you about. He's agreed to talk to you. He's interested in young talent. I'm sure he'll be very helpful. C'mon, get in."

"Right now?" Angela still felt doubtful.

"Yes, right now. You need to seize an opportunity when it appears."

Finally, intrigued by the idea of meeting her mother's friend, enough to push aside her reservations, Angela opened the door, threw in her backpack and climbed inside.

Lily wrestled the pickup into second with a

grinding of gears. Instead of taking the road that went out to the rez, she turned the vehicle onto the road that led to the main highway bordering the town.

"Where are we going?"

"Somewhere nearby." Lily smiled. "So you can talk privately. It's no one else's business."

Angela became concerned when the old truck passed the town limits and picked up speed. "How far is this?"

"Oh, uh… Milwaukee."

"That's sixty miles. How long are we going to be gone? Gran and Dad will be worried." Not to mention angry. Angela slid her phone out of her pocket. "I have to let them know."

Before she could punch in a number, Lily reached over to grab the phone and tossed it out the window.

Angela stared openmouthed. "Wha-at?"

"Live free for once. Artists don't schedule their lives."

With a thrill of fear, gazing at the blur of landscape as they sped along, Angela realized she had no control over her own life at the moment.

THE MORNING AFTER the attack on Fran Willowby, Grace talked to both Fran and Nellie, as well as to the police chief. A report was filed, since Fran had banged up her knee, though, luckily, the injury wouldn't require surgery. Grace was perplexed about who was out to make trouble for the green community. She didn't believe it was Angela, and she didn't want to think it was Kiki. Both girls would have to be questioned.

There were other, positive issues to deal with, including more calls from people wanting to look at condos. As she made notes and met with a couple of real estate agents, Grace couldn't help thinking on what exactly she was going to tell her father about the attack and the article.

Most important, she told herself, she simply had to change the way she dealt with her father. She needed to be straight about what she wanted, instead of avoiding confrontation. Caleb's remarks about not speaking up for herself had struck home.

Just before noon, her father arrived at the Walworth Builders offices. He waved at Grace, motioning for her to put aside whatever she was doing and come into his private office.

Okay, here goes. She assured him, "I've got everything under control."

He frowned. "Control? You don't even know what I have to tell you."

Not liking the intent look he gave her, she went on swiftly, "The article in the *Kenosha Journal* is actually bringing us business. We sold one townhome already and we're showing a couple of condos tomorrow."

"At Green Meadows? I don't care about Green Meadows."

"What are you riled up about then?" This threw a wrench in her plans. She had thought about what to say to him all morning.

"I'm dealing with something *important*," he said, emphasizing the word. "Green Meadows is just one of our ventures…and a small one at that." He leaned toward her. "We're having trouble with the board of directors. Bachman sold his shares to Davidson and he has a bigger vote on projects now. He wants to concentrate on commercial real estate, especially in urban areas."

His dismissive tone irritated her. "We're not abandoning Green Meadows. It's nearly ready to begin Phase 2."

"With you nursing it along like it was a private hobby," her father said. "But that's got to stop. You can put someone else in charge here and take your place as head of the business. I want to retire in January."

"You don't sound like you want to retire." As usual, he was giving orders. And he was so specific about what was going on with the company and where it might be headed that she had the feeling that he would still expect to have control, retired or not.

"I've made a definite decision. You need to move back to Milwaukee and take up your responsibilities. The transition from me to you has got to be smooth." Laying his briefcase on the desk, he sat down in his big black leather chair.

"I don't want to return to Milwaukee right now," was all she could say. She had thought about this moment often and was never sure what she would do. Faced with it now, however, she said firmly, "I have plenty to work on here."

"Delegate the work," he ordered, his voice clipped. "We have a meeting in Chicago tomorrow morning with a big wallboard supplier. I have a driver picking us up in another hour."

"I am not going to Chicago," she declared. "Not at the moment."

He pulled a pad out of his desk and started

making notes. "You'll need to pack a bag, since we'll be there overnight."

"You're not even listening to me!"

He looked up. "What are you yelling about?"

Her face warm, she spoke even louder. "I said you're not listening to me. I am *not* going to Chicago!"

He frowned. "Now is not the time for some petty rebellion, Grace. We have a lot on the line."

"Well, you'd better figure out how you're going to deal with it and with whom because it's not going to be me!"

He rose and actually looked her in the eye. "Grace! What is going on with you?"

It all spilled out. "I don't want to be president of the board. I don't want to be head of Walworth Builders. I want to finish the green community and—"

"Then what?"

"Whatever I think should be next. Another green community, maybe something bigger." She looked at him pleadingly, as if begging him to understand. "I want to be myself, Dad, not a clone of you."

"It's that professor you've been dating, isn't it?" he said with disgust. "He has you all mixed up."

"No, it is not that professor, although he has helped me think about things more clearly." She gathered her courage. "I've never wanted to be president of the board or CEO of Walworth Builders, Dad. I guess I never told you that directly, though I've indicated as much in other ways."

"I've planned for a family legacy all these years."

"I know that you have." And she felt a mix of pain with her anger. "But that's what *you've* wanted. What about me? You've never asked what I wanted. I would be miserable cooped up in those meetings all day."

His face was growing red. "What *you* want? You're shirking your responsibility! You are a spoiled girl, Grace."

Spoiled? That made her even angrier. "How much responsibility are you talking about? We aren't the royal family of England, Dad. And, even so, the monarch has the freedom to abdicate. Walworth Builders is just a business."

"*Just* a business? What about all that I've taught you? Why do you think I helped you get yourself straightened out?"

She couldn't believe he'd gone there. He'd helped her as a troubled teen so he could train her to be a business leader? "How about you helped me because you wanted me to become the best person I can be? Or maybe because you loved me?"

"Well, of course, I love you, Grace. But being CEO of the business *is* the best person you can be."

"No, it isn't. I hate board meetings."

"It isn't just board meetings."

"I hate pretty much everything else that goes along with being a CEO."

"This is a fine time to decide that."

"I always thought that I'd hate being a CEO. I've even indicated that while trying not to hurt your feelings. You don't listen."

"Well, what am I supposed to do? Just abandon my plans? I can't work forever."

"It sounds to me like you're nowhere ready to retire, but if you really are, then give the job to someone else. You have several people, one vice president that I know of, who would probably jump at the chance to run this company."

He started to pace, hands behind his back. "I can't do that right now. It will take time."

"You'll have to do it or keep on working," she insisted. "I'm not going to step in today.

That would make it even more difficult to get out later."

"Grace, I don't know what's going on with you." He stopped pacing, taking a deep breath. "You were fine until you started dating that man and trying to help his delinquent daughter."

"Don't blame other people."

He ignored her. "If you want to get married, you can find plenty of suitable men who would support your career."

"That's pretty cold." Was that how he'd thought of her mother? Suitable?

"Marriage should be practical, not just a love match."

The mention of marriage made her wonder if she was thinking of Caleb so seriously. Maybe she was. Their relationship had definitely made an impact on her. The idea of leaving him and going back to Milwaukee made her feel empty inside.

"Thinking about what you want, right now, is petty," Dad continued. "It will pass. You have to look at the big picture."

"I am looking at the big picture, and it's obviously very different from what you see. I don't want to be CEO of the company. I don't want my life revolving around business every moment."

"Then you certainly aren't the daughter I raised."

"You don't *know* the daughter you raised."

He stood still, just gazing at her. His face was drained of color and she thought she saw his mouth twitch.

Finally, he said, "Well, I know enough to disown you if you don't come around. And you're not starting another green community, Grace, or finishing this one with Huber resources." Then he picked up his briefcase and strode for the door. "If you come to your senses, you can find me in Chicago."

Grace watched him leave, deeply upset. Her father had never talked about disowning her before. She might have her freedom but she guessed she could kiss Phase 2 of Green Meadows goodbye. Not to mention her only familial relationship.

She burst into tears.

GRACE WAS IN no mood to see anyone, but she and Caleb had made plans to have pizza for dinner at a place in town, so she went ahead and met him there. Maybe she would feel better being with him. When she arrived, he didn't ask her how her day had gone, and he seemed distracted.

After they'd ordered, she said, "You look like you've had the same kind of day I have."

"Sorry, I'm just concerned that Angela didn't go to her grandmother's place right after school like she told me she was going to."

"Do you think she took off with Kiki again?"

"I don't know. Kiki has been hiding out ever since we visited her foster home." He slid his phone out of his pocket and sighed. "Of course, Angela doesn't answer my calls." He looked at her, his brow creasing as he finally noticed her subdued expression. "Did you talk to the police about the attack at the condo complex?"

"I spoke with Alex Novak. He's looking for Kiki, too."

"I don't think Angela had anything to do with it." He glanced at the phone as if willing it to ring. "Unless she sneaked out of the house at night."

"I already assured Alex he could rule her out."

Though she still wasn't sure of Angela or the effect her behavior would have on her and

Caleb. Given her own father's attitude about Caleb and her potential future with him, it seemed the fates were against them.

The food arrived and Caleb helped himself. Not that hungry, Grace just sat looking at her plate until he put a helping of salad and a slice of pizza on it.

"You need to eat," he told her.

She nibbled at the tasteless food. Caleb still didn't seem to realize anything was wrong with her, so she decided to tell him about her horrible afternoon.

"I had a huge fight with my dad about the company and his retirement."

"Oh? I hope you took a stand for what *you* want."

"I sure did. And, guess what? He talked about disowning me if I didn't take over the company for him."

"Come on, he's just throwing a tantrum."

"It didn't sound like it. He's cutting off funds for Green Meadows. Now that we have interest from new customers, I was ready to move to Phase 2."

"You'll just have to change his mind."

"What makes you think I didn't try?" And why was Caleb telling her what to do yet again? "You don't know him."

"You've gone through this before. Doesn't your dad find a way to make up, but not lose face?"

"Usually."

Grace couldn't believe he was just dismissing the matter.

He started talking about Angela again, where she could be.

"It's not just Green Meadows, Caleb," she interrupted. "He actually told me he only got me out of trouble when I was a girl so he could mold me into a super executive. I've never heard Dad speak that way before." She couldn't stand the thought of a rift between them. "If I don't do what he wants, I'll lose him."

"Grace, you are an adult," he said calmly. "You just have to take a stand and stop backing down."

She insisted, "I don't want to lose my father."

"You're not losing anything. If anyone is losing, it's him…intentionally, through his own doing."

Grace stared at the man who had made her think about a future with him. If Caleb truly cared about her, he would find a way to help her work through this. Instead, he was criticizing her for being reluctant to put a rift between her and her dad.

"It doesn't matter who is at fault," she said. "The result is the same."

"So you're going to buckle down to your father's will because otherwise he'll kick you out of his company?" He gestured with his fork. "You could work for someone else. Or start your own company."

"Making such a drastic change without a significant amount of forethought and planning is not that easy." She stared at her pizza, which was growing cold on her plate. "Maybe there's another way I could have handled it. *Could* handle it." The fact she couldn't come up with a solution really troubled her.

"Your father has to realize that you're an adult with dreams of your own. If you don't tell him, how is he supposed to understand what you want?"

He finally got to her. "You know, Caleb, I'm tired of you just giving me directives, as if you know the way everything should be handled."

His eyes widened in surprise. "You've been asking my opinion."

"And you've been giving me that opinion even when I *don't* ask for it."

"I didn't mean to put you in a bad mood."

"Being threatened with losing the relationship that means the most to a person tends to do that."

"Your relationship with your father means the most to you? What about a relationship with someone else, someone you can share the rest of your life with?" He glanced down at his phone again when it rang. "Nope, not Angela."

She couldn't believe it. Why couldn't he listen to her rather than tell her to ignore her father's orders, as if it were easy, while giving her yet more orders? Angela seemed to be the center of Caleb's world and business was the center of her father's. Where did she, Grace, fit in?

Disgusted, she threw her unused napkin on the table and rose. "I've heard enough for today. I only wish life were as simple as you seem to think it should be."

"Grace?"

Ignoring him, she headed for the door. "I'm making tonight simple. I'm leaving."

"What? Wait a minute, please!"

Which was all she heard before stalking out to her car. Pulling away, she saw Caleb standing in the doorway of the restaurant, but she just stomped harder on the accelerator.

GRACE DROVE AND DROVE, not even thinking about where she was going. The highway unfurled before her, a wide silver path leading somewhere, anywhere. Finally, noticing a large road sign, she realized that she was headed for Milwaukee. That was okay. She had an apartment there and could rest up, think about what she wanted to do next. She wouldn't let her father know and would lie low. She had to take care of herself, since nobody else seemed interested in the job.

The phone in her purse rang yet again. And she ignored it yet again. It was probably Caleb and she had no desire to talk to him.

Disappointment made her stomach whirl and her throat tighten. Caleb might be a responsible parent and a generally good man, but was he the one for her? Right now, overwhelmed by the day, she couldn't say for sure.

Once in the city, she barely had to pay attention to where she was going. Taking the correct exit, she made her way down familiar streets until they ended at the shores of Lake Michigan. There she entered the garage for the large condo building perched beside the lake, and parked. Then she took the elevator upstairs.

When she opened the door to her quiet abode, she immediately went to the French doors in the living room, opening them wide to the terrace outside. She took a deep breath, enjoying the fresh lake air, then threw herself down on a chaise lounge. Below, she could hear the gentle lapping of waves and, in the distance, the gentle hum of night traffic. A moon glowed overhead. She would simply shut the phones off entirely and relax. Tomorrow and thoughts of the future—both professional and personal—would come soon enough. About to turn off her cell, she realized she'd left her purse with her phone in the car.

Well, it could just stay there. As soon as she felt like moving from where she sat, she'd also tear out the jack for the apartment phone. There was no one she wanted to talk to tonight.

CHAPTER EIGHTEEN

"SHE HAS TO be somewhere nearby, Caleb," his mother said. "I don't think she's in physical danger."

"We can't be sure about that."

It had been hours since Angela had been due at her grandmother's. Caleb and his mother had driven all over town looking for the girl but hadn't caught a glimpse of her. Now they were taking a break in Caleb's kitchen for some coffee, since they seemed to be headed for an all-nighter.

"She could be up to her old ways," said Mom.

"Why? There's no reason. She hasn't been so angry lately. She has an idea, a good one, for the mural at Green Meadows." Which made him think of Grace with a pang. "She's almost done with school. She's been meeting with Lily."

"And, unfortunately, we don't know what has been said in those meetings." Mom frowned. "I wish we could trust that woman, but she isn't even answering her phone now."

"Should we go to the police? Report her as being missing?"

"That would be a good idea."

Which scared him. When Mom encouraged him to take the most extreme step in a situation, he knew she thought it was serious.

"Did you phone Grace?" his mother asked.

"Yes. Though she doesn't have anything to do with this."

And wasn't reachable anyhow. They'd had a fight and then she'd just walked out on him before he'd even had a chance to smooth things over. If he could talk to her, he would apologize for upsetting her, but he couldn't help feeling hurt and angry himself that she hadn't stayed and talked it through.

"I think Grace might make you feel better."

"She would."

Caleb had grown used to having Grace's support and understanding. He really would appreciate her presence right now. His daughter was gone. And his woman was gone, too. He'd thought he was being supportive with Grace, but he'd simply managed to drive her away. It seemed as if he was doomed to have almost all the females he loved desert him.

Wait. Did he *love* her?

Caleb was considering the idea that he was in love with Grace Huber when the doorbell rang.

Glancing at the kitchen clock, which announced two minutes past midnight, Caleb strode toward the front door. Outside, her wild hair sticking out in all directions, stood Kiki.

"Mr. Blackthorne?" she asked, sounding a little uncertain.

He immediately asked, "Do you know where Angela is?"

"That's why I'm here. I saw her get into an old pickup with her mother."

His heart plummeted. "When?"

"About four. They drove off but I have no idea where they were going." Kiki looked genuinely worried. "I've tried to text and call Angela over and over, but nothing. Not answering isn't her style."

Mom came up behind him. "Let the poor girl in, Caleb."

He obligingly moved aside.

"Are you hungry, dear?" Mom asked Kiki. "How about some cookies and milk?"

Caleb couldn't believe his mother was offering the girl food at a time like this. He said,

"If neither Angela nor Lily is answering their phones still, this could be a kidnapping."

"True." Mom sat Kiki down and poured her a big glass of milk, then set a plate of cookies in front of the girl. "We'll have to let the police know." She looked at her son. "Cookies for you?"

"The last thing I want is food right now," he said gruffly. "I have to find Angela!" He looked down at Kiki. "Thank you for coming to tell us you saw her with her mother. We appreciate your help."

Then, with Mom saying she'd stay at the house, in case Angela showed up or tried to call, Caleb left Kiki with her and headed for his truck. He drove straight to the police station to see Alex Novak. If the man was at work, that is. If he wasn't awake, he soon would be. Caleb wouldn't rest until a search was under way.

Parking in the station's lot, he made one last try to phone Grace. As he feared, it went to voice mail. He said, "Angela's missing. There's a chance she's been kidnapped, Grace. I really miss you. I need you. I'm sorry that I upset you. I didn't mean to, honestly. If you can find it in your heart to call me, please do. Anytime, night or day."

"This truck is going to run out of gas," Angela muttered under her breath when Lily turned down another dark country road lined with trees. They'd been driving for hours without stopping.

"We'll make it a little farther."

What in the world was her mother's plan? Angela wondered. Her suspicions had been growing since the woman had thrown the cell phone out of the car.

"We aren't going to see that artist at all, are we?" she asked.

"Not today."

"Then why are you bringing me here?"

"What is wrong with a mother and daughter spending some time together?"

"Out in the woods? In the middle of the night? And if everything's cool, then why can't I tell my dad where I am?"

Should she be afraid? Was her mother willing to do something desperate to get whatever it was she wanted? Angela was really getting jittery now.

Lily said, "I know of a cabin around here."

"You still didn't answer my question. Why are you doing this?"

Lily simply asked a return question. "Think

your dad will be worried? If so, I've accomplished my goal."

"You're doing this to worry my dad? Unbelievable." Angela was beginning to think she was lucky her mother had abandoned her all those years ago.

The country road turned into mere tire tracks through the grass. The pickup bumped along, the springs squeaking and complaining.

"You're a kidnapper," stated Angela.

"I'm your mother. I can't kidnap you."

"You don't know the law then. A parent can kidnap a child."

"I don't think your dad will want to go there. He'll just pay up."

So that was it? Her mother had taken her to get money out of her father?

"I hope he doesn't give you a penny," said Angela bitterly. "You don't deserve it. And there's no way I would ever want to live with you."

"I'm pretty sure I can get custody, at least partial custody anyway."

"A judge wouldn't be that stupid."

In the feeble light of the old dashboard, Angela saw Lily turn to look at her. "You are not a very nice girl at times, Angela. I'm your mother and I love you. I will do what I have to in order to be with you."

"I think the child support money is more appealing to you than having me in your life."

It was only a short while longer until Lily brought the old pickup to a stop under a big oak tree. Nearby, in the moonlight, Angela could make out the dark shape of a building.

Lily turned off the ignition with a roar and several chugging backfires. Finally, the truck gave a last wheeze and Lily removed the keys. "Let's go inside and see what we can pull together as far as sleeping and eating. I came up here a few weeks ago and left some canned goods and blankets."

"I'm not getting out."

"Yes, you are."

"I want to go home!" Angela demanded.

"We'll go home in the morning. Right now, I'm tired."

"Will this thing start in the morning?"

"Of course it will."

"I bet it won't. You don't even know if you have enough gas." Lily had said the gauge was broken.

"It will start," said Lily, pushing the keys back in and turning.

The truck merely groaned once, then became silent.

"See, I told you it wouldn't start," Angela said.

"Well, let it cool off. We'll try again tomorrow. Meanwhile, we have nothing else to do, so let's go inside."

Angela needed to stretch her legs so she followed her mother into what seemed to be an old fishing cabin. Lily lit a kerosene lantern, which illuminated the sparse furnishings, a couple of cots, a table and an old rocking chair. Several fishing poles hung on one wall and there was a large glass jar full of hooks on the table.

"Can I have a drink of water?" Angela asked.

"Use the pump over there," Lily told her, nodding to a makeshift sink. "There's a cistern."

There was also an outhouse. The place had no running water.

The women opened a can of tuna from a box of groceries that Lily had left on an earlier visit and spread it on some crackers.

After eating, Lily lay back on one of the cots. "I'm tired. Why don't you go to sleep? There's nothing else to do until morning."

Angela could think of a few things she could do. Even in the dark. First, she went outside to gaze at the stars to get her bearings. And then she planned her escape.

CHAPTER NINETEEN

THE NIGHT FLEW by once Caleb talked to Alex
Novak, who, in turn, notified the county sher-
iff and the state police. An Amber Alert went
out on Angela's whereabouts. Despite having
been seen in a vehicle, Angela could still be
hiding nearby, so police went through the re-
quired procedure of searching Caleb's house,
the grounds and the rez. They questioned the
friend who'd given Lily shelter, but she didn't
know anything. His mother kept Kiki close
and said the girl was helping her. The cops
had no time to question what the teenager
was doing there but they jotted down the information she gave them. Her description
identified a decrepit vehicle that belonged to
an elder on the rez. The old woman hadn't
known the pickup was gone until the police
came calling.

By dawn, an electronics expert placed the
GPS of Angela's phone in a location north
of Sparrow Lake. But when a state trooper

checked on the site, she found only pieces of the device scattered along the interstate.

Caleb was running on adrenaline and caffeine but he still could not sit at home and wait. "Lily could have taken Angela to the big rez up north," he told Alex. "The interstate runs by it. I could go up there and check things out."

"Not a bad idea," agreed the police chief. "Keep your phone handy. I'll advise you of what's going on."

In the parking lot, Caleb checked to make sure he had a flashlight and a jacket and his wallet. The phone charger was plugged into the truck's lighter outlet. He made a mental note to pick up some bottled water and snacks when he filled the truck up with gas. No telling how long he would be gone.

Looking for Angela by himself.

No Grace to keep him sane.

Nearly ready to leave, Caleb glanced up to see a well-dressed older man approaching him from across the parking lot.

"Professor Blackthorne?"

Caleb nodded, thinking the man looked familiar.

"I'm Henry Huber." He held out a hand for Caleb to shake.

"Grace's father, right?" They had the same bright blue eyes.

"Correct. Speaking of Grace, have you seen her?"

Caleb's gut knotted. "Have *you*?" knowing the man wouldn't be asking such a question if he was aware of Grace's whereabouts.

"I thought she might have contacted you," said Huber. "She won't pick up her phone when she sees it's me calling."

No wonder, after the argument they'd had. "She's not speaking to me either."

Would she ever speak to him again? Or was he destined to make his way through his current mess of a life alone? Without the woman he realized he loved?

"Hmmph." Huber stared at the state trooper squad car entering the lot. "Quite a bit of activity. I couldn't help notice as I was driving down Main Street. Is something the matter?"

"Nothing is wrong with Grace." Caleb knew the man would be concerned about his own flesh and blood. "At least I hope not. But my daughter Angela's likely been kidnapped."

Huber seemed taken aback. "Oh? That's terrible."

"Her mother has her but we don't know

where they went. Or whether they intend to come back."

"Grace doesn't know about it?"

"She left before it happened." Caleb added, "If she did know, she'd be here. She cares about Angela." If not about him. In spite of all the grief his daughter had given her, Grace was on Angela's side. "You raised a very good human being, Mr. Huber. You should be proud of her."

Now Huber sighed. "I am proud. I shouldn't be so hard on her."

"Unfortunately dads are not always the best listeners." Caleb recalled what his mother must have told him a million times. "Kids aren't clones who should do everything the way we would."

"A hard lesson to learn."

That remark sounded promising. But Caleb needed to look for Angela, with or without the woman he loved at his side. "Look, I have to go, Mr. Huber. I'm driving up north to see if my daughter might be there."

"And I guess Grace will answer her phone when she's ready."

"I guess so," agreed Caleb. "I had a fight with her, too. Two in one day must have been too much for her."

Huber didn't say anything for a moment, then looked straight at Caleb. "If I can do anything at all, let me know. Walworth Builders has a small plane, you know, if you need it for a search."

"Thank you."

Caleb climbed in his truck and left. When he stopped to fill up on gas before leaving town, he tried to reach Grace again. And left another message.

"I think your dad is sorry about the fight, Grace. Me, too…about ours, that is. Still miss you. Please give me a call."

WHEN GRACE AWAKENED, the sun was already up. She couldn't believe the light hadn't jogged her out of sleep earlier. She must have been really tired. She had certainly been stressed. As memories of the horrible day before came back to her, she slid her legs off the chaise and groaned. Having slept in her heels, she noticed her feet were swollen. Gingerly, she pulled the shoes off and padded stocking-footed to the kitchen.

"Oh, great," she said, opening the cupboard to find that she hadn't restocked the coffee. She'd have to pick up a cup at a drive-through.

Staggering into the bedroom with its attached en suite, she took a shower and changed into a loose shirt, jeans and running shoes. After coffee, maybe she'd go for a stroll in the nearby park. Nature always made her feel better.

On her way out, she started to grab for her purse, which she usually left on a table in the foyer. It wasn't there. Oh, right, she'd forgotten it in the car.

Downstairs, in the garage, she found her purse lying on the seat when she opened the door. She took out the cell and glanced at her messages and calls. Four messages from Caleb, two calls without messages from her father, then two more messages from Caleb. Hesitating, wondering if she wanted to hear what Caleb had to say, she contacted voice mail.

"Angela's missing…been kidnapped…miss you…please call me…" shocked her to attention. Her heart sped up immediately.

Without thinking, Grace started the car and accelerated out of the garage, intending to return to Sparrow Lake as fast as she could.

THE TRUCK STOP where Caleb agreed to meet Grace was a short turnoff near the interstate.

Driving north, she found it easily, a service station with a huge sign advertising diesel fuel and an attached lot where truckers could stop and spend the night. There seemed to be about a hundred semitrucks parked or moving in and out of the establishment.

She spotted Caleb's vehicle and pulled in next to it. He was standing near the door of the café a few yards away. Despite their argument of the day before, she immediately gave him a hug. He hugged her back, his touch comforting her. It felt like something she needed. That she couldn't do without.

"I'm so sorry, Caleb. Is there any news?" He had told Grace about the official search when she called him that morning.

"Not yet. While waiting here I remembered an old fishing cabin Lily and I used to go to with other kids back in the day. It was a place where we could escape our elders."

"Did you tell the police?"

"Not yet. I think we ought to go there ourselves. Let them know if we find anyone."

"Let's do it."

They got in his truck and left her car to be picked up later. On the road, he asked, "Where have you been anyway?"

"Milwaukee. At my condo."

"Forget your phone?"

"Actually, I did. I left it in my car all night."

They discussed what had happened the previous evening until Alex Novak called to say state troopers had not spotted the vehicle as yet. After telling Alex where they were going, Caleb turned the truck off the highway onto country roads.

Grace unfolded a map. "Where is this cabin exactly?"

"I can't say for certain. I know it's near a lake. I think Shale Lake."

"I don't see it on the map."

"It's there. It's just not very big. Don't worry, I know where I'm going."

"You remember after all these years?"

"Some things stick with you. It was the place where Lily and I…uh, decided we loved each other."

He didn't have to be embarrassed about it, she thought, if that's why he'd hesitated. Too bad they didn't have a place to claim as their own in the future. If they even had a future.

"So you think Lily remembers this place, too?" she asked.

"Probably. If no one has spotted them on the highways, it's likely she's hiding somewhere."

In another hour or so, Caleb turned off the bumpy dirt road. He followed tire tracks leading through brush and weeds. Trees grew denser and Grace could see the glimmer of water ahead from time to time.

"Shale Lake?"

"Right."

Rounding a copse of trees, they came to a weathered cabin with a beat-up blue pickup parked nearby.

"Bingo!" cried Caleb. "That's the vehicle."

They got out and rushed into the cabin to find Lily nonchalantly sitting in an old rocking chair, acting as if she was waiting for them.

"Where's Angela?" Caleb demanded immediately.

Lily shrugged. "I have no idea."

"I know you took off with her," Caleb said.

Lily remained cool. "I brought her here. She left."

Caleb stormed, "You had no right to do that."

"I'm her mother."

"No excuse," said Caleb. "You don't have custody of her."

"So you think I was going to demand a ransom or something?"

"Weren't you? Which direction did she go?"

Lily sniffed. "I told you I have no idea. We stopped here overnight. She was gone when I woke up in the morning."

"Hiking?" asked Grace.

"Maybe." Lily then addressed Caleb. "What's she doing here?"

"Grace is helping me," Caleb said. "She cares about Angela."

"Even though Angela hates her," remarked Lily with a tight smile.

Grace felt the pang Lily intended.

"Angela might very well change her mind," said Caleb. "Now, since you don't know where my daughter is, we're going to go looking for her." He took out his phone. "I'm going to call the police to come pick you up."

"Police?" Lily appeared startled.

"You *kidnapped* someone," Caleb said, emphasizing the word. "You're going to answer for it."

Lily rose, obviously beginning to feel upset. "I just wanted to be with my baby. Why is that so awful?"

Caleb made the call. "Hi, Alex? We found Lily in that old fishing cabin that I was looking for." He gave the directions.

Lily glanced around, as if looking for escape. She slid off, heading for the door.

Caleb caught her by the arm. "No, you don't."

Grace hoped she wasn't going to have to watch an actual battle between the pair. But Lily settled down as Caleb led her to a post in the middle of the small cabin.

"Can you look for some rope?" Caleb asked Grace, indicating an old dusty chest in one corner.

"You're going to tie me up?" asked Lily.

"I want to make sure you don't go anywhere."

"The pickup doesn't start."

"That won't stop you. You've got feet."

But securing Lily wasn't necessary since a state trooper arrived a few minutes later. A squad car must have already been in the area. Lily was cuffed, sobbing and sniffling. It almost made Grace feel sorry for her.

Caleb appeared regretful as well, but he was all business. "Let's go, Grace. I want to see if there's still a trail by the side of the lake. Angela would have taken that first."

"You two are going alone?" asked the trooper. "There's some rough country out there. If you wait for a bit, we can organize an official search."

"They can catch up with us," Caleb said. "I don't like to think of my daughter being by herself."

Outside, Grace followed Caleb down a trail by the lake that had pretty much grown over. Some yards on, Caleb found a footprint of Angela's sneaker. He set off, motioning for Grace to come along.

"She went this way."

Soon they had made their way into the woods surrounding the lake.

"Who knows where she might be," said Grace. "Even if we're going the right direction, she had hours to have gotten way ahead. Why do you think she left anyway?"

"Why would she stay? She didn't know what her mother was going to do."

"I'm glad I got your message in time to help you," she said.

"I appreciate that."

Farther on, the trail all but disappeared into a thicket of evergreens. Caleb circled the area and found another footprint. "Lucky it rained a couple of nights ago. Shady areas are still damp."

Still. "I bet a police helicopter would help."

"Yeah, it would. It takes a while to get a police search organized, though." He thought a moment. "Walworth Builders has a plane?"

"Yes, it does. A small one." But how did he know? "Did I mention that?"

"I saw your father before I left Sparrow Lake. He told me if he could help, he would."

"You looked him up?" That was curious.

"He found me. He noticed all the activity at the police station and wondered what was going on."

"He stayed in town then." And after the things he'd said to her. "I thought he was going to Chicago."

"He'd been trying to get hold of you."

Having checked her phone, Grace knew that.

"Did he say we could use the plane to search for Angela?"

"Something like that."

Touched that her father had made the offer when he'd seemed so negative about her and Caleb, she was already calling the Milwaukee office.

CALEB FIGURED HE and Grace had been hiking for several miles when the plane showed up.

They could hear the engine overhead before they could see it.

Grace got a call from the pilot. "Yes, we know she went this way. But it's hard to see anything, the woods are pretty dense." She looked at Caleb. "What color clothing was she wearing?"

"I think she had on a blue hoodie," he said. "And probably jeans. Sorry, I can't be more specific." He'd seen his daughter only briefly, yesterday morning before school. "She had a purple backpack, that I know for sure."

Grace relayed the information, then said, "He is? Okay, I'll talk to him." There was a pause. "Hello, Dad. I can't believe you came out here. I really appreciate your helping us."

Her father cared enough about her to do it, Caleb thought. "Tell them she's heading south and east. That way she could orient herself by the sun's position."

Grace passed on the information, then slid the phone back in her pocket.

"This way." They came to a creek that appeared too deep for wading but Caleb pointed out a log spanning the water a few yards along. "Looks like we've got a bridge."

He hopped on the log to test its strength, then took some running steps to reach the other side. Grace was staring at him questioningly.

He held out his hand. "Get on and hold yourself steady. Then take hold of me and I'll pull you across."

"I can make it."

She managed the log quite well.

"I always forget how accomplished you are," he said, wondering if he'd gotten too bossy again. "I keep telling you what to do."

"Well, you do have more hiking experience than me."

"You just don't like it when I advise you on relationships."

"Or push food on me when I don't want it," she said with a smile.

"I'm sorry about that. In fact, I'm sorry, especially because it seemed like I didn't care about your feelings. I hope you can forgive me."

There was a clearing on the other side of the creek where they could walk side by side.

"Thanks. I appreciate that." She let out a big breath. "What my dad said about disowning me… I just can't get the words out of my head."

"I don't think he meant them." Hearing

an engine, Caleb glanced up as the company plane flew overhead.

"It was cruel of him to say it. I should have told him how I felt a long time ago." Grace frowned. "I guess I've taught myself to avoid dealing with difficult situations."

"I noticed that when you left the restaurant. Then when you wouldn't answer your phone. I thought that was it for us. That would have broken my heart."

"Really?"

"The only other woman I ever loved left me, remember." He reached out to her and pulled her into his arms. "If I'm going to love someone, I want to know they will stick with me, not give up and run at the first sign of trouble."

"Are you saying you might love me?"

"I *do* love you, Grace." And he was absolutely certain, Even though he still had to deal with his problematic daughter, he wasn't going to let her get between them.

"I love you, too."

Grace planted a kiss on his lips, flooding him with warmth. Until this moment, he hadn't been sure they would be able to work things out. Now he couldn't see a future without Grace at his side.

They stood there entwined, forgetful of where they were or the task at hand. Until Grace's phone rang.

She answered, a little breathless. Then she disentangled herself. "It's the pilot. They've spotted smoke about a half mile east."

"Let's go!"

A short time later, they came upon what seemed to be a deserted camp. A crude shelter made of bent boughs stood to one side of a pit where a fire was crackling and a fish was frying on a slab of stone. But Caleb recognized the blue hoodie stretched across the top of the shelter and the purple backpack lying inside.

"Angela!" he yelled, glancing in all directions. "Where are you, Angel?"

She emerged slowly from some bushes near the shelter. "I know you're angry, Dad, but it wasn't my fault."

Heart uplifted, he immediately strode to her and pulled her up in a huge bear hug. "Angela!"

"Don't break my ribs, Dad!" Though her voice told him she was smiling.

He put her down, relieved and ecstatic. "I'm not angry. I already talked to your mother."

"Did the police arrest her?"

"Yes, they did." He held her by the arms and just looked at her, a sight for sore eyes. "Why did you take off anyway?"

"I was tired of sitting around and watching Lily," Angela admitted. "I didn't know what she was going to do. She wasn't even sorry for tricking me into coming with her."

"I don't think she considered the consequences," said Caleb. "But she will now."

Then more details spilled out. Angela told him about this artist Lily had promised she'd meet, the only reason she'd gotten in the truck. How Lily said he, Caleb, was too practical and wanted to spoil her creative dreams.

"That's not true," Caleb objected.

"Well, you are practical."

"It seems you can be practical, too." He smiled, gesturing to the shelter. "Pretty self-sufficient. Not bad for a place to sleep. You need to put some branches over the top, though."

Angela's grin was bigger than he'd seen in months. "Want some fish? I was hungry, so I caught it with some line and a hook I took from the cabin." Then her gaze focused over his shoulder.

Grace stood some feet away. "Hi, Angela." Ready for a snarky remark, he was surprised when his daughter replied simply, "Hi. Thanks for helping my father."

Maybe the relationship he craved with Grace wasn't going to be as difficult to manage as he'd feared.

CHAPTER TWENTY

"This is so lovely," said Gloria Vega, one of the most prominent members of Nellie's quilting group. "Just big enough for you and Olive."

Nellie showed her guest both bedrooms of her new condo, the smaller of which Nellie used as a sewing room.

"Of course, you had to have space for fabrics and a table," remarked Gloria. "You've fit everything in nicely." She looked around at the shelves where sewing items were stored. "Did you say these floors are bamboo?"

"Sure are," said Nellie. "Sustainable material."

Gloria seemed impressed, just like Nellie expected. "Your living room is big enough for most of the quilters. You'll have to have the whole group over some time."

"I plan to," Nellie told her as they returned to sit down on the living room couch. She introduced the woman who was already seated there. "This is Fran Willowby, my neighbor."

"Hi, Fran," Gloria said, dark eyes sparkling. "Do you sew, too?"

Fran shook her head. "No, I don't, but I really admire all the work you ladies do."

Nellie had hung one of her nicest quilts on the living room wall and decorated her dining table with a beautiful runner she'd also designed and sewn.

The three women sat down to enjoy a glass of wine from the bottle Gloria had brought as a housewarming present.

"I meant to have you over weeks ago," Nellie told Gloria. "I've just been so busy."

Gloria laughed. "Right. I've heard about the ghost you've been chasing around out here."

"There's no ghost," said Nellie, irritated the topic had come up again.

"Well, there's something," Fran said. "I have a twisted knee thanks to whatever or whoever it was."

"Somebody's pulling high jinks," insisted Nellie, staring toward the window from which they could see the area where Fran had her run-in. She frowned, punching at her glasses. "Every once in a while, I still think I see something white moving about in the trees."

The women continued to chat as night fell

and shadows flitted here and there under the lights of the complex. Nellie was pleased that Gloria and Fran seemed to have so much in common. It turned out Fran had lived in Gloria's neighborhood before moving to Green Meadows.

Nellie got up to return her glass to the kitchen, passing the window with the view of the area where Fran had confronted the mystery assailant. She stopped short when she glimpsed something white moving outside. Her eyes widened. A large white figure appeared to be emerging from behind the wall of a town house.

"I can't believe it!" Nellie's cry startled the other two women. "There it is! Speak of the devil…"

Gloria and Fran both hurried to the window to stare but Nellie was already grabbing her broom to rush outside.

"It's not getting away again!" shouted Nellie, whipping open the door.

"Wait, be careful!"

Fran's warning didn't slow Nellie at all. She hurried down the walkway, aware that Gloria was running after her.

"There it goes!" shouted Gloria as the bulky white figure slid into view and made haste to escape in the opposite direction. It had two black spots on its back and seemed to be dragging a tail.

Up ahead, Mr. Cassidy suddenly opened his door…and his mouth at the sight of the invader. "Hey, you!"

The apparition slowed enough that Nellie was able to give it a good whack with her broom.

"Ugh…"

Then Mr. Cassidy faced off with the creature and punched it in the face.

"Yah!" The figure groaned, fell to its knees, then collapsed on the sidewalk.

Mr. Cassidy hefted the intruder onto its back, revealing the round bearded face of a man dressed in a fuzzy polyester cow suit. It was one piece with a hood from which white ears protruded, along with two rubber horns.

"It's that ghost tour guy!" cried Nellie. "Vincent Pryce!"

"Please," begged Pryce, raising one white-gloved hand. "I didn't mean any harm."

"No harm?" shouted Nellie. "You've scared the heebie-jeebies out of us with your prowling around."

"And knocked me down!" cried Fran, who'd managed to make it over from Nellie's condo.

"What do you think this is?" Mr. Cassidy took in the costume, including the rubber udder in front. "Halloween?"

Pryce didn't answer the question. Instead he pleaded, "Can you help me? The zipper's stuck. I've been in here for hours."

"Good," said Nellie, raising her broom for another blow. "Suffer some more."

Mr. Cassidy laughed and blocked Nellie's arm before she could strike the fallen man again. Behind Nellie, Gloria laughed, as well. The "ghost cow" splayed out on the sidewalk did look ridiculous, Nellie had to admit.

But she remained serious. "Call the police. This guy is finished scaring people."

"I just wanted to drum up business," Pryce pleaded. "I stayed off the property whenever I could."

"But you're here now," said Mr. Cassidy. "That's trespassing."

Gloria already had her cell phone out. "I'm calling 911."

"Unless you'd rather we just quilt you into that cow suit forever," said Nellie. "I have the tools."

Again, the group laughed. Nellie smiled grimly.

"Can't we just take this as a joke?" asked Pryce.

"No, we can't," said Nellie. "We're putting an end to this nonsense once and for all."

AS GRACE EXPECTED, they spent a lot of time at the police station once they got back to Sparrow Lake. Alex Novak wanted to talk to everyone, especially Caleb and Angela. Paperwork had to be filed. The state trooper who'd arrested Lily at the cabin had already arrived and she had been booked. Grace wasn't certain if Lily now occupied a jail cell, but she didn't ask. She still felt bad for the woman but not bad enough that she thought Lily should have been let off. The outcome of the kidnapping could have been far worse, with Lily leaving the state with Angela. Caleb had been so worried.

To her surprise, while they were waiting in the lobby of the station, Grace got a call from a deputy who'd been called to Green Meadows. A prowler had been caught.

The deputy and his prisoner arrived a few minutes later and Grace recognized Vincent Pryce! The ghost tour operator appeared far less energetic than he had the last time Grace saw him, when he was entertaining customers at The Busy Corner. Clad in some sort of Halloween cow costume, he looked extremely silly and ashamed. Both his moustache and the mouth beneath it drooped. He could hardly meet Grace's eyes.

A couple of troopers standing around burst into laughter, one of them quipping, "Yeehaw, looks like there was a roundup, pardner!"

Grace wasn't sure how she felt. A crowd of residents from Green Meadows swarmed in a few minutes later. They must have followed the squad car in their own vehicles. Both the station and the parking lot outside were buzzing.

Nellie was among the Green Meadows group. "We caught him!"

"Vincent Pryce and his ghost tour," breathed Grace. "I can't believe he thought he could get away with it."

"He didn't get away," said Nellie, sounding victorious.

As he was led past her to the front desk, Pryce caught Grace's eye. "Look, Ms. Huber, I'm sorry. I didn't mean to cause any trouble."

"But you did cause trouble, Mr. Pryce," Grace said. "Your outfit may be funny but you weren't trying to amuse anyone."

"And you're pressing charges, right?" the deputy asked Grace. "If nothing else, he was trespassing."

"Yes, I'll press charges," Grace told him. "He also injured Fran Willowby. Is that assault?"

"Battery," said the deputy. "Probably at the misdemeanor level."

Caleb came out of Alex Novak's office to sit down beside her. "I bet he built the scare cow across the road, too."

"But that wasn't on our property." Though Grace planned to ask the police chief about it.

A half hour later, the crowd had thinned a bit, though plenty of people were still coming and going at the police station. Returning from getting herself a drink of water from the cooler in the lobby, Grace spotted her dad arriving. He must have driven down from Milwaukee, where the plane was based.

"Some kind of hullabaloo going on here," her father remarked, looking around. He was dressed in casual clothes, something rare for a man who lived in suits.

"It was even busier earlier," said Caleb, rising to shake Henry's hand. "We can't thank you enough for your help with the plane."

Grace wasn't sure if the "we" meant Caleb

and daughter or if she counted, as well. When Caleb came closer to slip his arm around her waist, she thought maybe she did.

Her dad smiled. "You're only too wel-come."

"There have been a lot of mysteries solved this afternoon," Grace told her father. "Residents caught the prowler at Green Meadows."

"There *was* a prowler?" said her dad. "I heard about the vandalism, then the kid on the skateboard. I've kind of lost track of all the incidents out there."

Grace told him about Vincent Pryce and how the ghost tour operator had dressed up as a cow.

"I wouldn't have minded seeing that," said Dad. "Ghost cow, huh?"

"They got him out of the cow suit," said Caleb. "Maybe he's locked up."

When Angela finally came out of the inner offices, Caleb went to see how she was.

At the same time, her dad pulled Grace aside. "Can I talk to you?"

"Now?"

"I don't know when I'll find you next."

"Okay." She strolled with him to a quiet corner. "You don't have to worry about me disappearing again." She hoped they would never have another terrible argument. At first he seemed to be at a loss for words, so she said, "You're going to tell me that I'm just finding myself and you forgive me, right?"

"No." He actually looked sheepish. "I was out of line. I would never disown you, Grace." He paused for words again, proving the admission was difficult for him. "I thought it over afterward and was horrified at what I said. I was upset and went too far." His gaze slid to Caleb. "It's not easy losing my little girl."

Did he mean losing her to a man or to another profession?

Regardless, she said, "You'll never lose me, Dad. No matter what I do or who I'm with. We'll always be family."

"I'm proud of you, Grace. Especially that I raised such a caring and wonderful person."

They hugged and she pretended she didn't see the tears in his eyes. She'd rarely seen him so emotional.

He said, "And you're right about someone else in the company being interested in taking over when I retire. Is that a relief for you?"

"It is. But you're not retiring right away, are you?"

"No."

"And I'll help you with the transition.

Again, I appreciate your volunteering the plane, Dad. We found Angela faster because you sighted the smoke."

"How is she?"

"She seems to be fine. And her mother was arrested."

Caleb and Angela approached, and Caleb thanked Grace's father again.

The older man said, "Hey, since everything is all right, how about some refreshments at the café? The check's on me."

"I don't know if I'll let you pay but I could use some grub." Caleb admitted, "I haven't had anything since that bit of fish that Angela cooked out in the woods."

"She cooked a fish?" Dad asked.

"And built a shelter," Grace added.

Caleb smiled proudly, then looked from Grace to her father. "Is it okay if my mother and a friend of Angela's joins us? I thought we'd celebrate."

"Sounds good to me," said Grace and looped an arm in her dad's to bring him along as they headed for the door.

A celebration was definitely in order.

GRACE WAS THANKFUL she'd made up with her father but she still wasn't sure how secure her relationship with Caleb was. They might love each other, but she refused to stand between a father and daughter.

They'd both been exhausted the night before, so after eating, Caleb had taken Angela home. Maddie had left with Kiki, saying she would let the girl stay with her while she tried contacting her grandmother.

Grace still felt a bit worn out herself the next day, but she'd gone into her office anyway and spent the morning trying to get caught up. Early in the afternoon her cell phone rang. She saw that it was Caleb and tried to tamp down a thrill of excitement.

"Have you recovered yet?" he asked.

"That may take a few days."

"Why don't you take some time off right now—if you can—and drop by to see Angela's new design for the green community's mural?"

"She has something already?"

"Already? It's been a while. She had the sketches done before the kidnapping."

Grace smiled. "I'd love to see them." Though being around Caleb would again remind her of how much she wanted a commitment from him.

She drove to his house and parked. As

usual, he met her at the door. He slid his arms around her and kissed her soundly.

She murmured his name, bringing him in closer, not expecting this much enthusiasm.

"I'm so happy to see you," he said, ushering her inside. "How are you? I canceled my class today to sleep in. Angela skipped school."

"I'm fine. Better now, actually."

The sketch pad lay on the table as they entered the kitchen.

"Angela?" Caleb called, pulling a chair out for Grace.

The teenager came in from the other room.

"Hello," said Grace. "I hope you're recovering from your ordeal."

"I'm okay." Angela made minimal eye contact and her tone was neutral. She opened the pad and withdrew a sketch, a landscape.

"Wow," said Grace, immediately liking the drawing.

In broad strokes, the landscape featured birds flying over a great expanse of trees, a lake and hills in the distance. A path led inward and on, disappearing into the horizon. The colors were rich, if muted, like nature.

"That's beautiful," remarked Grace. Exactly what she'd hoped for.

Angela smiled shyly. "I'll be ready to execute it in another week, as soon as school's out."

"Perfect."

"Can I have an assistant?"

"That's up to you," Grace told the girl. "Remember this is community service." In case the other person wanted to be paid.

"I know. She sort of owes you something, too."

"Kiki?"

"She's a good artist, too."

"Will Kiki be around long enough to finish the mural?" Caleb asked, then informed Grace, "She managed to contact her grandmother."

"She did? When did all this happen?"

"Today," Angela said. "She's really excited."

"I guess the reason we couldn't get hold of Mrs. Hartl was because she was so busy getting ready to move out of her big old home into someplace smaller."

"Now, she might even move here," said Angela.

"Well, we don't know that yet," warned Caleb. "Don't get your hopes up."

"At least she's coming to Sparrow Lake to

see Kiki." Angela added, "And Kiki will help me with the mural for as long as she can."

"Wonderful," said Grace. "I hope she can work out something with her grandmother. She needs a family."

"I know you helped Dad try to find her grandmother," Angela said. "I appreciate that."

It was the second time the girl had thanked her since they'd found her in the woods. She said, "Let me know what you need. Your dad has a discount at the art store but I want Green Meadows to pay for the materials. I want the mural to be done professionally, so it will last."

"I can apply a finishing varnish," Angela told her. "Matte, of course. I don't think you'd want it shiny."

"And make sure you put your name on it," said Grace. "People will be looking at it every day. You might get more work."

"Speaking of work," Caleb said. "Margaret Becker offered to talk to Angela about art careers. I had a conversation with her last week and she said there are fields that look for art degrees. And talent."

"That sounds like a good idea." Grace told

Angela, "Hopefully, you could work at something you really like."

Grace knew how important that was. She felt as if a weight had been lifted off her shoulders ever since she'd put her foot down about not taking her dad's job.

"We hope so." Caleb picked up the landscape sketch. "So once you get started with this, Angela, don't you think you should meet with Grace from time to time until it's finished?"

Angela nodded. "Sure."

"It's only professional," said Caleb, "to converse with a customer when you're creating something for them."

"I want it to be Angela's individual creation." Grace couldn't help recalling the girl's initial ideas. "As long as we avoid ghostly designs."

"That's okay. I'm over that." Angela snickered. "Didn't that crazy ghost tour guy look funny in that cow suit?"

"Yes, he did," Grace admitted.

Angela said, "I heard him say he was stuck and the police had to cut him out of that silly costume."

"He deserves to have gotten stuck," said Caleb. "Now, changing the subject." He turned to Grace. "How about we retire to the deck for some lemonade?"

"Sounds good."

Grace noticed that Angela hadn't been invited, but she didn't seem angry about it. In fact, she had been in such a good mood today that Grace felt inordinately happy. She helped Caleb with the pitcher of fresh lemonade from the refrigerator and they went out on the deck to sit in comfy chairs.

Or, rather, Grace sat in a chair. Caleb plopped himself down on the two-person glider and waggled his finger at her to join him. When she did, he slid his arm around her.

"Isn't it beautiful out here?"

"Gorgeous," Grace agreed, admiring the open yard that reached back to a tall stand of trees. "Are those wildflowers over there?"

"Some late bloomers. I planted them with prairie grass that'll grow tall by summer."

"Only indigenous species, right?"

"Of course. I don't want to be kicked out of the environmental studies profession," he said, joking. "I'm going to need some help with that, though."

Was he asking her to do it? "I'm just a beginner as far as landscaping goes."

"I'm sure you'll do fine under my tutelage."

Then he raised his brows. "Oops, I mean my senior partnership."

She had to laugh.

"Seriously, Angela has no interest in plants. She refused my invitation anyway."

"When do you need this help? Now?"

"Mostly next spring."

"Next year?"

"Something like that."

She became even more thoughtful. "Well, I am going to implement Phase 2 for Green Meadows."

"And you'll be too busy?"

"No." She tried to carefully choose her words. "It's just I'm not sure I can be around you and not…well, the way I feel…"

"Not be around me and what? Want to be paid in kisses?"

He leaned closer as if he intended to kiss her right now but she placed a hand on his chest.

"Caleb. We really have to think about this."

"The fact that we love each other?"

"Whether or not we can make plans. When I love someone, I expect some sort of commitment." She had to be honest. "And, well, we've had a lot of trouble with your daughter not liking me in your life. I don't want to be a point of contention between the two of you. It would be too difficult."

"You noticed a different attitude today, though, didn't you?"

"She seemed much more friendly."

"I talked to her about us, about my being with you on a long-term basis."

She couldn't contain her surprise. "You did? When?"

"Last night, before we went to sleep."

She met his eyes, warm and brimming with emotion.

Emotion bubbled up in her as well when she asked, "What did she say?"

"Angel said she thought she could deal with it."

"*Deal with it?* I—is that supposed to be good?"

"In my book it is. She also told me that at least you're someone she can respect. That's good, believe me."

After all the emotional upheaval the teenager had been through, that was as much of a compliment as the girl could give, Grace thought, acknowledging it was okay with her.

"So what kind of a commitment are you looking for?" he asked.

"At least a year...till we get the foundation built."

"I'd say the foundation is already started. We have good materials."

"You think we're ready for Phase 2?" She smiled.

"I'm ready for Phase 5."

"That's going to be some kind of structure we're building."

"It better be. I want it to last forever."

And he sealed his words with a resounding kiss.

* * * * *

LARGER-PRINT BOOKS!

GET 2 FREE
LARGER-PRINT NOVELS
PLUS 2 FREE
MYSTERY GIFTS

Love Inspired®

Larger-print novels are now available...

YES! Please send me 2 FREE LARGER-PRINT Love Inspired® novels and my 2 FREE mystery gifts (gifts are worth about $10). After receiving them, if I don't wish to receive any more books, I can return the shipping statement marked "cancel." If I don't cancel, I will receive 6 brand-new novels every month and be billed just $5.49 per book in the U.S. or $5.99 per book in Canada. That's a savings of at least 19% off the cover price. It's quite a bargain! Shipping and handling is just 50¢ per book in the U.S. and 75¢ per book in Canada.* I understand that accepting the 2 free books and gifts places me under no obligation to buy anything. I can always return a shipment and cancel at any time. Even if I never buy another book, the two free books and gifts are mine to keep forever.

122/322 IDN GH6D

Name	(PLEASE PRINT)	
Address		Apt. #
City	State/Prov.	Zip/Postal Code

Signature (if under 18, a parent or guardian must sign)

Mail to the **Reader Service:**
IN U.S.A.: P.O. Box 1867, Buffalo, NY 14240-1867
IN CANADA: P.O. Box 609, Fort Erie, Ontario L2A 5X3

**Are you a current subscriber to Love Inspired® books
and want to receive the larger-print edition?
Call 1-800-873-8635 or visit www.ReaderService.com.**

* Terms and prices subject to change without notice. Prices do not include applicable taxes. Sales tax applicable in N.Y. Canadian residents will be charged applicable taxes. Offer not valid in Quebec. This offer is limited to one order per household. Not valid to current subscribers to Love Inspired Larger-Print books. All orders subject to credit approval. Credit or debit balances in a customer's account(s) may be offset by any other outstanding balance owed by or to the customer. Please allow 4 to 6 weeks for delivery. Offer available while quantities last.

Your Privacy—The Reader Service is committed to protecting your privacy. Our Privacy Policy is available online at www.ReaderService.com or upon request from the Reader Service.

We make a portion of our mailing list available to reputable third parties that offer products we believe may interest you. If you prefer that we not exchange your name with third parties, or if you wish to clarify or modify your communication preferences, please visit us at www.ReaderService.com/consumerschoice or write to us at Reader Service Preference Service, P.O. Box 9062, Buffalo, NY 14240-9062. Include your complete name and address.

LILP15

LARGER-PRINT BOOKS!

GET 2 FREE
LARGER-PRINT NOVELS
PLUS 2 FREE
MYSTERY GIFTS

Love Inspired®

SUSPENSE
RIVETING INSPIRATIONAL ROMANCE

Larger-print novels are now available...

WESTERN WP PROMISES

YES! Please send me **The Western Promises Collection** in Larger Print. This collection begins with 3 FREE books and 2 FREE gifts (gifts valued at approx. $14.00 retail) in the first shipment, along with the other first 4 books from the collection! If I do not cancel, I will receive 8 monthly shipments until I have the entire 51-book Western Promises collection. I will receive 2 or 3 FREE books in each shipment and I will pay just $4.99 US/ $5.89 CDN for each of the other four books in each shipment, plus $2.99 for shipping and handling per shipment. *If I decide to keep the entire collection, I'll have paid for only 32 books, because 19 books are FREE! I understand that accepting the 3 free books and gifts places me under no obligation to buy anything. I can always return a shipment and cancel at any time. My free books and gifts are mine to keep no matter what I decide.

272 HCN 3070 472 HCN 3070

Name	(PLEASE PRINT)	
Address		Apt. #
City	State/Prov.	Zip/Postal Code

Signature (if under 18, a parent or guardian must sign)

Mail to the **Reader Service**:

IN U.S.A.: P.O. Box 1867, Buffalo, NY 14240-1867
IN CANADA: P.O. Box 609, Fort Erie, Ontario L2A 5X3

* Terms and prices subject to change without notice. Prices do not include applicable taxes. Sales tax applicable in N.Y. Canadian residents will be charged applicable taxes. This offer is limited to one order per household. All orders subject to approval. Credit or debit balances in a customer's account(s) may be offset by any other outstanding balance owed by or to the customer. Please allow 4 to 6 weeks for delivery. Offer available while quantities last. Offer not available to Quebec residents.

WPBPA16R

LARGER-PRINT BOOKS!
GET 2 FREE LARGER-PRINT NOVELS PLUS
2 FREE GIFTS!

HARLEQUIN

super romance®

More Story...More Romance

READERSERVICE.COM

Manage your account online!

- Review your order history
- Manage your payments
- Update your address

We've designed the
Reader Service website
just for you.

Enjoy all the features!

- Discover new series available to you, and read excerpts from any series.
- Respond to mailings and special monthly offers.
- Connect with favorite authors at the blog.
- Browse the Bonus Bucks catalog and online-only exculsives.
- Share your feedback.

Visit us at:

ReaderService.com